advance praise for *three shoeboxes*

"*Three Shoeboxes* will force y[...] [...]f
and about the comfortable l[...] -
sitive, and extremely well wr[...] |
make you think and stay with [...]e
book down. Grab it immediate[...]
– Rachel Van Dyken, #1 New York Times bestselling author,
The Bet

"In *Three Shoeboxes*, Steven Manchester chronicles a seem-
ingly strong marriage and loving family that suddenly begins
to crack and fragment under the weight of guilt and old
secrets. It's psychologically accurate, well-plotted, and a sen-
sitive, honest portrayal of what it's like to have a long-buried
past finally surface, and what that reckoning does to everyone involved."
– Mark Sullivan, #1 *New York Times* bestselling author,
Beneath a Scarlet Sky

"Raw, moving, and brutally honest—Steven Manchester
takes you on an emotional rollercoaster. Grab your tissues
for this heart-wrenching story—better yet, grab a box full!"
– Tanya Anne Crosby, *New York Times* and *USA Today*
bestselling author, *The Girl Who Stayed*

"*Three Shoeboxes* is a compassionate, accessible portrait of
a vitally important topic, PTSD, how it affects the sufferer
and the family—and how to find hope and healing."
– Jenna Blum, *New York Times* and international bestselling author, *Those Who Save Us* and *Storm Chasers*

"*Three Shoeboxes* will linger in your thoughts long after
that last page. Steven Manchester has brilliantly woven a
story that will touch your heart, twist your emotions, and
remind you why he is easily one of your favorite authors."
– Steena Holmes, *New York Times* and international bestselling author, *Emma's Secret: A Novel*

"Steven Manchester is a master author of human emotion. You will come away from his tales having been fully engulfed in his fictional world and also having learned something about yourself."
– Heather Froeschl, reviewer, *BookReview.com*

"Grab the Kleenex. You'll need them handy. *Three Shoeboxes* starts off on an incredibly honest picture of the downward, spiraling effect that post-traumatic stress, anxiety attacks, and depression can have on a man's life. To get the details so vividly accurate, I would assume that Steven has had first-hand experience with these disabling conditions. Amazing!"
– Tracy Farnsworth, Editor, *Roundtable Reviews*

"Author Steven Manchester has a way of using his gift of words to remind us of our own humanity and the simple truth that people in pain can hurt others in ways we don't always consider. *Three Shoeboxes* is a novel that shows that, no matter who we are, we have a connection to each other that can bring out the best and worst in us. This is why we have to work so hard to show up for each other at all costs. *Three Shoeboxes* is the kind of heartfelt reminder we all need."
– Cyrus Webb, media personality/Amazon Top 500 Reviewer

"*Three Shoeboxes* is Steven Manchester's most powerful work to date. He doesn't pull any punches in this brutally honest story about a man suffering from PTSD. His protagonist doesn't understand what triggered his recent panic attacks, but they're violent enough to cause him, a successful man with a perfect marriage, a great job, and three beautiful kids, to descend into alcoholism. And to lose everything he holds dear. The author digs deep and shares raw, terrifying emotion. His protagonist spins out of control and winds up in a dirty motel room with a pistol pressed against his temple. This is terrific writing. Manchester's protagonist's life becomes nightmarish, his rage palpable, and his ultimate redemption breathtaking. It was enough to bring this reader to tears."
– John Lansing, #1 bestselling author, *The Devil's Necktie*

"*Three Shoeboxes* is a story of a husband and father who, due to things he doesn't quite understand himself, loses everything: his wife, his children, his job, and, worst of all, himself. However, the story doesn't stop there. It is a story of love and faith, as well. After losing his family and realizing just how low he has fallen, Mac sets about rebuilding his life and regaining at least part of his family the very best he can. This story is another testament to Steve Manchester's skill as a writer."
– Carol Castellanos, reviewer, *Midnight Reviews*

"*Three Shoeboxes* by Steven Manchester is probably the best of his works thus far! As I read, I could sense the love of one father for his children. Though Mac had a loving relationship with his wife and three children, everything seemed to fall apart at once. But through the author's wonderful pen, he shows the reader just how this man's faith restores it all."
– Noonie Fortin, 1SG, USAR (Ret), Author, *Colonel Maggie*

"Throughout *Three Shoeboxes,* Manchester guides the reader on an inspirational and emotional journey. Weaving a story around serious topics such as PTSD and losing a spouse, this story is hard to put down. *Three Shoeboxes* immediately captures your attention—and holds on to it—long after you've finished the last page. Manchester's work is addicting. He's mastered the art of involving his readers and pulling at their heartstrings until they laugh, cry, or both."
– Kim Wilson, co-author/co-editor, *Living Miracles: Stories of Hope from Parents of Premature Babies*

"At a time when such topics as family, love and old-fashioned human kindness have become taboo, along comes a story that threatens to turn the world on its cold, deaf ear. If *Three Shoeboxes* does not bring you to tears, I'm not sure anything will."
– Russell N. McCarthy, Esq., C.F.O., *Rising Tide Entertainment, Inc.*

three shoeboxes

steven manchester

THE
ST●RY
PLANT

The Story Plant
Studio Digital CT, LLC
P.O. Box 4331
Stamford, CT 06907

Story Plant Paperback ISBN-13 978-1-61188-260-5
Fiction Studio Books e-book ISBN-13: 978-1-945839-19-1

Visit our website at www.TheStoryPlant.com

First Story Plant Paperback Printing: June 2018
Printed in The United States of America

For my children

"How can someone take something from you
when it lives in your heart?"
– Dr. Faust Fiore

chapter 1

It was their fifteen-year wedding anniversary. *Fifteen years*, MacKenzie Anderson thought, feeling the weight of the special occasion. *I should've waited until this year to give Jen the diamond bracelet*, he thought, cursing himself for his premature decision the year before. *I'm going to be making payments for the next couple of years anyway.*

In the hopes of being creative or original, MacKenzie—Mac, as most people called him—abandoned his mind and ventured into his heart, where he hoped the answer to his dilemma could be found. It didn't take long for the only obvious choice to hit him. *I got it!* he thought. *Rather than the usual material token, I'll give Jen a peek into the future. For our fifteen-year wedding anniversary, I'll give her a promise.* His mind raced for more details. *I'll also fill a box with...* He nodded, a smile filling his handsome face. *I know exactly what to do.*

Mac awoke earlier than Jen, as he had for the better part of a decade and a half. Sitting up, he took the few precious moments needed to confirm how much he really loved her. Though he'd memorized it years ago, he studied the soft contours of his wife's face framed by a full head of chocolate locks. Working his way down, he focused on her full lips. She smiled; it was the slight-est grin, but enough to steal away his yawn. He inhaled deeply. Her smell was so sweet, so distinct. *I'd recognize it in either heaven or hell*, he decided. She stirred once, and again, before struggling to open her eyelids and reveal a pair of light hazel eyes that sparkled with life. Mac never budged; he was inches from her face when her senses registered his presence. "Happy anniversary, beautiful," he whispered.

With a low purr, Jen pulled him to her. They hugged for a long while. "I love you," she finally breathed into his ear.

He squeezed her tighter. *After all these years*, he thought, *she still owns my heart.*

While she lay in a mountain of warm cotton blankets, he dressed for work. "I'm really sorry I have to work late on our anniversary," he told her.

"Will you stop apologizing," she said. "I told you, I understand."

He nodded. "I promise, we'll celebrate next weekend. We'll get a babysitter and go out."

She smiled, kissed him again and watched him hurry out the door.

Unlocking the car door, Mac slid behind the steering wheel and looked back at the house. *What a trooper*, he thought, *pretending it doesn't bother her*. But she was disappointed and he knew it. After being together for so long, even the best acting wouldn't have fooled either of them. *Wait until she finds out what I've got planned for tonight*, he thought chuckling. He looked back at the house again, unsure about the last time he'd been this excited to go out on a date.

∞

"Stay out of my stuff," Bella yelled at her little brother, her screech traveling down the stairs from her bedroom.

"I wasn't in your stuff, Beans," Brady yelled back.

Jen shook her head. *Now there's a lie*, she thought. As she went about her normal morning routine—primarily cleaning up after the three hurricanes she called Jillian, Bella and Brady—she spotted a young man dawdling around the front of her house. Back-stepping into the shadows, she watched the kid for a moment from the living room window. Carrying a long white box, he was clearly searching for a specific house number. And he looked more stressed than anyone his age should have been. *He's making a delivery*, Jen decided, smiling, *from Mac.* The boy finally confirmed the address and rang the Anderson's doorbell. Jen answered the door.

"A delivery for Mrs. Anderson," the kid said.

"That's me," Jen said, signing for the package and giving him a well-deserved tip. "Thank you."

He half-nodded before sprinting away.

Cradling the white box in her arms, she watched him with amusement. *I wish my kids had something they took that seriously.* She closed the front door and slid the bow from the box. It was a lovely bouquet of long-stemmed roses, fifteen in all. *One for each year*, she thought. She'd told Mac, "No flowers this year. We can use the money elsewhere." But she'd never been so happy he'd ignored her wishes. She plucked the card free and read, "Thank you for fifteen great years, three beautiful children and one incredible life." *There's the man I fell in love with*, she thought, her smile lasting until the moment her thoughtful husband returned home.

Both of Mac's feet weren't in the house when he announced. "We have dinner reservations tonight." He winked at her. "And you have a half hour to get ready."

She hugged him. "I love you," she said, "but a half hour?"

He laughed. "Hurry," he said, patting her on the backside. "It's all arranged. I'm bringing the kids to your sister's so we have all night." He smiled.

All night, she repeated in her head. *Now that's something different.*

It was just past twilight when they pulled up to D'Avios, a fancy restaurant located at the bottom of the posh Biltmore Hotel in Providence. The young valet attendant opened Jen's door. In one swift motion, he caught Mac's keys, along with a promise for a good tip.

"I'll get you on the way out," Mac said, grabbing his wife's hand to escort her into the restaurant.

Jen tucked a wrapped present under her other arm, surveying her husband's free hand. *He must have gotten me something small enough to put in his pocket,* she figured.

The ambiance was perfect, the service reached beyond doting, yet neither of these could compare to the meal. The filet mignon swimming in béarnaise sauce melted like ice cream in July.

"Surprised?" he asked, grabbing for her hand.

"I actually am this time," she admitted. After so many failed attempts at keeping a secret, she was impressed her husband hadn't leaked a word—*especially to the kids*, she thought. "Thank you."

14

A pink hue spread evenly across his boyish face. "You're welcome."

Jen studied her husband, wondering, *How did I ever get so lucky?* Beyond his dark hair and penetrating eyes, he was the definition of a devoted husband and father who considered spending time with his three children a favorite pastime. And he'd worked hard for years, finally reaching a point in his life—at thirty-eight—when he could start breathing easier. "How's work?" she asked.

"Ross just assigned us a pretty big project," he said and stopped. "But I don't want to talk about work tonight."

What about talking about me returning to work then? she asked in her head. "The kids then?" she teased.

"Nope," he said. "I couldn't love them any more than I do, but even they can survive without our attention for the next few hours."

She was taken aback. *With all our day-to-day responsibilities, I can't remember the last time we shared a night like this*, she thought, her chest feeling warm.

They'd just ordered coffee and dessert when the pianist stopped playing and made an announcement. "I'd like to ask everyone to join me in wishing Mr. and Mrs. Mac Anderson a happy anniversary. Fifteen years ago today, they took each other as man and wife, and we're honored to have them celebrating with us tonight."

There was a buzz of polite applause.

Stunned, Jen looked across the table to catch the blush of a little boy paint her considerate husband's face again. Before she could say a word, the pianist broke into his next song—their wedding song. Her chest filled with emotion, causing her eyes to swell. "Thank you, Mac," she whispered past the lump in her throat. "I..."

He leaned across the table and grabbed her hand, interrupting her. "Happy anniversary, babe," he said.

15

For whatever reason, she expected him to reach into his pocket and pull out his annual token of love. He didn't, so she grabbed the wrapped present from the empty chair beside her and handed it over to him. "This gift is the one thing that means more to me than anything else in the whole world," she told him, her eyes swelling more.

While the pianist filled the room with a nostalgic melody, Mac tore through the wrapping. In one magical moment, he reached the prize. It was a framed photo of them and the kids—Jillian, Bella and Brady. "Our family," he gasped.

Before he could react any further, she hurried over to kiss him.

"God, do I love you," he said.

"And I love you too," she said, hugging him tight and ignoring a room full of stares.

"So, I get another fifteen years then?" he asked.

She never answered. Their shared embrace said it all.

After a few moments, he pushed her away to look into her eyes. "You're not going to ask me where your present is?" he asked, smiling.

She half-shrugged. "I hadn't thought about it," she fibbed.

He laughed. "I'll give it to you at home. It was too big to bring here."

"Oh, I bet it was," she said, giggling.

He laughed again, quickly raising his hand to call for the check.

As they stepped out of the restaurant, Mac stopped short on the sidewalk and turned to face her. "Hey," he whispered.

"Yeah?" she said, stepping into his arms.

"I really love you, you know."

"I know."

"Do you?" he asked. Her lips parted to reply when he pulled her even closer. "I mean it," he said. "I love you, Jen."

She felt overwhelmed by this genuine display of affection. She knew this proclamation went far beyond the three words they exchanged each day—a nice little habit they'd established from the beginning. This was intended as a confirmation of all they were—*and will be forever*. It was as though they were young again and he'd professed his love for the first time—sincere and unashamed.

She grabbed his face in both her hands and considered all they'd been through together. They began as any first love—filled with innocence and thrills—before life eventually ushered in reality. *Back then, our romance was so intense, burning as brightly as the sun*, she thought, *and twenty-four hours in a day wasn't nearly enough time to be together.* "I know," she told him, "and I love you more today than ever before, more than I have the words to describe." A ball of raw emotion choked her.

He kissed her long and hard. "I do," he said.

"What?" she asked.

"I still do," he repeated with a smile. "After fifteen years, I promise to take you as my wife in good times and in bad, in sickness and in health—all of it. I want you, no, I need you as my wife for the next fifteen years and the rest of my life after that."

She kissed him back, matching his fervent passion for her. "I still do, too," she vowed, feeling like she was being reborn.

When they reached the car, she turned to him. "There's no way you're ever going to top this one," she said, grinning. It was the best memory she'd ever been given. "So, what's the big gift waiting for me at home?"

He winked. "The consummation," he said.

∞

After gazing at his beautiful wife, Mac looked up and slammed on the brakes. The car in front of them had stopped short. "Jackass!" he barked, his heart racing.

Jen leaned forward in the passenger seat. "I think there's been an accident," she said.

Once the rubbernecker in front of them had inched past the scene—never even considering to stop—Mac slowed to a crawl and surveyed the scene. Two cars had been involved in the wreck. "It looks like it just happened," he told Jen.

She nodded. "I hope everyone's all right."

The windshield of one of the cars had been shattered, half of it now covered in crimson red. *That's a lot of blood*, he thought, his own blood turning cold. *Should I stop?* Almost involuntarily, he pulled off to the side of the road. "They need help," he said to his worried wife. *And someone really needs to help them*, he thought, trying to steel himself to be that someone. His body's fight or flight response, however, pled for him to drive on and avoid the gruesome scene.

As Mac swung open the driver's side door and took one step out of the car, a siren wailed in the distance. Leaning to his right, he peered into the rear-view mirror. Flashing red and blue lights strobed into the dark night behind them. "The cavalry's arrived," he said aloud, more for himself than for Jen.

"Thank God," she said, nodding. "I just hope no one's hurt bad."

As the siren got louder and the flashing lights brighter, Mac glanced at the blood on the windshield one last time. *Someone's definitely hurt*, he thought. *There's nothing worse than a friggin' car accident.*

Chapter 2

Jen sat at the kitchen table, drinking coffee and reading the newspaper, her oversized bouquet of flowers sitting before her in a crystal vase.

Mac entered the room, grunting and pounding on his chest like a silverback gorilla. "Be honest," he said, "last night was amazing, wasn't it?"

Jen dropped the paper and kissed him. "You were an animal, babe. It was the most incredible eight minutes of my life."

Mac grabbed for his chest, pretending he'd just been wounded.

Jen laughed. *Goofball.*

His eyes drifted off for a moment. "Eight minutes?" he muttered. "I didn't realize it lasted that long." He shrugged. "That's not bad after fifteen years, right?"

Laughing, Jen handed him a cup of coffee. "You know I'm teasing," she whispered, kissing him again. "Last night was amazing. You were very sweet for putting so much thought into it." She gazed at him. "And I'm holding you to that promise."

"Ditto," he said.

"And I really love my treasure box."

Mac smiled. "And I love the framed photo, Jen." He took a sip of coffee before looking at the kitchen clock. "Oh, I need to go pick up the kids from Diane's."

Jen shook her head. "I already talked to her this morning and she's offered to drop them off."

"Really?" he said, shocked. "What time?"

"I told her any time this morning would be fine," Jen said, shrugging.

"Your sister's such a sweetheart," Mac teased. "I never know whether to hug her or throw her into a headlock."

"Be nice, Mac," she said. "If it wasn't for Diane, you wouldn't have had your eight minutes of glory last night."

Mac nodded. "That's true, I guess."

Jen glanced up at the kitchen clock. "I'm going to head upstairs and get showered. We need to start getting ready for Brady's party." Kissing Mac once more, she left for the bedroom.

Mac watched her walk away and smiled. "Mac Anderson," he said to himself, "you are one lucky son-of-a-bitch." As he sipped his coffee, his breathing suddenly became short and quick. He stood, freezing in place. A moment later, he stumbled from being dizzy and grabbed for a kitchen chair to brace himself. He then grabbed for his chest before reaching up to his neck to check his erratic pulse. "What the hell," he gasped, trying to catch his breath. *What the hell's happening?* he thought, before heading for the bathroom to splash cold water on his face.

After being dropped off, the kids barged into the living room.

Jillian was the spitting image of her father, with dark hair and eyes. Dressed in her usual baggy clothes—an earth-toned outfit that drew attention away from herself—she looked toward the stairs leading to the bedrooms. "Just keep it down, guys, so Mom and Dad can sleep," she whispered.

"Okay," Brady said, "but I don't know how long I'll be able to *keep it down*."

While Jillian shook her head, Bella laughed. The three claimed their usual spots on the couch. Jillian picked up the remote control and clicked on the television.

"I don't want to watch this show," Bella complained.

"Leave it on!" Brady yelled. "I like this show."

Bella pushed Brady's shoulder. "Shut your mouth, Brady. Mom and Dad are..."

Brady pushed her back. "You shut your mouth, Beans!"

"Stop fighting," Jillian warned through gritted teeth, separating them, "and we're going to watch something else." *The last thing I need is for Dad to get after me because these two can't shut up.*

Taking a few deep breaths to compose himself, Mac was still in shock when he stepped into the living room.

Excited to see him, the kids immediately ceased their squabble.

"How did it go, Dad?" Bella asked right away. With her mother's chocolate curls and light eyes, this girlie-girl had recently turned eight—an age when pigtails and Barbie dolls had just started to lose their attraction.

"Yeah, was Mom surprised?" Brady squealed.

Pushing aside the terrifying episode, Mac took a seat beside them. "Mom was definitely surprised," he said. "We had a wonderful night. Thank you, guys, for giving us the time."

"I still say you should have cooked her dinner," Jillian teased.

Mac grinned. "Ummm..."

"Yeah, you should have," Bella agreed.

"I suppose I could have picked up dinner," Mac said, "but I still would have had to heat it and serve it to her."

Bella grinned. "And the way you cook..."

"...it was probably best you went out to eat, Dad," Brady added, finishing his sister's thought.

The kids all laughed.

"Very funny, guys," Mac said.

"So, what did you give Mom for an anniversary gift?" Jillian asked, becoming serious.

"Let me show you," Mac said proudly, sliding a wooden box in front of them and opening it.

Excitedly, Jillian plucked a card out of the treasure box and read it aloud, "Jen, thank you for fifteen great years, three beautiful children and one incredible life."

"Awww," Bella said, "that's so sweet, Dad."

Nodding, Mac began pulling out some of the gifts. "I got Mom some of her favorite music, some chocolate, perfume and English tea." Picking up the lingerie, he tucked it under his leg. *Maybe they didn't notice*, he told himself.

Brady reached into the box and pulled out a small teddy bear. Looking it over, he shook his head and tossed it back in.

Mac continued pulling items out of the box. "...candles, some lotions, bubble bath and wine."

"You gave all this stuff to Mom?" Bella said.

Mac nodded. "Well, it is our fifteenth anniversary." He studied his daughter's innocent face and smiled. "You don't think she deserves it?"

Both Bella and Brady shrugged, while Mac and Jillian laughed.

Jillian dove back into the box and pulled out a homemade booklet. "Mommy's coupon book..." she read before opening it. "I'll wash the dishes," she read, flipping the page. "Extended foot massage." She flipped to the next page. "Whatever your filthy imagination can..."

"All righty then," Mac said, snatching the booklet out of her hand and throwing it back into the box with everything else. "So, what did you guys do at Aunt Diane's last night?" he asked, changing the subject and closing the box.

"We watched TV," Brady said, "that's all."

Mac snickered. "Of course you did."

"What did Mom give you for an anniversary gift?" Bella asked.

Mac looked down the line at each of them and smiled. "You guys," he said and, before they could question it, he showed them the back of a framed photo. "Before Mom handed this to me, she told me that my gift is the one thing that means the most to her in the whole world." He grinned. "When I tore off the wrapping paper, this is what I found." He turned the framed photo around for his children to see.

"It's a photo of me, Bella, Brady," Jillian blurted, "and..." She stopped. "...it's our family."

"Awww," Bella cooed again.

"Were you surprised, Dad?" Brady asked.

"I was, buddy. I even told her that she might be able to hang out with us for another fifteen years," he teased.

Bella slapped her father's arm, while Jillian and Brady laughed.

"Okay," Mac said, "now who wants to help me get everything ready for Brady's party?"

Jillian clicked off the television, while Brady rushed to his father's side. Bella stood. "I'll make a birthday banner," she said, heading off to her bedroom.

"I'll get the cake frosted," Jillian said, going off to the kitchen.

Mac patted the cushion beside him for Brady to take a seat.

Grabbing a balloon from the end table, Mac began blowing it up. "So, are you ready to turn seven, little man?" he asked his son between breaths.

The dark hair, light-eyed boy shrugged. "I haven't thought a lot about it, Dad. I just wish..." His small face was filled with worry. Even though Brady was the baby of the family, this rough-and-tumble tyke had a high emotional IQ.

Mac stopped inflating the balloon. "What do you wish, buddy?"

"I just wish my friend, Drew, was coming to my party," he said sadly. "His family had to move away, so we're not friends anymore."

"Not friends anymore?" Mac repeated, pinching off the air in the half-inflated balloon. "How's that even possible?"

Brady shrugged again. "Well, we can't see each other anymore, so..."

"Brady, you don't have to be *with* someone to care about them," Mac interrupted, shaking his head. "Everyone I love lives right in here..." he pointed toward his chest, "...where they're safe and sound." While his young son gave it some thought, Mac inhaled deeply to drive his point home.

Brady followed suit and smiled. "That means me and Drew can be friends forever," he squealed. "Thanks Dad."

With a wink, Mac started inflating the balloon again when his heart skipped three beats and his breathing came to a sudden halt. He leapt to his feet and immediately grabbed for his chest, while the air emptied from the balloon. *I can't breathe*, he thought, feeling terrified. *I... I...*

"You okay, Dad?" Brady asked, equally alarmed.

Is it a heart attack? Am I dying? An onslaught of macabre feelings and fragmented thoughts began rushing through him.

"Dad?" Brady repeated.

"Go upstairs," Mac gasped, unsure of what was happening, "and help your sister with the banner."

"But Dad..."

"Now, Brady!" Mac snapped, trying to sort through a thousand jumbled thoughts racing through his mind.

While the small boy hurried off to his sister's bedroom, Jillian stepped out of the kitchen to see what the commotion was all about.

"Go back to your cake," Mac barked in a voice much louder than he'd wanted. But he couldn't help it.

Jillian rolled her eyes. "Whatever," she said under her breath before disappearing behind the door.

Wave after crushing wave of adrenaline raced through Mac's veins, making his extremities tingle. *What the hell...*

The terrifying episode was just starting to subside when Jen entered the living room. She looked around. "The kids home?" she asked.

"Beans and Brady are upstairs, making a banner for the party," he said, breathing away the last of his menacing symptoms. "Jill's getting the cake frosted in the kitchen."

"Getting the cake frosted?" she repeated. "I was going to finish the cake."

Mac took another deep breath, trying to steady himself.

"What's wrong?" Jen asked, searching his face.

"It's probably nothing," he said, shrugging.

"What is it?" she asked, stepping closer to him.

"I don't really know. I was blowing up a balloon when all of sudden I started having trouble breathing."

"From blowing up a balloon?" she asked in disbelief.

He shrugged again. "My heart skipped a few times and..."

"Then we need to go to the Emergency Room!" she interrupted, her face instantly changing from confused to fearful. "We'll reschedule Brady's party for another..."

"No, no," Mac said, shaking his head, "we're not rescheduling the party." He took a deep breath. "Look," he said, grinning, "I feel better already. Like I said, it was probably nothing."

"But what if it wasn't *nothing*?" she asked, wrapping her arms around him and looking up into his face.

"If I don't feel well after the party, I'll go get checked out."

She stared at him. "Promise?"

"Promise."

She kissed him. "And you'll tell me if it happens again?"

"You'll be the first to know," he said, adding a grin.

She didn't smile.

"I need to go get ready for the party," Mac said before kissing Jen and starting for the bedroom. "People will be here before we know it."

∞

Colorful balloons, tied to the mailbox of the Anderson's colonial home, blew in the soft summer breeze. The quaint New England street was filled with parked cars on both sides. In the backyard, Mac stood on the deck, enjoying the company of his and Jen's many guests, and cooking enough hamburgers and hot dogs to feed a small army.

He looked up to see that Sarah Chin, Bella's best friend, had just arrived. "Hi Sarah," he called out.

"Hi, Mr. Anderson," Sarah called back, her big rosy cheeks engulfing her face and closing her eyes when she smiled.

Mac chuckled at the sight of the sassy young girl.

Wearing pointy party hats, the children ran and played games. They took turns chasing Sophie—a four-pound teacup poodle with the attitude of a grizzly cub—

in and out of the house. Adults congregated in small groups, sipping fruit-garnished cocktails and pretending to pay attention to their screaming children. Hidden speakers played pop music, everyone celebrating the birthday of Mac and Jen's young boy, Brady.

As a band of screaming children chased Sophie back into the kitchen—being careful not to squish her—Mac walked in behind them to grab some more sliced cheese from the refrigerator. The wall calendar showed the words *BRADY'S BIRTHDAY;* the date was August 24. Sophie led the kids into the living room where she ran in circles. Mac laughed. On the mantle above the fireplace, family photos in mismatched frames smiled from behind spotless plates of glass. Mac and Jen's wedding picture was surrounded by photos of them and the kids: shots taken at Disneyland, the beach, a picnic, New York City and the aquarium, just to name a few. Though the settings changed, the themes remained the same. The entire Anderson family was together, and they were smiling. "Go play outside," he told the kids.

Jen took a seat between her sister, Diane Nedar, and her mother, Sue. Although Diane was the younger sister, she had already experienced enough life to be terribly and thoroughly jaded. And Sue, being recently divorced from their dad, showed all the signs of newfound freedom. She was already inebriated.

"You got here a little early," Jen said to her bitter sister.

"At least I'm here," Diane replied, snickering. "Did Dad even call Brady to wish him a happy birthday?" she asked, still clutching her nephew's present.

"Yes, he called," Jen said, rolling her eyes, "and he said he'd swing by during the week when his hateful daughter wasn't around."

Diane's nostrils flared. Within seconds, a grin replaced her sour puss—as she obviously realized she was wrong for bringing up their father.

"For someone who swears she doesn't care about Dad," Jen added, sipping her cocktail, "you spend an awful lot of time talking about him."

Diane sighed heavily. "Some habits are harder to break than others." She shrugged. "It's a lot more fun to hate him."

Both women looked toward their mother.

Sue took another sip of her cocktail. "To tell you the truth, girls," she said, shaking her head, "I'm not sure I could ever stop caring for someone—especially when you've shared a love as deep as mine and your father's." She smiled. "But for now, it's a lot more fun for me to hate him too."

The three women were sharing a laugh when Bella and Brady approached, carrying a birthday banner. After kissing their aunt, Diane handed Brady his gift.

"Thanks Auntie Diane," the boy said.

"You're welcome, Brady," she said, "and you can open it now. You don't have to wait until later."

Brady was tearing into the present when Mac walked past. "Hi, Diane," he said. "Thanks for helping us out last night."

She nodded. "Always happy to help my sister."

He let it go. "Okay, well, I'm glad you made it today."

"And why wouldn't I, Mac?" she asked.

Mac shook his head. "Always a pleasure talking to you," he mumbled under his breath. Ignoring his sister-in-law's dirty look, Mac solicited Jillian's help to hang the large banner that read *HAPPY BIRTHDAY BRADY* in big bold letters.

The slider door opened again, followed by Brandt Swanson, Scott Gervasio and Roland Dube stepping onto the back deck, each of them holding a wrapped present.

"Thanks for coming, fellas," Mac told them.

"I wouldn't have missed it, Mac," Roland said.

"I would have," Brandt joked, "but I know I'd never hear the end of it."

Mac laughed. "Can I get you guys a drink?"

"It's five o'clock somewhere," Scott replied.

Mac headed back toward the kitchen to mix their drinks. The party was completely underway.

∞

While the kids played, the adults gathered in two small groups: Jen, Diane and their mom sat together, while Mac, Brandt, Scott and Roland huddled off in another corner of the deck.

"So how did last night go?" Sue asked, grinning.

"That's right," Diane said, "I forgot to ask."

Jen looked at her sister and shook her head. "Mac planned the most incredible dinner for our anniversary," she said, talking directly to her mother. "We even renewed our vows..."

"You did?" Sue asked, slurring both words.

Jen nodded. "More or less." She couldn't stop smiling. "It was the most amazing night." She looked toward the grille. *I wonder how he's feeling?*

"Good for you," Sue said, sipping her drink.

Jen found Mac peering over at her. He winked. She returned the playful gesture. *He must be feeling better,* she thought, *because the beer bottles are really starting to pile up near that grille.*

"Yeah, good for you," Diane repeated. "It's so nice that your happiness is reliant on a man..."

Jen stood, cutting off her sister. "Thanks, Mom," she said, bending to kiss the intoxicated woman's rosy cheek. "I should go check on my other guests." She looked down at her sister. "You really do need to get over your daddy issues, Diane," Jen said. Shaking her head at her sister's absurdity, she started for the kitchen to warm up more appetizers.

While Sue laughed, Diane opened her mouth to reply. Nothing came out.

∞

Wearing his *Kiss the Cook* apron, Mac flipped another batch of charred burgers onto the plate of buns being held by his wife.

"Feeling okay?" she asked him in a whisper.

"Never better," he replied, and then lowered his tone. "Maybe it was just the result of eight minutes of intense physical activity?"

Feeling relieved, she grinned. "Well if that's the case, then maybe we should cut that timeframe in half going forward?"

"I could definitely make that happen."

They both laughed and, before Jen turned to leave, he stole a kiss from her. In turn, she stole a swig of his beer. "Hey, get your own," he teased.

She put the platter of burgers down to grab his smiling face. "My dear, in case you've already forgotten, everything that's yours is mine."

He wrinkled his nose in a display of playful disapproval. Jen took the opportunity to pat his backside, earning her another wink.

"And I wouldn't have it any other way, beautiful," Mac whispered. "Okay kids," he called out in a comical screech, "come and get it!"

The children stampeded toward the grill. As they lined up for their food, Mac teased each one, affectionately patting the heads of Jillian, Bella and Brady.

Although Bella and Brady clearly appreciated their father's attention, Jillian violently jerked her head to avoid his touch.

Jen laughed before rejoining her mother and sister at their plastic patio table.

As the day progressed, so did Mac's level of intoxication. Even still, he took charge of the children's games, hosting several chaotic rounds of musical chairs and one nearly lethal game of pin the tail on the donkey.

When the hired clown finally arrived, the big-shoed prankster performed magic tricks before twisting balloons into vague animal shapes. Mac took it one step further and filled some of the balloons with water, arming each child for battle. As their laughter turned to wondrous squeals, the excitement spilled through the yard and contagiously rubbed off on the adults. Before it was over, even Sue was soaked from head-to-toe.

Once Jen finally stopped laughing, she returned from the kitchen with Brady's birthday cake. As the sun dove for the horizon, she lit the candles. Arm-in-arm, she and Mac joined their family and friends in a strong rendition of "Happy Birthday to You."

"I wish...I wish..." Brady whispered, his eyes closed tight. He blew out seven candles. While everyone applauded, Jen and Mac kissed. As fast as he could shred through the paper, Bella passed one gift after the other to her little brother. It didn't take long before the smiling boy was sitting in front of a pile of new clothes and shiny toys.

Mac approached his young son. With a proud smile, he handed Brady his last gift.

He's going to love it, Jen thought, excited for her little guy.

Brady ripped through the wrapping and opened the box, pulling out a small white sailor's hat. "Dad, does this mean...?" he began to ask.

"It sure does, Brady," Mac confirmed. "You're now an official crew member of the Anderson sailing team. We ship out in the morning."

"Yes," Brady squealed, "my wish came true!"

Applause echoed through the yard for the second time.

While the boy donned the tiny white hat, Mac took a knee and spoke to his son about safety. "Sailing can be a lot of fun, but it can also be very dangerous. Like everything else in life, you'll be fine if you show respect; respect for the boat, for the water, and for me."

A set of wide eyes remained glued on the beloved teacher.

"As the captain," Mac continued, "you have to listen to everything I tell you out there on the water. If you don't, somebody might get hurt." He searched Brady's eyes. "So, when I tell you to do something, don't question it. Just do it. We can always talk about it later, okay?"

"We know, Dad," Jillian and Bella sang in chorus.

"I know you do," Mac said, "but it's important that Brady knows, too."

As if on cue, Brady saluted. "Aye, aye Captain."

Everyone, except Brady, laughed.

Darkness swallowed the last hint of light before all the party guests bid their farewells.

"That yard's a disaster," Jen said. "I'd better go clean up." She turned to her children. "I'll be up in a little while to kiss you guys goodnight."

"Thanks for the party, Mom and Dad," Brady told them.

"You're welcome, son."

While Jen headed for the yard, the kids lined up before their father.

"Goodnight, Dad," Brady said before sprinting for his bedroom.

"Goodnight, buddy," Mac called out after him. "Love you."

"Love you too," the boy yelled back, already halfway up the stairs.

Bella approached Mac next. "Goodnight, Daddy," she said.

He pulled her in for a tight hug. "Sweet dreams, angel. I'll see you in the morning."

The young girl kissed his cheek.

Watching her walk away, Mac called out, "Love you..."

"Love you more," she said without turning around.

At the base of the stairs, Jillian said, "Night Dad."

"Night Jill." He looked toward the ceiling. "Listen, the monsters don't have to go right to sleep, but please make sure they don't kill each other up there."

"No worries. I got it," she said.

"Love you, Jill."

"I know," the smirking tomboy said, heading for her bedroom.

What a fun age you're at now, he thought, and grinned.

Mac joined his wife in the yard. It looked as though an angry twister had passed through just hours before. Streamers and broken balloons covered the lawn. Cake frosting was smeared on the patio furniture. He looked at Jen; they shared a laugh over the mess.

While crickets chirped, they worked together to clean up, a comforting silence hanging between them. Jen yawned, causing Mac to do the same. They chuckled again.

"So, an early wake-up call, huh?" Jen said.

Mac nodded. "Taking the kids sailing at first light."

"Brady made out like a bandit today," she said, yawning again.

"He sure did," Mac agreed. "It's funny. I was just thinking the same thing— about how blessed we are for the family and friends we have."

Jen nodded. "I agree, but it's the other stuff that makes me feel blessed. The way you play with the kids... how they laugh."

Taking a break from the cleaning, Mac took a seat. "You know, Jen, I don't even remember what our life was like without the kids around." He thought about it and smiled. "And I'm glad I don't."

With a kiss, she took a seat beside him and studied his face. "How are you feeling?" she asked.

"Stop worrying, babe," he told her, "I'm fine."

She smiled. "Good, then why don't you finish this yard," she suggested, "while I go tuck in the kids and then take a shower."

"I get another eight minutes tonight?" he asked.

She started for the house. "If you think you can handle it," she called over her shoulder.

Oh, I can handle it, he thought, hurrying to finish his chore.

After checking in on the kids, Mac slid into a pair of pajama bottoms, while Jen threw on the matching top. They eased into bed.

"Well," she said, "it looks like in a couple of weeks I can pick up where I left off with my career."

Yawning, Mac locked eyes with his wife. "What's that?"

"Come September," she said, "all the kids will be in school full-time and I can finally return to work," she whispered. "It's always been our plan and I'm so excited to..."

Mac rolled over and landed on top of her where he kissed her passionately. "You sure you want to talk about work right now?" he asked.

She didn't respond. Instead, she slid off her top and pulled Mac onto her. Heavy breathing and faint moans quickly changed the subject.

As though he'd been buried alive, both car doors closed in on Mac. He struggled and struggled but he still couldn't break out of the dark, crumpled box. *I'm trapped*, he thought, *I'm trapped and...and there's no escape.*

Suffocating on a pair of empty lungs, Mac shot up in bed. His eyes suddenly thrown open, he searched for the cause of his anguish. There was nothing there. It suddenly dawned on him, *It was just a stupid nightmare.* Even still, he continued to gasp for air, while a frigid film of sweat covered his trembling body. He looked to his side to find Jen sleeping peacefully. He considered waking her. *No*, he decided, *she worried enough about me today.* Slowly pulling the covers off his legs, Mac tiptoed out of the bedroom.

Alone in the living room, Mac took a seat on the couch and was going to click on the TV when a powerful wave yanked him erect, making him gasp for air again. *I can't friggin' breathe*, he thought, his mind racing for an answer. While he held his chest, his hand trembled uncontrollably. "What the hell is happening to me?" he whispered, his pathetic voice quivering in the silence.

But as quickly as the inexplicable episode began, it passed over him. *I should go tell Jen*, he thought, but considered the sailing trip in the morning. *No.* He took a few deep breaths. *Maybe it's just from a lack of sleep?*

Chapter 3

Jen was deathly afraid of water, so she always stayed home when the family went sailing—usually with Brady. *She'd nearly drowned as a child,* Mac thought, *and has never been able to face her fears of the water.* Strangely, this always bothered him. *Jen's very logical,* he thought, *so it doesn't make sense that she can't get past it.* He'd never made an issue of it. *I suppose some things are better dealt with alone,* he thought. *Besides, I kind of like the idea of sharing my passion for sailing with just the kids.* It was his favorite way to bond with them. And as an added bonus, he was happy to give his wife the precious gift of being able to sleep in. *She holds down the Anderson fort every day,* he thought. *She deserves a break.*

The sun was yet to rise when Mac—exhausted from the previous night's peculiar event and the lack of sleep that followed—turned the mini-van onto the highway. He juggled the steering wheel in one hand and a hot cup of coffee in the other. They weren't two miles down the road when he realized, *It's been too long since I've taken Jillian and Bella sailing.* He glanced into the rearview mirror and smiled. All three kids were very much awake for the early hour, squirming with excitement. Brady beamed the brightest, thrilled to be embarking on his first watery adventure. *I've become so busy with work deadlines,* Mac thought, *that I've forgotten the blessings of innocent fun.*

Trees flew by the window and, as the sun finally made its grand entrance, Mac began a chorus of songs. "Row, row, row your boat, gently down the stream. Merrily, merrily, merrily, merrily, life is but a dream..." He peered back into the rear-view mirror again and the warmth of unconditional love filled his soul. *My life really is a dream*, he thought.

The adventure began as soon as they pulled up to the marina. With shoes unlaced, only the kids' breathing could chug faster than their feet. Each one beat Mac to the long, wooden dock.

They might be smaller than me, he thought, *but they sure are quick.*

At the sailboat slip, the children donned their bright-orange life vests. "Okay guys," Mac said, taking a knee and speaking to them again about safety, "do you remember what I told you at Brady's party, that sailing can be a lot of fun, but it can also be very dangerous?"

Three heads nodded, each set of wide eyes focused on their teacher.

"Safety must come first," Mac continued, "so you have to listen to everything I tell you out there today."

"We know, Dad," Jillian and Bella replied in symphony. "You already told us that."

"And it's worth repeating," Mac said.

Wearing his most serious face, Brady saluted his dad. "Aye, aye, Captain."

Jillian and Bella burst into laughter. Brady, however, maintained his intense demeanor.

Mac assisted each child onto the boat. After untying the ropes from the slip and throwing them onto the boat, he jumped aboard. "Okay then," he said, "let's go have some fun."

∞

It was a calm, sunny day, with only a few clouds bringing about slight winds; *it's a perfect day for Brady to
break into sailing*, Mac thought. Jillian, Bella and Brady
sat at the rear of the boat, listening attentively as their
dad worked the sails. After tying off a rope, Mac began
pointing out the animals that foraged on the shore,
birds gliding in the sky, and so on.

Brady's face was frozen in awe. The boy scanned the
world around him before his eyes finally met Mac's.

*He obviously wants to describe what he's feeling,
but can't articulate it,* Mac realized. With a smile, he
answered the question that his little boy could not put
into words. "It's the feeling of freedom, Brady, that's
what you feel." After a thoughtful pause, he spoke to
them all. "But guys, you don't need to be happy to feel
free. Like everything else in this world worth living for,
freedom lives right in here." He pointed to his chest,
inhaling deeply to drive his point home. The kids followed suit. After a proud nod, he returned to working
the main sail—but not before he saw the kids look at
each other and exchange smiles. The deep breathing
continued.

"Why doesn't Mom come with us?" Brady eventually asked.

"Because this is my thing with you guys," Mac
answered, "and she's very considerate for letting us
have the time together."

The small boy shook his head, unconvinced.

"Have you always liked to sail, Dad?" Bella asked.

"Yes," Mac said, realizing that he felt completely at
peace; whatever was plaguing him at home hadn't followed him out here. "But I didn't even try it until I was
much older than you guys." Taking in their tranquil sur-
roundings, he added, "I wasn't able to do a whole lot

when I was a kid, but it's not..." He stopped to find the right words.

"What Dad?" Jillian asked.

"It's all about finding something that brings you peace," he explained. "For me, it's being outdoors, close to nature." He inhaled deeply. "Being on the water feels like time spent in heaven for me."

"Then why don't you do it more?" Bella innocently asked.

"Yeah," Brady added, "instead of working all the time."

Mac chuckled. "Because when you're an adult, you do what you have to do before you can do what you want to do."

"That's stupid," Jillian blurted before looking up with a face that expected to be scolded.

Mac grinned at her. "I agree."

Brady shook his head. "It doesn't sound like being an adult is too much fun."

"It's what you make it, son," Mac said, smiling.

Throughout the magical day, Brady told stories that made no sense. The four of them ate fast-melting popsicles from a small, red cooler and laughed under the sun. For everyone's entertainment, Bella described each person on every passing boat with great fictitious detail. "That one's a real princess," she said, "and the man with her is an astronaut." As they lay in the boat, looking up to watch big puffy clouds float by, they took turns pointing out the obvious pictures painted above. *So many games I've forgotten*, Mac thought.

"I don't think I want to become an adult," Brady commented out of nowhere. "I've been thinking about it and I think I'd rather stay a kid."

"Me too," Mac replied.

The kids laughed.

"Like I said," Mac added, "it's what you make it, buddy." He looked at his children, each of them giving him their undivided attention. It was rare. "The thing to remember is that we're each responsible for our own lives, so it's important to take charge of yours and…"

"We know Dad," Jillian interrupted, her reply sounding like it had been practiced a thousand times.

Mac ignored her. "There are people," he continued, "very sad people who go through life blaming everyone but themselves. They complain about their troubles and all the things they want and don't have. The problem with that is, as soon as you consider yourself a victim in this world, you've lost control of your own life." He peered into his children's eyes. Although they looked confused, they were still with him. "We're given one life," he said, lowering his tone, "so take accountability for it and make it a great one."

They each nodded.

As the sun touched the flat horizon, Mac studied his children closely and pondered who they were. *These three are the wisest people I've ever known*, he decided. With messy hair and wrinkled clothes, they didn't care one bit about success or wealth. Their only job was to laugh all day, which kept them in good health. *Their minds are sponges in search of right,* he thought, *and their hearts are pure, which they have no qualms about sharing.* In their eyes, Mac saw peace, feeling so grateful for the rare opportunity to be reminded of what meant most in life. *I am blessed.*

Tanned by the sun's smothering kisses, Mac and the kids took their last lap around the lake for the day. While

Jillian, Bella and Brady talked about their lives, Mac listened attentively.

"So, are you guys happy summer's almost over?" he asked, teasing them.

"No!" they sang in unison.

"I just hope I get Mrs. Parsons this year," Bella said. "All the kids say that she's so much better than Mr. Rego."

"She is," Jillian confirmed. "I loved Mrs. Parsons."

"I don't care who I get," Brady said, "as long as we have recess."

Everyone laughed.

"What about you, Jill?" Mac prodded his teenage daughter. "Are you excited to get back to school?"

"Hardly," she fired back. "I hate..."

Mac's penetrating gaze stopped her from finishing the sentence. He gestured with a slight nod toward the two younger ones.

"I hate that we don't get recess anymore," she concluded, cleverly covering her tracks.

"Well, at least they still give you lunch," Mac teased, winking at her.

Everyone laughed—except Jillian.

"For whatever it's worth, it's okay to be a little bummed that summer's over," Mac said. "Just remember that doing well in school and getting a good education is one of the most important ingredients toward being successful and living a comfortable life. As adults, we..."

"...do what we have to do before we can do what we want to do," Jillian interrupted in a tone that usually accompanied rolling eyes.

"That's not what I was going to say," Mac responded, letting her off the hook for her age-appropriate sarcasm, "but that works too."

After docking the boat, they raced to the top of the hill. Mac beat them back to the car. Looking back one last time, he realized that he'd just enjoyed one of the best days of his life. *Although we did nothing but laugh, somewhere through it all something very important happened.* He'd been reminded that he was still alive—alive to play and forget his worries—*if only for a few moments.* Wearing a proud grin, he shook his head. *I still have a lot to learn,* he thought. *Some days, I honestly think my kids know more than I do.*

On the ride home, Mac returned to the rear-view mirror and made a wish: *When they get older, I hope all three of them remember the days when they had all the answers—* his eyes filled—*and were good enough to share them with their dad, who sometimes forgot the important things in life.*

He set his gaze back upon the road before them.

"Row, row, row your boat," they all sang out of tune, "gently down the stream. Merrily, merrily, merrily, merrily, life is but a dream."

Looking fully rested, Jen stood at the foot of the king-sized bed, wearing a see-through nighty. "Thanks for the quiet time today," she told Mac. "I didn't realize how much I needed it."

"Well deserved, babe," Mac said, stifling a yawn. Although he desperately needed sleep, his mind—and body—were already laser-focused on other matters at hand.

"But there is one more thing I need," she whispered, tugging on the lace ribbon of the lacey negligee, "that is, if you still have the energy to..."

Mac pounced like a jungle cat, enveloping his playful wife in one swift motion. Within seconds, he had her on her back where he could explore every inch of her quivering body with his mouth. *I could be in a coma and still be able to ravage this woman,* he thought. After all the years they'd been together, Jen still brought him to heights of pleasure he never imagined he could climb. "Let's see what I got left in me," he whispered in her ear before embarking on the love-making session with the commitment and vigor of a man half his age.

Unashamed by each other's wants and needs, the happy couple moved as one—until they were glistening in sweat and struggling to take in air.

Mac lay beside his grinning wife. "Well, that's everything I got," he teased, shrugging.

Kissing his lips one last time, Jen got up to shower. "And I couldn't ask for more," she said, still breathing heavily.

After taking his turn in the shower, Mac's head wasn't on his pillow for more than thirty seconds before he was out cold.

There was a loud bang, followed by the horrible sounds of broken glass and mangled steel. "Oh God, no!" Mac screamed, the strong smell of gas filling his sinuses.

Mac jumped up, panting like an obese dog suffering in a heat wave. His heart drummed out of his chest. Startled from a sound sleep, he didn't know what was wrong. He leapt out of bed and stumbled toward the bathroom. He couldn't breathe. He couldn't think. *There's something wrong,* he finally thought, *I...I need help.* He searched frantically for an enemy. There was none. As he stared at the frightened man in the mirror, he considered calling out to his sleeping wife. *She has enough to worry*

about with the kids, he thought, but was already hurrying toward her. "Jen," he said in a strained whisper.

She stirred but didn't open her eyes.

The constricted chest, sweaty face and shaking hands made Mac wonder whether he was standing at death's door, cardiac arrest being his ticket in. *I have to do something now*, he thought, *or I'm a goner.* "Jen," he said louder, shaking her shoulder.

One eye opened. She looked up at him.

"It's happening again," he said in a voice that could have belonged to a frightened little boy.

Jen shot up in bed. "What is it?"

"I...I can't breathe. My heart keeps fluttering and I feel..."

"I'm calling an ambulance," she said, fumbling for her cell phone.

"No," he said instinctively, "it'll scare the kids."

She looked up at him like he was crazy.

"I'll go to the emergency room right now!" Grabbing for a pair of pants, he started to slide into them.

Jen sprang out of the bed. "I'll call my mom and have her come over to watch the kids. In the meantime, Jillian can..."

Mac shook his foggy head, halting her. "No, I'm okay to drive," he said, trying to breathe normally.

"But babe," she began to protest, fear glassing over her eyes.

"I'll text you as soon as I get there," he promised, "and then call you just as soon as they tell me what the hell's going on."

Jen's eyes filled. "Oh Mac..."

He shot her a smile, at least he tried to, before rushing out of the house and hyperventilating all the way to the hospital.

∞

I'm here, Mac texted Jen before shutting off the ringer on his phone.

The scowling intake nurse brought him right in at the mention of "chest pains." Within minutes, the E.R. staff went to work like a well-choreographed NASCAR pit crew, simultaneously drawing blood while wiring his torso to a portable EKG machine.

As quickly as the team had responded, they filed out of the curtained room. A young nurse, yanking the sticky discs from Mac's chest, feigned a smile. "Try to relax, Mr. Anderson. It may take a little bit before the doctor receives all of your test results."

For what seemed like forever, Mac sat motionless on the hospital gurney, a white curtain drawn around him. *I hope it isn't my heart*, he thought, *the kids are still so young and they need...*

"Who do we have in number four?" a female voice asked just outside of Mac's alcove.

Mac froze to listen in.

"Some guy who came in complaining of chest pains," another voice answered at a strained whisper. "Test results show nothing. Just another anxiety attack."

No way, Mac thought, not knowing whether he should feel insulted or relieved.

"Like we have time to deal with that crap," the first voice said. "Can you imagine if men had to give birth?"

Both ladies laughed.

No friggin' way, Mac thought before picturing his wife's frightened face. *She must be worried sick. But I can't call her without talking to the doctor. She'd...*

The curtain snapped open, revealing a young man in a white lab coat with a stethoscope hanging around his neck.

This kid can't be a doctor, Mac thought, the world suddenly feeling like it had been turned upside down.

"Your heart is fine, Mr. Anderson," the doctor quickly reported, his eyes on his clipboard. "I'm fairly certain you suffered a panic attack." He looked up and grinned, but even his smile was rushed. "Sometimes the symptoms can mirror serious physical ailments."

Mac was confused, almost disappointed. *So, what I experienced wasn't serious?* he asked in his head.

The young man scribbled something onto a small square pad, tore off the top sheet and handed it to Mac. "This'll make you feel better," he said, prescribing a sedative that promised to render Mac more useless than the alleged attack.

"Ummm...okay," Mac said, his face burning red.

The doctor nodded. "Stress is the number one cause of these symptoms," he concluded. "Do you have someone you can talk to?"

Mac returned the nod, thinking, *I need to get the hell out of here.* Although he appreciated the concern, he was mired in a state of disbelief. *I'm a master of the corporate rat race*, he thought, unable to accept the medicine man's spiel. *If anyone knows how to survive stress, it's me.*

"That's great," the doctor said, vanishing as quickly as he'd appeared.

My problem is physical, Mac confirmed in his head, *it has to be.* He finished tying his shoes.

Pulling back the curtain, he was met by the stare of several female nurses. He quickly applied his false mask of strength and smiled. *A panic attack*, he repeated to himself. When put into words, the possibility was chilling.

The nurses smiled back, each one of them wearing the same judgmental smirk.

With his jacket tucked under his arm, Mac started down the hallway. *Sure*, he thought, *I have plenty of people I can talk to.* He pulled open the door that led back into the crowded waiting room. *That is, if I actually thought it was anxiety.*

Mac sat in the parking lot for a few long minutes, attempting to process the strange events of the last several days. Although he felt physically tired, there weren't any symptoms or residual effects of the awful episodes he'd experienced—*not a trace of the paralyzing terror I felt. And they just came out of the blue.* He shook his head. *How can it not be physical?* He thought about the current state of his life. *Work is work, it's always going to come with a level of stress, but that's nothing out of the ordinary.* He shook his head again. *I just don't get it.* He grabbed his cell phone and called Jen. "Hi, it's me."

"Are you okay?" she asked, the worry in her voice making him feel worse.

"I'm fine, babe."

"Fine?" she said, confused. "What did the doctor say?"

"He said it's not my heart."

"Oh, thank God."

Her reaction—although completely understand-able—struck him funny, making him feel like the boy who cried wolf.

"So what is it then?" she asked.

He hesitated, feeling oddly embarrassed to share the unbelievable diagnosis.

"Mac?"

"The doctor thinks it was a...a panic attack."

This time, she paused. "A panic attack?" she repeated, clearly searching for more words. Then, as a born problem solver, she initiated her usual barrage of questions. "Did they give you something for it? Is there any follow up?"

"Yes, and maybe."

"What does that mean?"

"He gave me pills that I'd rather not take if I don't need to. And he suggested I go talk to someone."

"Talk to someone? You mean like a therapist?"

"I'm pretty sure that's what he meant."

"Oh," she said, obviously taken aback. "Then that's exactly what you should do."

"I don't know..."

"Is there something bothering you I don't know about, Mac," she asked, "because you can talk to me, too, you know."

"I know, babe. But there's nothing bothering me, honest." He took a deep breath. "For what it's worth, I don't buy the anxiety attack diagnosis."

"Well, whatever you were feeling this morning was real enough, right? I could see it in your face. It wouldn't hurt anything for you to go talk to someone." She still sounded scared and he hated it.

"Maybe not," he replied, appeasing her. In the back of his head, though, he was already contemplating how much he should continue to share with her—*or protect her from.* "I need to get to work," he said.

"Why don't you just take the day off and relax?" she suggested.

Here we go, he thought. "I wish I could, babe," he said, "but we have way too much going on at the office right now."

"And maybe that's part of your problem," she said.

"I'll be fine, Jen," he promised. "We'll talk when I get home, okay?"

"Okay."

"Love you," he said.

"And I love you," she said in a tone intended for him to remember it.

∞

Mac arrived at New Dimensions Advertising. As an executive at the pinnacle of his impressive career, he was energetic, in control and one step away from the next big promotion. An early meeting had been scheduled with his creative team. He walked in late, a tray of hot coffees in one hand and a box of donuts in the other.

"I know. I know," he began in his even-tempered demeanor, "I expect everyone to be here on time, except for me, right?" He smiled at his handpicked crew. "Okay, now that we have that cleared up..." Except for several laughs over the donut box, there was no response. He went on. "Oh yeah, and Brady wanted me to thank everyone again for their generous gifts." He smirked. "Well, everyone but Scott."

Scott, an entry-level consultant, peered up from the box. White powder covered his half-open mouth. He was clearly confused by the comment.

"No, I'm sorry Scott," Mac said, his smirk growing into a full smile, "I have that wrong. Brady loves the monster truck you gave him. It's me who has the problem with it."

Scott still couldn't respond, his mouth stuffed with sugary dough.

Mac leaned in close to his young prodigy. "My friend, never ever buy a child a toy that can scream louder than the child's father." There was a comical pause, followed by Mac's wink. "Trust me, when you have kids you'll know exactly what I'm talking about."

Scott's smile displayed his relief. The three women and two men seated at the conference table all laughed. From the look in their eyes, they held a deep respect and admiration for their affable boss.

As everyone dove back into the donut box, concepts at different levels of development began flying around the room. Mac controlled the flow, occasionally jotting down some of the ideas into his leather notebook.

Receiving a nod from Mac, Scott took the floor. "I've done the legwork on this one, boss. The way I see it, Woodpine Furniture is competing with three major retailers, each one located within a ten-mile radius of the other. With such a concentration, they can't..."

"Competing?" Mac asked, jumping in. "I disagree. In fact, it's been my experience that a rising tide carries all ships."

Scott—along with the rest of the team—awaited an explanation.

Mac chuckled. "It means that when people are looking for furniture, they'll shop around—especially if it's only within a ten-mile radius. And we can use this knowledge to give our client the edge." Mac's eyes drifted off into a creative world that few people ever got the chance to witness. "That's our ace, Scott. We'll monitor the other stores' advertising and find a way to capitalize by enhancing our own."

"Love it," Brandt blurted, while the rest of Mac's team sat in awe.

Scott cleared his throat. "Ingenious," he said, "then we can..."

Mac's eyes glassed over and he suddenly realized his mind was floating away—and it wasn't promising to be a pleasurable experience. His knee bounced from nervous energy. Although he tried to stop it, he couldn't. Aware of the fact that he couldn't stop fidgeting, a clammy sweat began to form on the back of his neck.

"Blah...blah...blah..." Scott said, his voice no more than an annoying hum now.

Mac pulled at his collar a few times before getting to his feet. *I can't friggin' breathe again*, he thought, his mind being thrown into a death spiral. He could feel everything inside of him turning dark, like he was being taken over by some evil force. *I...I can't breathe...*

"Everything okay, boss?" Scott asked.

Mac shook his head. "If...if you'll all excuse me... please."

Scott halted his presentation, while Mac took the opportunity to hustle out of the room, shocking everyone.

Mac rushed to the management washroom. Before the door had completely closed behind him, he was bent at the waist, struggling to take in oxygen. *Oh God,* he thought, trying desperately to calm down and center himself. As he began to slow his breathing, he caught his own reflection in the mirror. This scared him more. Instead of finding the confident man that normally grinned back at him, he was looking into the terrified face of a man he barely recognized—the poor guy's wide eyes searching frantically for answers. "What the hell..." Mac managed, his pitiful voice echoing off the subway tile walls. *Am I really having panic attacks?*

Fifteen miles away—an entire world—in the Anderson home, Jen went through her normal routine. After breakfast, she broke up a quarrel that was turning physical between Bella and Brady. "I've just about had it with you two and your fighting. School will be starting soon and you won't have as much time to play together. I suggest you make the most of the summer you have left."

"But Brady's always in my stuff, Mom," Bella complained. "He...

"Na...ah!" Brady countered.

"He is, Mom," she said, "and..."

"I've heard enough from the both of you," Jen yelled. "Now either go outside and find a way to get along, or go to your rooms where you can stay for the rest of the day. It's up to you." Placing her hands on her hips, Jen's right eyebrow rose for an answer.

"Mom?" Jillian called out.

As Jen turned, Bella and Brady exchanged slaps under the table. Jen's head snapped back to them. The two little ones took their cue and headed for the great outdoors, hooting and hollering as they left. Jen turned to her eldest daughter and shook her head. "What are we going to do with those two?" she asked.

"Let's just get rid of them," Jillian said.

Jen laughed until she remembered Jillian wanted to talk. "Something on your mind, Jill?" she asked, still straightening up from the breakfast rush.

Jillian shrugged. "Last year, I had a problem with some tool at school."

"Tool at school?" Jen asked, amused by the rhyme scheme.

"A bully," Jillian translated.

"Oh," Jen said, taking a seat and gesturing that her daughter do the same. "What's her name?"

"It's a boy and he kept calling me a lesbian because of the way I dress." Her eyes swelled with tears. "But I'm not a lesbian, Mom. I like boys. I'm just not..."

Jen placed her hand on Jillian's leg, prodding her to go on.

"I'm just not a girlie-girl," the teenager finished.

Jen searched her daughter's eyes. "I know who you are, babe. And if you were a lesbian, it wouldn't make a difference either way to me and your father."

"But I'm not, Mom."

"I know, Jill," Jen said. "Why didn't you tell me last year when it was happening?"

"Because I talked to him about it and he finally stopped."

"And?"

"And he just started up again online."

"Online?"

"On social media," Jillian said. "Snapchat and Facebook." The girl wiped her eyes. "Should I tell Dad about this punk?"

"No," Jen said instinctively, "I wouldn't. Your dad's going through a tough stretch at work right now," she fibbed. "I'll be happy to call the *tool's* parents and..."

"No," Jillian snapped back, shaking her head. "That would only make things worse. I'll handle it. I just wanted you to know what's going on."

"And if the bullying doesn't stop, Jill, then you need to promise me that you'll let me know."

"I'll let you know, Mom."

"Okay," Jen said, picking her next words carefully. "We've all been through it, babe, but it doesn't make it right. Bullies are insecure people who have to put other people down in order to feel better about themselves."

Jillian stood. "I don't really care what this tool's issue is. If he doesn't cut the crap, he's going to be sorry."

Jen started to respond, but stopped. Something inside her preferred that her daughter be angry rather than accept the role of victim.

With his office door closed and locked, Mac sat at his desk and stared at the three pages of therapists listed in the HMO catalog. *How am I supposed to know who's who?* he wondered, eventually picking the one located between work and home—*Dr. Shelley Lawrence.* Reaching into his pocket, he pulled out the prescription the E.R. doctor had written for him. *Maybe I should get this script filled?*

Chapter 4

I've been spilling my guts to this clown for nearly two weeks now, Mac thought. Seated in the high-back leather chair, he faced Dr. Lawrence, his muted therapist. *And the panic attacks have only gotten worse.*

"So, tell me how you're feeling," she asked.

Like always, he thought, *like my heart's about to explode.* "Well, the attacks haven't stopped."

"They haven't?" she said, sounding as surprised as ever. She jotted some secret note into her mint green journal.

Jackass, he thought, but said, "I think they've gotten worse." Although Mac had experienced his fair share of reservations about therapy, he'd gone into it with an open mind. It hadn't taken long, however, before his mind slammed shut. *This therapist provides no answers,* he thought, *and no relief.*

"Really?" she said, writing another note.

"Yeah, really," he said, sounding more sarcastic than intended.

She quickly looked up from her book.

Mac dove right into the same explanation he delivered every session. "Sometimes it starts during a bad dream, but not always. My heart races. I can't catch my breath and I feel like I'm suffocating. My fingers and toes start to tingle and then the worse feeling of fear—doom, I think is the best word to describe it—comes over me."

"Hmmm," she sighed, her hand bobbing inside the mysterious notebook. "Have the pills helped?"

"I don't think so," Mac said, being honest. "They just make me tired and unable to think clearly. And I need the full use of my brain for the work I do." *Unlike you*, he added in his head.

"Have you been drinking?"

"No," he lied, and they both knew it.

"How often do the attacks occur?" she asked.

"There's no schedule, if that's what you mean. Sometimes they come one right after the other..." He swallowed hard. "...even on top of one another. And sometimes they're spread out. Either way, I'm left feeling terrified of the next one that I know is right around the corner."

"Hmmm...terrified," she repeated, making another notation.

What a waste of friggin' time, Mac thought. and sat for the remainder of the session engaged in some strange staring contest—until his breathing became shallow and his fluttering heart began to thump out of his chest.

∞

It was nearly one o'clock when Jen pulled the mini-van into the drive-thru line at Sonic.

"Why are we in the drive thru?" Brady asked over the front seat.

"Yeah," Bella added, "Dad always lets us order from the car port."

"Forget it," Jen said, "I'm not even dressed and if we see someone..."

"Please Mom?" Brady pled.

"The car port's our favorite," Bella added.

Jen looked at Jillian, who was slouched in the passenger seat.

The teenager shrugged. "Whatever," she muttered, offering her signature answer to everything.

Jen shook her head. *We'd better not see anyone we know*, she thought. "Fine," she said, surrendering to the kids, and drove around the drive-thru line to find an empty car port.

The kids screamed their orders past their mother's ear into the crackling speaker, which inevitably turned into another back seat yelling match. To avoid confusion, Jen spun to threaten her tribe into silence before ordering two kid's meals, as well as a chicken sandwich for Jillian.

Minutes later, an awkward teenage boy on roller skates delivered the food. The transfer of three bagged lunches was shaky at best. Jen checked to ensure that the orders were correct. *Close enough*, she thought before distributing the fast food to her hungry pack.

While Jen stole a few fries, she heard a loud knock, making her jump in her seat. She looked up to find an old colleague, Abigail Rose—a glimpse of her previous life—standing at her window. *Oh shit,* Jen thought, *this is what I get for leaving the house looking like a bum.* She took a big breath, threw on her best smile and rolled down the window.

"Hi Jen," Abigail said, "it's so funny to run into you today."

Taking another deep breath, Jen smiled wider, awaiting an explanation.

"Your ears must have been ringing this morning," the pant-suited professional added.

Just land the plane already and spit it out, Jen thought, hoping Abigail couldn't read minds.

"During this morning's team meeting, my boss was asking if any of us knew someone who might be looking for a staff position," she explained, displaying her toothy smile. "And, of course, you were the first person to come to mind."

"Oh...wow..." Jen fumbled, at an unusual loss for words.

Bella and Brady, on the other hand, were not; they started fighting over their bagged lunches.

"The tater tots are mine," Bella barked, "you asked for fries."

"But I wanted tater tots too," Brady retorted.

"Bella, get your fist out of your brother's face," Jen hissed, dancing between an adult conversation and reprimanding her children, "now!"

"Mom," Brady whined, "why doesn't Beans..."

Jen raised her index finger for him to stop. "Brady, honey, Mommy's trying to have an adult conversation right now, okay?"

Jillian turned her body completely around in the passenger seat and threatened her siblings—through her practiced glare—into silence.

While Jen blushed with embarrassment, Abigail smiled. "Sorry about that, Abigail," Jen said, giving her kids the evil eye, "but my children are testing my last nerve today."

"It certainly looks like your plate is full," Abigail said, condescension dripping from the words.

Jen had begun her journalism career with Abigail, a woman who was not nearly as talented. *And now she's a senior correspondent*, Jen thought. The truth of it left a bad taste in Jen's mouth. "It is funny that we've run into each other today," Jen agreed. "I've recently given a lot of thought about coming back to the newspaper."

The tone of the conversation surprisingly changed. "That's great," Abigail said. "I have to tell you, I've seen very few who have a way with words like you do. You really are one of the best, Jen." The veteran reporter glanced at the kids in the back seat and then back at Jen. "You should think about coming back and doing what you love. There's nothing wrong with balancing both, you know." She grinned. "It might not be as fun as this," she teased, winking, "but we'd love to have you back."

Jen blew an unruly wisp of hair from her make-up free eyes. "You know, with my husband's help, there's no reason I can't balance both." She thought about it and smiled. "I'll talk to Mac and then give you a call sometime next week."

"Fantastic!"

"Thanks Abigail. I really appreciate the vote of confidence," Jen said, feeling bad about wanting to avoid the woman.

With a final nod, Abigail walked away from the van, half-waving at the kids.

Jen sat parked for a while, eating a handful of fries and thinking about the incredible offer. She looked sideways to Jillian.

"I think it's great," the teenager said. "You should go back, Mom."

Jen smiled so wide she could feel her jaw muscles stretch. *I should,* she confirmed in her mind.

The two in the back seat confused the moment of silence as an invitation to start in on round three. "Those are my tots," Bella hissed, "you have French fries, Brady."

"Enough already!" Jillian wailed.

"Guys, let's get going," Jen said, her calm demeanor halting the verbal joust, "Dad will be home from work before we know it."

Mac breathed through the final onslaught of another anxiety attack. Dazed and confused, he sat at his desk like some post-apocalyptic zombie. The attacks were starting to bring about their own set of symptoms, causing Mac to retreat into himself—making him sullen and uncommunicative. Even when the telephone rang off the hook, he didn't bother to answer it. Instead, amidst the framed colorings of his children's artwork, he picked up a picture of his family. No sooner did he have both hands on it when there was a knock at the door. He sat still, almost paralyzed.

Ross Panchley, the agency's V.P., slowly opened the door and stuck his head in. "Mac, have we brushed in the final touches on the Woodpine project?" he asked, looking for an update.

Mac gawked at his boss like the sleepwalker he was becoming.

The wise man shut the door behind him and took a seat across from Mac. "All right," he said, "let's talk about it."

Mac shook his head. "There's not much to talk about, Ross. Scott has a few good ideas, but we still have some bugs that need to be worked out. We're going to need another solid week."

"I wasn't referring to work," Ross said.

Mac looked at his supervisor with confusion until he remembered that Ross was also a friend. "I don't know, Ross," he fibbed, trying to keep his personal business personal. "I suppose I just feel a little run-down lately." He shrugged. "I can't really place my finger on it."

Ross squinted. "Have you seen a doctor?" he asked, shifting in his seat.

Mac nodded. "I...I have," he admitted, feeling his face flush, "but you know me with doctors."

Ross stood to leave. "Mac, make sure you get yourself squared away. In the meantime, no pressure but..." He was already at the door when he turned and smiled. "...but the Woodpine proposal has to be in the bag soon, or the firm's going to lose more money than it can afford to." He shut the door behind him.

Mac returned to his family photo. "Yeah, Ross," he snickered, "no pressure." As he admired the photo, he could feel the weight of his responsibilities pressing down hard on his once-broad shoulders.

∞

Mac returned home, disheveled and exhausted. Although Jen noticed, the kids missed it. They were too busy taking turns smothering him in hugs and kisses.

"How was your day, hon?" Jen asked, trying to initiate a conversation.

He didn't answer. She waited for him to inquire about her day, but he never reciprocated the same concern. Instead, he grabbed a beer from the fridge.

"How was your session with Dr. Lawrence?" she asked in a little more than a whisper.

"Another wasted hour of my life that I'll never get back," he groaned.

That's not good, Jen thought, but decided not to dig deeper until the kids were in bed. "I saw Abigail Rose today," she said. "She told me..."

With a few simple nods of his head, Mac ignored her completely.

Jen stopped and watched as her husband drank heartily from the shiny can, his eyes distant. *Now that's unusual for a weekday*, she thought. For the time being, she decided to let it go. "Come on, guys," she yelled at the kids, "dinner's ready."

A small stampede entered from the living room.

"Go wash your hands," she instructed her merry band, "all of you."

"We did," they claimed.

"Then wash them again. And this time, use soap."

Throughout dinner, besides the children's bantering, a strange silence hovered over the table. Mac was clearly in his own world, removed from the entire scene.

"So, how's the new project going?" Jen asked him.

He grunted once before taking another sip of beer.

"That good, huh?" she said, growing agitated.

Another guttural noise escaped from him.

No matter how hard I try, Jen thought, *I just can't reach him.*

Jillian exchanged several looks with her mother, clearly taking it all in.

Wiping her mouth, Jen gazed at her husband. "Mac," she said, waiting a few moments until he acknowledged her presence, "I'd like to talk about..."

"Sit on your bum at the table!" Mac yelled at Brady in a tone much angrier than seemed appropriate.

The little boy jumped from his knees to his backside, knocking his dinner plate off the table in the process. Food flew everywhere, making Mac's face turn crimson.

Oh shit, Jen thought, hurrying to her knees to start the clean-up.

"Let him do it," Mac roared, making everyone freeze. "It's his mess," he barked, "let him clean it up."

Jen looked up from her knees. "It was an accident, Mac," she said, continuing to slop the food back onto the plate.

"You baby him too much," Mac hissed, taking in breaths like a freight train preparing to derail.

The kids sat in timid silence, while Jen finished the clean-up and fetched another plate of food for Brady.

Some time passed before Mac cleared his throat, breaking the awkward silence. "I'm sorry," he said to no one in particular, "it's just work." He looked toward Jen. "That big deal we have going has to be wrapped up soon. Either that, or we lose the client entirely and I start delivering newspapers for a living." He offered a weak smile.

Okay, Mr. Hyde, Jen thought, feeling chilled by her husband's drastic mood swing. At this point, she didn't know whether or not to buy his casual demeanor. "Well then," she replied, choosing optimism, "it's a good thing Ross has you on the project." She returned the grin. "From what I hear, thirty-eight-year-old newspaper boys are a dime a dozen."

Mac's smile was even weaker than before, leaving her at a complete loss. *What the heck?* she thought, not knowing what to make of it. "Eat," she told the kids, rushing them through dinner. While Mac stared off into nothingness, Jillian's stare was burning a hole into the side of Jen's head.

Once the dishes had been dried, the family retired to the living room where they fell into their normal nightly routine. Jen picked up a book. Mac clicked on the TV. The kids played a board game until they could no longer interact peacefully.

As the bickering got loud, Mac slid to the edge of his recliner. "That's enough," he barked, his tone as sharp and angry as earlier, "put it away!"

The kids froze in place again.

Taking a deep breath, he eased back into his chair. "If you think you can behave," he said, softening his tone, "then you can watch TV with me and Mom. But if you can't do that, then you can all go to bed. Am I understood?"

Jen closed her book and gave the kids a look that said it all: *It's not a good night to test Dad.* Although they quickly did as they were told, a short time passed before she stood. "I think we need to call it an early night, guys."

Grumbling under their breath, each stopped at their dad's recliner to kiss him. "Good night, Dad," they said.

"Goodnight, guys," Mac said, his attitude instantly flipping from cranky to cuddly, "I love you."

Jen made another mental note of the sudden swing. *He's even short with the kids now,* she thought, studying his blank face, *and that's nothing like him.*

Bella, the last in the kissing line, grabbed his face. "Daddy, I hope you have a better day tomorrow," she whispered, "'cause I really love ya and I hate when you're sad."

"Thank you, princess," he said, looking ready for tears, "and I really love you, too."

Jen escorted their sweet daughter off to bed.

Mac felt bad for snapping at Brady, but the onset of another attack had cornered him into a really bad place. *I'll make it up to him,* he thought, and was already tucked in when Jen slid beneath the covers beside him.

"Bad day?" she gently asked, placing her head on his chest.

"Yup," he said, enveloped in a darkness he'd never known. Although the horrid attacks had kicked off his nightmare, he was now mired in a constant state of frustration and anger and didn't know who or what to blame.

"Dr. Lawrence isn't helping?"

"She's useless," he said, the bile rising at the back of his throat.

"If you think it's a waste of time, Mac, then why are you still going?" she asked, innocently.

"Because I'm still living in hell every day," he snapped.

Jen came off his chest and met his glare.

"And if you gave a shit," he barked, "you'd come with me and see what it's like." At last, he'd revealed a fraction of what he was feeling.

"Of course I'll come with you," she said, sounding sorrowful. "I didn't realize you wanted me to."

"And why would you?" he said, cutting her off. "You'd have to give a shit about me." Something deep inside him knew this wasn't true, but he also knew that he was suffering alone and, although it was illogical, he wondered why his wife wasn't helping him.

"That's just not true, Mac, and you know it."

"Do I?" he said, trying not to sound desperate. "From what I can tell, everything else is a priority for you."

"What, like taking care of our kids?" she said defensively, but went silent just as soon as the words left her lips. "I want to go to therapy with you, hon," she added, softening her tone, "I really do."

"You know what, don't worry about it," he said, turning his back to her, "Dr. Lawrence sucks anyway." He felt so incredibly torn; although a part of him wanted to reach out to his wife for some much-needed support, the greater part of him feared that she would discover he wasn't the man she thought he was. "Night," he mumbled.

"Goodnight," she said, and wrapped her arm around his shoulder, squeezing it tight. "I'm here for you, Mac," she whispered. "You don't need to do this alone."

Mac never uttered a word and he never budged, unable to grab hold of the lifeline his wife had just thrown him. *But I do*, he thought.

Chapter 5

In the quiet of the late hours, Mac tried to get some sleep in his leather recliner. In the distance, he thought he could hear the moans of a boy in trouble—carried on the whistling wind. He listened closely and the moans grew louder. *I have to help*, he thought, but his legs were anchored and he couldn't move. *I have to...* Suddenly, the moans turned to blood-curdling screams. "Help me," the boy shrieked. "Please...I don't want to die!" Still, Mac's legs wouldn't budge.

Gasping for air, Mac was vaulted from the chair. For a few horrid moments, he nearly screamed out to Jen for help. Instead, he stood paralyzed, bent at the waist, terrified by a world of darkness that only he could sense. While it felt like bolts of electricity were ripping through him— one shock after the next—he fought to hold on, exerting more will than he'd ever mustered. *I may not even make it to the hospital alive*, he thought. The feeling that he was going to die washed over him like a heavy acid shower. He could feel his entire existence—his very essence— plunge into a freefall. While his sweaty, quaking hands gripped the telephone receiver, he tried desperately to catch his breath as he contemplated an ambulance ride. *It's probably just a panic attack*, he heard the young E.R.

doctor say in his head, followed by the giggles of nurses. He tried to slow both his heart rate and his thoughts. *It's no use,* he realized. He could feel the damage scar his very core. *I'm in trouble.*

Then, five eternal minutes later, it was over. Exhausted, he collapsed back into his chair. Though he might have been afraid to close his eyes again—for fear of being awakened the same brutal way—he felt a strange pride that he'd never made the call. *Jen has enough to worry about with the kids,* he thought, wiping his eyes. *At least she and the kids don't have to suffer because of it.* He felt grateful for that.

Mac sat alone in the darkness for hours. Although there were so many unanswered questions, he now understood that this nightmare was going to play out the next day and each day after that. *And the symptoms are going to grow more powerful,* he realized, *until I can no longer bear them.* Like a predator in the darkest night, fear stalked nearby. Hours of blissful slumber had been replaced by the most demented reality. The nightly attacks were a rough, intense experience, testing him each time to his limits and beyond. While the rest of the world peacefully snored away, he feared blinking for too long. Living was starting to give way to basic survival, while any terrifying dreams he now experienced were replays of his actual life.

Am I losing my mind? he wondered.

Jen stepped into the living room to find Mac out cold in his recliner. She looked at the wall clock. *Great,* she thought, shaking him. "Why did you sleep out here last night, Mac?" she asked, as he struggled to open his eyes. "You realize you're already late for work, right?"

Mac flew up from the recliner. "Oh shit..." He hurried off to their bedroom to get changed.

Jen followed him, staying in the hallway. "We need to talk about me returning to work, Mac," she said through the closed door. "I was trying to tell you over dinner that I saw Abigail Rose yesterday."

"I don't have time for this right now, Jen," he yelled through the door. "I need to get to work."

"But I really need to talk," she said.

"Then talk."

"I've been thinking about Abigail Rose's offer and..."

"What offer?"

"She suggested I come back and work for the newspaper."

"Just what I need right now," he muttered.

"What's that supposed to mean?" she asked.

Mac emerged from the bedroom, half-dressed for work. "Jen, I have to get to the office." He adjusted his tie. "We'll talk when I get home, okay?"

"Okay," she said, thinking, *No more excuses.*

After the front door slammed shut. Jen started in on her morning chores. Within the hour, the kids had destroyed the breakfast table before their voices spilled through the screen door out into the back yard. Taking a seat at the kitchen table, Jen stared at the phone as if she were expecting it to ring. *Am I really ready to go back, Abigail Rose?* she thought, and looked up to find Jillian standing before her.

"What the hell's wrong with Dad?" the teenager asked.

"Watch your mouth," Jen said.

"Well, is there," Jillian asked, "something wrong with him?"

"Why do you ask?" Given her husband's recent behavior, the question seemed silly as soon as she asked it.

Jillian shrugged, clearly struggling to articulate the change she was witnessing in her father. "I don't know," she said, "something's not right with him."

"I think he's just been swamped at work," Jen said, the suggestion as much for herself as for her daughter. *Though I hope the anxiety isn't anything more than work stress,* she thought.

"Maybe," Jillian said.

"You can talk to him about it, you know. I'm sure he'd be happy to know that you're concerned about him."

"Whatever," Jillian said, indicating that she was through with the conversation.

Jen sighed. "Are you sure you don't mind watching Bella and Brady for a few hours while I have lunch with Grandma and Auntie Diane?" Jen asked. "I can just as easily cancel and..."

"Go," Jillian said. "I told you, we'll be fine."

"Are you sure?"

The teenager nodded. "No worries. I'll take care of the monsters."

At the abandoned park across from the lake, Mac took a seat on a green wooden bench. For the first time in his life, he felt lost—and alone. His entire world was starting to unravel. Lifting his cell phone, he punched in a few numbers. "Good morning, Barbara. It's Mac. Would you please let Ross know that I won't be in today. Seems my little one's given me a touch of the bug." He listened. "Right. I'll call him later. Bye."

Set adrift on the lake in the family's small sailboat, Mac pulled out a pint of vodka and took a long drink. *My life's*

anything but a dream, he thought, tears threatening to break down his cheeks.

No matter how hard he fought against it, Mac's internal battles had gotten even worse until they actually began melting into his daylight hours. More vicious than any adversary, the rubbery legs, lightheadedness, cold sweats and nausea commanded most of his waking moments. *And even when I'm in the middle of one of these attacks, I'm more afraid of the next one to come.*

He was becoming too intimate with the absolute horror of it all. *The physical and mental toll is excruciating*, he thought, *this constant feeling of doom and gloom, of utter despair.* Each sudden impact was all consuming. It seeped into every aspect of his life and threatened to ruin him socially, career-wise, and financially. He tried to sever the feelings by drinking. *It helps momentarily*, he thought, *even if it does come back to bite me hard the next day.* For a while, Mac lay in the fetal position, realizing that even being on the water felt like hell now. *There's no escaping this nightmare*, he thought, *there's no reprieve.*

Jen met her mom and sister at the neighborhood bar and grille. While Jen and Diane considered the fresh fish, Sue concentrated on the drink menu.

"The blackened salmon looks good," Diane suggested.

"And so do the margaritas," Sue added.

Jen snickered louder than she'd intended.

Sue's head flew up from the menu. Without uttering a word, she studied her daughter's face. "You want to tell me what's bothering you?"

Jen shrugged. "It's nothing."

"It's not nothing," Sue said.

Diane placed her menu on the table, more interested in the conversation.

"I really shouldn't complain," Jen said. "It's just that..."

"Just that what?" Sue prodded.

Jen took a deep breath. "Mac's been so different the last few weeks," she confessed, shaking her head. "He hasn't been his usual funny and attentive self. Even the kids are starting to pick up on it."

"Really?" Sue asked, surprised.

Jen nodded. "He doesn't want anyone to know, but..."

"But?" Diane asked, leaning in to get the scoop.

Jen's glared at her sister. "You swear you won't say a word?"

"I swear."

Jen looked at her mother.

Sue held her middle three fingers into the air. "Scout's honor."

"Mac's been having panic attacks and started seeing a therapist."

"Oh, that's awful," Sue said, "I suffered from panic attacks years ago. There's nothing worse."

"Any idea why?" Diane asked, appearing concerned.

Jen half-shrugged. "He thinks it's work stress." Her eyes welled up. "I feel so bad. I wish I knew how to help him."

"Just be there for him, Jen," her mother said. "Trust me, there's not much more you can do."

Jen nodded. "It's definitely been a little darker at the house, walking around on egg shells when Mac's in one of his moods. I've tried talking to him about me returning to work this fall, but..."

"I thought you guys had a plan?" Sue said.

"We do...or did anyway," Jen said. "The plan was to have me back on the newsroom floor once Brady started school full time. As you know, we ended up waiting another year, but the plan was, once the kids hopped on the school bus this year..." She shook her head again. "I've tried talking to Mac a couple times about it, but I think he's avoiding the subject."

"Screw that," Diane blurted.

"It's odd," Jen continued, ignoring her sister. "Mac's always supported the dream completely. In fact, it was originally his idea." She half-shrugged. "I know he's had a lot of pressure at work lately. Maybe it's just..."

"Typical man," Diane interrupted, "completely self-absorbed."

"He's suffering from panic attacks, for Pete's sake," Sue snapped back.

"Mac's an incredible husband," Jen quickly added before taking another deep breath. "He's just a little distracted right now."

Sue placed her hand on Jen's forearm. "I agree. Mac's a good man and, even if you tried, you couldn't have picked a better father for my grandchildren." She nodded. "And that's coming from someone who isn't very fond of the opposite sex right now."

Jen nodded, feeling better.

"As long as there's communication, respect and trust, love can find its way out of any problem," Sue added before giving Jen's arm a good squeeze. "Talk to him sooner than later, though," she suggested, lowering her tone. "It's important that you guys stick to the plan, or I promise that you'll end up resenting him for it."

"Yeah, you need to make sure your husband's life doesn't completely consume yours," Diane said. "To hell with any man who thinks he can just..."

"Give it a rest, Diane," Jen snapped.

Diane was often wrong, but never in doubt. Although she went silent, she could only remain in that space for a moment. "Just don't let Mac's problems pull you under," she added in a quieter tone.

Jen shook her head. "You really do need to get laid, Diane," she said.

While Diane's mouth hung open, Sue laughed so hard she nearly fell out of her chair.

The waitress arrived at the table. "Do you ladies know what you want for drinks?" she asked.

With a huff, Diane picked up her menu, concealing her scowling face behind it.

Finally composing herself, Sue asked, "What kind of tequila do you use in the house margaritas?"

Without truly knowing how he got there, Mac was perched on a barstool at the Progressive Club, just two streets up from the park. Although the lack of light in the seedy bar took his eyes a few minutes to adjust, the strong smells punched Mac right on the nose. It was like stepping into a giant ashtray that had been filled with stale beer. Pat Ruggiero, a mountain of a man with bear paws for hands and thick glasses that made his eyes look like they belonged to a walleye, was taking inventory behind his pock-marked bar. Peering up from his bottles, he shook his head at Mac, who was already wrestling with his fourth drink. Mac's upper body was nearly lying on the bar, as he gulped as much vodka as was necessary to take a break from the horrific attacks.

"Drinking for effect, I see," Pat commented in his baritone voice.

Mac slammed his empty glass on the bar, making Pat's eyes grow even larger from behind his spectacles. "I'll take another," Mac slurred.

"Someone's having a good day, huh?" the big man said, pouring another drink.

"I really don't want to talk about it," Mac said.

"Good," Pat said without missing a beat, "because I really don't want to hear about it." He half-shrugged. "It ain't that kind of joint, you know?"

While the callous bartender returned to his half-empty bottles, Mac gulped his vodka. *Then why even mention it, you stupid bastard,* he thought before swallowing hard. *You wouldn't believe what I'm going through anyway.*

Jen pulled into the driveway, feeling better. *Mom's right,* she thought, *if I don't pursue this plan of returning to work, I'll be filled with resentment. I'm definitely talking to Mac about it tonight.*

The sound of children playing in the backyard announced that her kids were okay. *At least Jill didn't let them kill each other,* she thought before taking a seat at the table. She looked at the wall phone; she couldn't help but stare. Finally, she stood, picked up the receiver and dialed. "Hi, may I speak with Abigail Rose, please?" Listening, she nodded. "I understand. Can you please tell her that Jen Anderson called. I'm available on my cell phone whenever she has a moment." She smiled. "Thank you so much."

Jen had returned to cleaning the kitchen when the telephone rang. *Wow, that was quick,* she thought, rushing to the phone. She took a deep breath. "Hello?" she answered, feeling excited.

"Hi Jen, it's Ross Panchley."

She was struck with surprise. "Oh, hi Ross," she replied, concealing her disappointment. "What's up?"

"I need to talk to Mr. Hooky for a minute," he said.

"Mr. Hooky?"

"Yeah, Mac. Could you put him on, please? I have a quick question and he's not answering his cell phone."

While Jen's stomach flopped sideways, she could feel her face flush. As she scrambled for an answer, there was an awkward moment of silence. "Actually, Ross," she babbled, "Mac stepped out for a moment. Should... should I have him call you when he gets back?"

"No, just tell him to come and see me first thing tomorrow morning," Ross said, his tone changing from playful to disappointed. He'd obviously picked up on her confusion, putting the puzzle together.

As Jen hung up the phone, a thousand bad scenarios played out in her head. *Where could he be? What if he's in trouble or hurt?* She called Mac's cell phone—twice. Both calls went directly to voicemail. With trembling hands, she picked up the receiver again and punched in some numbers—while a thousand dark thoughts ambushed her mind. "Mom, it's me. Mac didn't go to work today." There was a pause. "No, he never said where he was going." The tears were already starting to blur her vision. "I'm...I'm worried sick about him."

Jen's entire day was spent in a state of grave worry. Several times, she felt waves of fear so deep within her core that she thought she was going to vomit. She called Mac again and again—no answer. *Please God,* she silently prayed, *please let him be okay.*

A week fit itself into a day before Mac returned home, intoxicated and broken. It was well past dusk, but enough natural light remained to reveal a dent on his car's left front fender. Jen was waiting on the doorstep, her arms folded across her heaving chest. *Oh shit*, he thought. As he approached the stairs, his wife's worry was evident in her eyes. *Shit,* he repeated in his head.

"You've been out drinking all day?" she managed, her voice shaking.

"Not all day," he replied, attempting to slip past her.

She threw out her arm, stopping him at the door. "Where've you been, Mac?" Her eyes were swollen with tears. "Will you *please* talk to me and tell me what's going on."

"I'm fine, Jen," he slurred. "I needed some time to myself, so I went to the lake." He offered the embarrassed shrug of a little boy who knew he was in trouble. "Then... then I had a few drinks at the Progressive Club."

"What's going on with the panic attacks?" she asked.

"They're not as bad," he lied, "or at least...at least they're not as often."

He saw a hint of relief seep into her eyes.

I'm the one who's always solved problems, he thought, *but now I am the problem.* He wanted so badly to protect Jen and his kids from the invisible beast that stalked him.

Jen stepped into the house. He staggered in behind her and saw that all three kids were in the living room, a dreadful concern swimming in their eyes.

"Go outside and play, guys," Jen told them. "Mom and Dad need to talk."

"But our show's coming on," Bella said.

"Yeah, we want to watch the show," Brady confirmed.

"Now," Jen said firmly.

"Isn't this just great," Jillian mumbled. With an exaggerated snicker, she got up and stomped out of the room. Like two timid ducklings, Bella and Brady followed their big sister.

Jen turned to face her husband. "You told me this morning that we'd talk when you got home from work. Then, Ross Panchley called, looking for you."

Starting to sway, Mac stumbled toward their bedroom. "To hell with Ross Panchley," he burped.

"Oh, that's real nice, Mac," Jen said, close on his heels.

He collapsed onto the bed, his mouth hung open and his eyes flitting in and out of consciousness.

Jen sat on the foot of the bed. "I talked to Abigail Rose today."

He opened his eyes.

"I'm interviewing tomorrow for a reporter's position at the newspaper," she added.

He sprang up in bed. "You're what?" For reasons he didn't fully understand, even in his drunken haze the idea of his wife leaving the house petrified him. "Don't…" He hiccupped. "Don't be silly, Jen," he managed, "summer hasn't even ended yet. Besides, I've been thinking, we really don't need the money." He hiccupped.

Jen looked confused. "Babe," she said, clearly taken aback, "we had a plan. And I really need to return to work."

Collapsing back onto the bed, he let out a wounded grunt—and then a hiccup. *That's just great*, he thought, *exactly what I need right now.*

"Why is that a problem now?" she asked. "Talk to me, Mac."

He placed his forearms over his eyes. *Because I feel like I'm losing control of our life together*, he screamed in his head. He took a deep breath and hiccupped. "Of course you deserve to have your career back," he mumbled.

There was silence, and then he felt Jen's warm lips on his forehead. "Ross wants to see you first thing in the morning," she said. "And you might want to get an estimate on the fender you dented."

He listened as her footsteps drifted out of the room and, even in his drunken stupor, the heart palpitations returned.

Chapter 6

Mac's head throbbed; it was a punishment for saturating his body with alcohol and assassinating a million healthy cells. Moving ever so slowly, he ran the brush through his short hair and placed it back into the medicine cabinet. As he washed his face, he could feel something tickle the back of his neck—sending a shiver down his spine and making his skin tingle. He reached to the back of his head and swiped three times before retrieving a long, light hair. Instantly, he was filled with fury. "Who used my brush?" he roared, making his head pound harder. He stomped out of the bathroom and into the living room.

Jen and all three kids looked at him in shock.

"Who used my brush?" he repeated even angrier, holding out the single strand of hair.

There was silence, everyone frozen in fear.

"I think you might be overreacting, Mac," Jen said, standing and moving toward him.

"Overreacting?" He was beside himself.

Jen stopped in mid-stride and squared up her body, instinctively blocking her husband from their children.

"I don't ask for much," Mac said, "but I hate the feeling of long hair on my neck." He shook his head in disgust. "You all know that."

"I used it, Daddy," a small voice quivered.

Mac was glaring at the couch when Bella stood, her tiny shoulders beginning to shake from her sudden sobs.

"I'm sorry," she cried, "I...I didn't know."

Jen's face turned from confused to furious. "Enough!" she yelled back. "You're making a big deal out of nothing."

Mac opened his mouth to retort, but discovered that his angry wife wasn't nearly done.

"I'll buy you a new brush, Mac, but you're done scolding these kids for something stupid."

His lips parted again, but his words were halted by the palm of Jen's firm hand.

"Done!" she repeated, her body now positioned in a fighting posture—like a mother bear.

Mac shook his head again. "I'm going to work," he said, storming out of the house.

Feeling torn—between understanding her husband's troubles and feeling the need to defend her children from him—Jen stepped into the kitchen, away from the kids.

Jillian walked in behind her and opened the refrigerator door. "Seriously, Mom, what the hell is up with Dad?" She grabbed a bottle of orange juice, unscrewed the cap and started to place it to her lips.

"Use a glass," Jen said, letting the curse word slide.

Jillian started for the cabinet but stopped. "He's always yelling for no reason," she explained in her bratty tone. "He yells all the time now at all of us."

"Listen, I know he was wrong just now but..."

"But?"

"Doesn't he usually have a good reason for yelling?" Jen asked.

"Most of the time—no, he doesn't." Shaking her frustrated head, Jillian screwed the cap back onto the juice and put it back into the fridge—without so much as a sip. "I can't even..." She stopped.

"You can't even what?" Jen asked.

"I can't even talk to him anymore," Jillian said sadly.

"He loves you, Jill. You know that." Jen shook her spinning head. "There must be a full moon tonight," she said, "because everyone's being a little dramatic today."

"Whatever, Mom. I just can't talk to him, that's all." With a huff, she left the room.

As Jen watched her daughter stomp away, she thought, *She's definitely got a point.* It was the first time she'd ever had to get between her husband and her children—and she hated it. *I need to get my head straight for this job interview*, she thought, *and this definitely isn't helping.*

Mac sat at his desk, feeling like a fresh cadaver. *Maybe I should look for a new therapist,* he thought, *one who can actually help me.* He took a drink from a pint bottle. There was a knock at the door—one knock. As Ross entered the office, Mac quickly tucked the odorless vodka into the top drawer of his desk.

"How are you, Mac?" Ross asked, taking a seat across from him.

"Fine."

"Listen Mac, I have no idea what's happening in your personal life," Ross began, unwilling to mince words, "but I'm warning you now, you need to take care of it before it destroys your professional life."

Mac nodded. He wanted to explain, but he could see that Ross was angry and incapable of listening at the moment.

Ross stood and started for the door. As he reached the threshold, he said, "And no more stalling on the

Woodpine project. I want it completed by Friday, or you're off the account. No more excuses."

Again, Mac could only nod.

Leaving behind the sigh of a disappointed parent, Ross exited.

Mac sat alone again, feeling more overwhelmed than he could ever remember. Pulling the vodka bottle from his desk, he took a long draw. He then picked up the framed photo of his family and studied it. "What am I doing?" he mumbled, disgusted with himself. Putting the frame down, he picked up the telephone and dialed. "Scott, it's Mac, come to my office." He listened for a moment. "Yes. Right away, please."

Halfway across the city, Jen was dressed in a new red power suit, interviewing for the newspaper reporter's position.

"When you were working, how many by-lines did you produce?" Joe Bigelow, the editor-in-chief, asked.

"Several dozen," Jen answered. Although she felt nervous, she was firing the answers back as quickly as they were being asked. "I covered everything from court reporting to human interest stories," she added.

"Any preference?" he asked.

She shook her head. "I love writing...reporting," she said. "Whatever the assignment, I feel an obligation to give it every bit of my attention and effort." She nodded. "Readers deserve at least that much."

While a subtle smile peeked out from the corners of his mouth, Joe fingered through her portfolio. He was clearly impressed. "It just so happens that I have an investigative reporter's position available right now," he said before looking Jen straight in the eyes. "So, when can you start?"

Jen's eyes grew wide. *Oh my God,* she thought, *I actually got it!* "The kids begin school in a week," she said, trying not to squeal. "I can get started just as soon as I see them onto the bus."

Joe stood and extended his hand. "Well then, welcome aboard, Jen Anderson."

"Mr. Bigelow, thank you so much for this opportunity," she said, shaking his hand, "I promise you won't be sorry."

"I have no doubt," Joe said. "I look forward to working with you."

I'm finally back in the game, she thought, and squirmed with joy over the truth of it. As she left the office, she suddenly felt a sharp pang of fear. *I wonder how Mac's going to react?* It didn't take long for the sensation to subside. *Mac has always supported my decisions,* she thought, *he'll understand.*

Jen was almost at her van when she checked her watch. *Oh, I need to get the kids.* Walking on air, she picked up the pace.

Mac spoke in hushed tones to Scott, who sat across from him. "I've been thinking, Scott. I really feel that you're ready for your first big test in the ad business."

Although Scott smiled, he appeared tentative about where this was going.

"I like your ideas on the Woodpine Project," Mac explained, "and I'm prepared to let you run with them. You know, prove yourself, so to speak."

Scott slid to the edge of his seat, his face excited.

Mac leaned in. "So, I'll expect the preliminary package by tomorrow evening and the finished proposal by Friday afternoon." Offering a wounded smile, he used his remaining energy to raise an eyebrow. "Think you can handle it?"

Scott leapt to his feet. "Consider it done!" He turned to get started, but stopped dead at the door. "Want me to keep this between us?" he asked.

Mac appreciated the loyalty, but cringed. His subordinate obviously knew there was something amiss. "No," he answered, reclaiming his seat, "this is my call."

Scott shrugged. "Okay, boss. Thanks for the shot. I promise you won't be sorry."

As the young man left, Mac dropped his forehead onto his desk and moaned. His brain felt like it might actually implode. Sitting erect, he grabbed the vodka bottle from his desk drawer and took a long swig, doing his best to beat back his relentless demons. Sliding the bottle into his pocket, he prepared to leave the office. On his way out, he caught his reflection in the office window and paused before it. "You are such an asshole, Mac Anderson," he told the hazy reflection, his soul filled to a new level of self-loathing. Two breaths later, the start of a new panic attack tapped him on the shoulder. *Oh God*, he thought, *I don't know how long I can take this.*

Sophie was the only one home when Mac stepped through the front door. The house was empty. There was a note on the table. *Jill has a dentist's appointment and then we're going shopping for school clothes. I'll bring home take-out.* The note wasn't signed.

After feeding the tiny dog, Mac grabbed a beer before taking an impromptu tour of their home. As if he'd never seen the place, he studied photos of his children, their colorings on the fridge, and other things he'd forgotten to miss. Gulping down the first beer, he grabbed another before heading off to the bathroom to relieve himself.

The telephone was on its fourth ring when he hurried to pick it up. The machine answered first. Mac listened, as Abigail left Jen a surprising message. "Jen, I just spoke to Joe and he told me he offered you the investigative reporter's job and that you accepted," Abigail said excitedly. "He said you discussed some child care concerns, but that they shouldn't be a problem." There was a brief pause. "I told Joe you're the best I've ever worked with and that I can't wait to work with you again. Congratulations." She was almost giddy. "I'm absolutely thrilled!"

"You've got to be friggin' kidding me," Mac groaned.

Sophie looked up at him but never answered.

Fear instantly consumed him. "Damn it!" he said before beginning to hyperventilate, starting in on another full-blown panic attack. *My life's crumbling down all around me and Jen wants to go to work*, he thought, pacing the kitchen floor. An onslaught of unwelcome adrenaline shot through his body, numbing his limbs while simultaneously striking terror in his heart and mind. *Here we go again*, he thought, and held on for another lap through hell.

It was well past dusk when Jen returned home with the kids. Although Bella and Brady were quarreling with each other, Jillian was quiet, her mouth visibly swollen. Jen fumbled with two bags of groceries and a cardboard box filled with Chinese food. As Mac grabbed the bags from her, Jen awaited a kiss that didn't come.

Bella and Brady also headed for Mac to kiss him but stopped short.

"When were you going to tell me?" Mac asked, angrily.

"Tell you?" Jen asked surprised. "Tell you about what?"

"About the interview at the paper?"

She felt confused. "I've been talking about returning to work for weeks, Mac," she said, "but you haven't been listening." She stepped closer to him. "I'd actually planned on having a quiet night together and celebrating. I was hoping…"

Turning his back to her, Mac started for the kitchen.

Her heart skipped a beat. "Go wash your hands for dinner," she instructed the kids, trying to remain positive. It wasn't easy. *For years, I've managed this house and raised our kids*, she thought, *and when it finally comes time for me to find my own success in the world, my husband's going to be my biggest obstacle?* She couldn't believe it.

∞

A shroud of silence hung over the dinner table. There was no hiding it; the termite of miscommunication had taken a few nasty bites.

"We need you here," Mac finally blurted, sounding desperate.

"I've been here, Mac," Jen said, trying to remain calm. "Besides, the kids will be in school while I'm at work." She studied him. "If we work together, there's no reason we can't…"

He popped to his feet, threw his chair under the table and stormed off, leaving Jen absolutely befuddled.

As she sat in quiet contemplation, trying to make sense of it all, it didn't take long to decide, *I'm taking the job. I need to. The health of my soul depends on it.* She shook her head.

There was silence, the kids squirming with the realization that their parents were engaged in another heated battle. "Why do you guys fight all the time now?" Bella asked.

"Don't worry about it, sweetheart," Jen said. "This is between your father and me. We'll be fine."

"Sure Mom," Jillian mumbled sarcastically, her mouth still swollen.

They all looked at their mom in disbelief.

"Just finish your dinner, please," she told them.

The anxious silence droned on.

After tucking the young ones in, Jen found her puffy-eyed husband sitting in his recliner staring off into space. *We need to talk this out*, she thought. "Ready for bed?" she asked Mac.

He nodded and, without a word, followed her into the bedroom. As she got changed, she watched him strip to his underwear, turn on the TV and sit at the edge of the bed, entranced. She took a seat beside him. "All right now, do you want to tell me what's going on? We've had a plan in place for years and now it's a problem."

He stared at the TV.

Momentarily abandoning her hope of discussing the newspaper job, she adjusted her focus. "Just because Dr. Lawrence didn't work out, that doesn't mean you shouldn't find a therapist who can..." She stopped.

He continued to stare at the TV.

She grabbed the remote, turned off the set and stood in front of him.

He gazed up, almost catatonically. "I'm fine, babe," he lied.

To her surprise, those three dismissive words unlocked an arsenal of dark emotions that she didn't realize she'd been keeping at bay. "You're not fine," she snapped back. "You won't tell me what's going on with you, but you stomp around this house angry at every-one. I don't even know if you're still getting the anxiety attacks. Or if you've completely swapped out your medicine for alcohol."

Mac could barely maintain eye contact.

Jen stared at him. "I've tried to figure out how I can help you, Mac, and make things better. I swear I have. I've asked again and again, but you won't let me in." She paused, trying to remove the quiver from her voice. "If you want to lock me out, then there's nothing..."

"I think my creative juices have dried up on me," he mumbled, an explanation that seemed to surprise him even more than her.

What? He's never failed at work, she thought. *Why does he fear it now?* "Don't be stupid," she told him, "you're the best in the business. I know it. You know it. And everyone else knows it, especially Ross."

Mac offered a half-smile in trade for her encouragement.

"Is that what this is all about?" she asked.

He looked into her eyes; it only lasted a moment but it was a glimpse of her husband, the man that hadn't been around for weeks.

"And I'm not sure you still remember," she whispered playfully into his ear, jumping at the chance to connect on a deeper level with him, "but work isn't the only thing you're good at."

His eyes had already drifted off. "Huh?" he asked. "What?"

Jen said nothing, a heavy sigh her only proof of frustration.

Mac returned to reality for a moment. "Come here," he said.

Almost involuntarily, she rolled onto him, where they started to play and become intimate.

Suddenly, Mac froze. "Wait," he said, "I... I can't."

Are you kidding me? Jen thought, releasing another sigh.

"I'm sorry, babe, but I just had an idea," he said, pushing her off him. "If I don't write this stuff down now..." He jumped up and headed for the door, leaving his wife half-naked.

"Fine," she said, hardly concealing her disappointment, "get to work then. I'm going to sleep."

Without accomplishing anything significant, Mac returned to bed a few hours later. He looked at his wife. *She's already sleeping,* he thought. *It must be nice.* He sat on the edge of the bed, preparing to face another bout with pain. *She has no idea,* he thought, never considering that this truth was of his own doing. His fear-inspired insomnia had become a nightly routine. *I can't get any rest or find any peace.* He looked at Jen again. *I can't feel anything but fear and sorrow now.*

Jen awoke early to find Mac already gone. Sitting erect, she slid up in the bed, pulling her knees to her chest. She stared at the empty pillow beside her, thinking, *I can't believe how much Mac has changed.* As much as she was concerned about him, she was equally bewildered. *He's become a shadow of the man I've always known,* she realized, but the real reasons for this remained a puzzle with several missing pieces. She'd never felt so frustrated and scared.

Jen's right, Mac thought on his way to work, *but the idea of her leaving the house now—* Panic plucked another cord in his heart, causing shivers.

On the drive, he pondered how much he'd changed. *What's odd is that daily stressors don't seem to be real factors at all.* In fact, he was so wired all the time that he actually felt comfortable under duress. *It's when I'm at ease that the world begins to unravel and I can't breathe or swallow or even walk.* If he was sitting still, he'd suddenly want to jump up and flee from some invisible enemy. *And when I'm in public, I feel like the walls are closing in all around me and I'm going to lash out and hurt someone.* He shook his head. *Even during prayer, I can't avoid the feeling of being in danger.* Often, he found himself alone in the living room, drinking vodka and wondering when and if his courage would ever return. *I probably shouldn't have stopped talking to Jen about all of this,* he thought, *but I'd rather she focus on the kids until I can get my shit together.* The idea of being a selfish father seemed much more painful than the torment he suffered alone.

Chapter 7

The Anderson family—minus Jillian—was seated at the kitchen table, preparing to dive into another home-cooked dinner.

"Where's..." Mac began to ask.

Without a word, Jillian took a seat at the table. Her face was flush.

She's been crying, Mac realized. "What's wrong?" he asked, as he reached for the bowl of mash potatoes.

"Nothing," Jillian said, trying to dismiss him with a subtle shake of her head.

"I asked you what's wrong," he barked, making her eyes go wide and her siblings sit up straight.

"The kid that's been bullying me," she began, clearly trying to contain her emotions, "no matter what I say or do, he won't stop."

Mac dropped the big plastic spoon. "You're being bullied?" he asked, feeling his own face burn red. A cauldron of rage bubbled just beneath the surface.

Jillian nodded. "And he's relentless," she muttered.

Mac studied his daughter's avoiding eyes. *She's legitimately scared*, he thought. Out of the corner of his eye, he saw Jen squirming in her seat.

"He keeps calling me a lesbian," Jillian added, "and..."

"Why is he calling you a lesbian?" Mac interrupted, distracted from his rising anger. "Not that there's any-thing wrong with..."

"I know that, Dad, but I'm not a lesbian," Jillian huffed. "He's just trying to hurt me and get other people to join in the fun."

Mac was now on his feet. "How long has this been going on?" he growled.

Bella and Brady began nervously fidgeting in their chairs.

"It started at the end of school last year," Jillian explained, "but then he started bullying me on Facebook this summer. I told Mom…"

"What?" Mac screeched, redirecting his attention toward his wife. "You knew about this?" he roared, spittle flying from his bottom lip.

Eyes wide, Jen nodded. "Yes, Mac, I did. Jillian told me that some punk was…"

"And you kept it from me?" he interrupted.

"I didn't keep anything from you. Jill and I talked about it, and she wanted to handle it herself."

"And you didn't think I needed to know about it?"

Peering into his eyes, Jen leaned in to Mac—as though she were about to speak in code—and said, "You had other things going on and didn't need anything more to worry about."

"I'm her father," Mac snapped back, unwilling to even entertain that his wife had been considerate. "It's my job to protect this family." He shook his head. "But I can't do my job if I don't know what's going on around here, can I?" He looked toward Jillian. "Who is this little bastard?"

Bella and Brady began to cry.

The panic in Jillian's eyes grew. "He's no one, Dad. I'll…I'll make him stop."

"Oh, I think we're beyond that now," Mac said. "I want his name and I want to know where he lives."

"No Dad, please," the teenager begged, "he's just a stupid kid."

"I'm not going to say a word to him, Jill. But his father and I are going to have a nice heart-to-heart talk." Mac could feel a river of adrenaline rushing through his throbbing veins.

"But Dad..."

"Mac," Jen interjected; she was now on her feet as well.

Whimpers from Bella and Brady played dreadfully in the background.

"What's his name, Jill?" Mac asked, ignoring his pleading wife and frightened young ones.

Jillian hung her head and began to cry. "Ronnie Stevens."

"And where does this Ronnie Stevens live?"

"You can't go over there, Mac," Jen protested. "There are other ways we can deal with this."

"Where?" Mac yelled, still focused on his teenage daughter.

"On...on Gifford Road," she whimpered, "the green house right on the side of the school."

Mac threw his chair under the table and marched toward the front door.

"Mac, don't," Jen yelled, on his heels. "It'll only make things worse."

"I'll never tell him anything again," Jillian called out from the kitchen before joining her sister and brother in a chorus of sobs.

Mac never looked back. "Let's see if the little bastard ever bullies you again," he said and, with a primal grunt, slammed the front door behind him.

∞

Before he knew it, Mac was standing on the front step of the Stevens' green house. He pushed the doorbell, never letting up.

The front door flew open, replaced by an annoyed man standing in the threshold. "What is it?" the home-owner asked, clearly not happy with the rude intrusion.

"Are you Ronnie Stevens' father?" Mac asked, getting right to the point.

"Who the hell are you?" Mr. Stevens asked.

"The name's Mac Anderson and my daughter, Jillian, just told me that your son's been bullying her."

Mr. Stevens' brow folded in disbelief. "That doesn't sound like Ronnie."

"Because he's a great kid," Mac jumped in, "and he'd never do something like that, right?"

"Listen buddy…"

"No, you listen, *buddy*. If you can't teach your kid to be a gentleman, I'm happy to come back and teach him the lesson myself."

"Is that a threat?" Mr. Stevens' stammered, his voice rising a full octave.

"Oh, not at all, *buddy*. It's a promise," Mac said through gritted teeth. Throbbing with rage, he took a step forward, causing Mr. Stevens to backpedal into his house. "Just make sure Ronnie leaves my daughter alone." Mac turned and started down the steps.

"If you ever come back here again," Mr. Stevens called out, trying to retain some dignity, "I'm calling the police."

Mac stopped at the bottom of the stairs, turned and glared at the wide-eyed man. "And if your son ever picks on my girl again, the cops won't be able to help either one of you."

Trembling from anger, Mac sat in his parked car for a long while. *What the hell was that?* he wondered, realizing that he'd completely lost control. *I've never threatened a person in my life.*

The next few days whipped by in some trance-like blur for Mac. On Saturday, the last family outing of the summer was planned for the local zoo. Even in the thick heat, a frigidness hung between him and Jen.

"Did you remember to pack the cooler with ice?" she asked him on the drive there.

"I don't remember you asking me to," he countered.

"I have to remind you to fill the cooler with ice now?" she said.

"How's that?" he asked, his blood pressure on the rise.

She never responded; she just looked at him with a blank face.

"If you have something to say, Jen, then..."

Jillian cleared her throat loudly in the back seat. "Another fantastic family memory," she mumbled under her breath.

The car returned to silence.

∞

As if they were on a mission, every animal from the white tiger to the three-toed sloth was visited. While Mac spent time explaining and discussing each species, Jen took charge of the picture taking and distribution of snacks. Toward the end of their concrete safari, Brady noticed one of the zoo keepers standing inside of the lion's enclosure.

"Hey look, Dad," the excited boy called out, "that guy's standing right near the lion and he doesn't even look afraid."

Mac wrapped his arm around his son's shoulder. "Now that's a brave man, huh? I bet if you wanted to, Brady, you could be a zoo keeper when you grow up."

Brady shook his head. "No Dad," he said with conviction, "when I grow up, I want to be just like you."

Jen walked away from the lion's enclosure with Jillian and Bella in tow.

Taken aback by the sincerity in his young son's voice, Mac's eyes watered. "No son," he whispered under his breath, "you can do a lot better than that."

"Can we get ice cream now?" Brady asked, hurrying to catch up with his mother and sisters.

"You can get anything you want, buddy," Mac called out, lagging behind the group.

The newspaper read *September 4*. Jen gushed over her first published by-line since returning to work. On his way by her desk, Joe Bigelow stopped. "It didn't take you long to keep your promise, Jen," he said. "Great piece on the Board of Health cover up. I'm not sure they appreciate it, but I do." He winked. "It's a fine piece of journalism."

Jen couldn't recall the last time she'd felt so proud— *or happy*.

Abigail Rose stepped up next and patted her on the back. "You've even made me look good," she whispered, "so I'm buying lunch."

Joel Ward, the newspaper's photographer, quickly joined in on the celebration. "Did I hear someone mention a free lunch," he teased, "'cause this diva's famished." He jammed his ring-clad thumb into his chest.

The girls laughed.

"Fine," Abigail said, "but Jen can order whatever she wants." She looked back at Joel. "And you're being held to a ten-dollar limit."

Laughing, the three of them headed off to the local pub. Even with all the excitement, Jen thought, *I can't wait to get home and share this with Mac.* Her proud eyes misted over. *He'll finally be able to understand what this work means to me.*

∞

It was nearly five o'clock before Jen arrived home, beaming like a kid on Christmas Eve. Her pocketbook wasn't even off her shoulder when she shoved her first article in Mac's face. "It just ran this morning," she said, unable to contain her excitement. "Joe told me he thinks it's a great piece."

While Mac slowly read the article, Jen spoke to Jillian about the "incredible" photographer who'd been assigned to her. "Joel's photography is the best I've ever seen," she said excitedly. "He's got such a way of expressing his passions through his work."

"Really?" Mac blurted. sarcastically.

"He's really good, Mac," Jen said, innocently.

"Well, good for Joel," Mac said before folding up the newspaper and handing it back to her. "Nicely done," he said before nonchalantly patting her arm. "Congratulations." His words echoed with emptiness.

She felt crushed. *If he was any more excited about my success, he'd be sleeping*, she thought and began to cry.

Ignoring her, Mac turned to his daughter. "Come on, Jillian, you need to finish your summer assignment. Get it out. I'll help you."

He's so cold, Jen thought, throwing a dishtowel across the kitchen and rushing out of the room. *That's the last time I share any of my writing with him*, she thought, the hurt and regret growing stronger. *I should've known better,* she cursed herself.

∞

In their darkened bedroom, Mac threw on a pair of pajama bottoms. Jen wore an old nightgown. Both bitter and exhausted, they slid beneath the bed covers.

Jen's cell phone rang. She grabbed the phone, looked at the caller ID and sent the call to voicemail.

"Who the hell's calling you at this time of night?" Mac asked, feeling his hackles rise.

"It was Joel, my photographer at work."

"Why is he calling you so late?"

"How do I know?" she said. "I didn't take the call, did I?"

"It seems strange to me that some guy…"

"Joel's not some guy," Jen said, cutting him off. "He's gay."

"Sure, he is," Mac responded, still on the defensive.

While moonlight illuminated Jen's silhouette, she rolled over, placing her back to Mac. "He is gay, Mac," she repeated. "Not that it should make a difference either way."

"What does that mean?" Mac asked.

"It means that there's no reason for you to be jealous. I would never…"

"I'm not jealous," Mac quickly countered.

"Okay," she said and lay motionless—her back still to him.

In the silence, he shook his head. "Well, goodnight," he muttered, stretching to give her a kiss.

Although subtle, she moved away from him.

"What is it now?" he asked.

"Nothing," she said, yawning, "I'm just not feeling well, that's all. Is that okay?"

"I guess it has to be okay, doesn't it?" he snickered. "Seems to me that you're the one who should go see a doctor," he continued. "You haven't felt well for a while." There was an aggravated pause. "At least not with me."

"What are you talking about? I tried to initiate love-making with you a few days ago."

He said nothing.

"And what does that mean," she exploded, "at least not with you?"

"Nothing," Mac muttered in a whisper. "Joel's gay, right?"

Sighing heavily, Jen shifted her weight, trying to settle into a comfortable position for the night.

While Mac placed his hands behind his head and stared into the darkness, Jen pretended to fall asleep—*again*. But her frigidness would prove no match for the unforgiving anxiety that was preparing to steal Mac's sleep. He was already filled with worry over Jen having an affair at work. *Jen claims Joel's gay, but he's definitely trying to get close to her.* In one part of his brain, the idea of his wife cheating was absolutely ludicrous. But logic wasn't actually in command most of the time now. *How does she know he's gay?* Mac wondered. His imagination was in high gear and his thought process wasn't about to take him to any place nice.

During breakfast, Jen never even looked at Mac. *She's still pissed off,* he thought. "No breakfast today?" he asked.

"There are bagels in the fridge," she said, finally acknowledging his presence. "They're easy enough to toast."

A sucker shot of anger made his face burn. He stood to leave the room.

"Where do you think you're going?" she asked.

"I need to get ready for work," he said, glaring at her.

"I told you," she said, shaking her head, "Joe set a ten o'clock deadline for me, so you'll have to truck the kids around today." She began writing instructions.

"Well, isn't that considerate of Joe?" Mac said, rage boiling up in him. "Doesn't he remember you still have kids? I don't understand why he can't assign the early assignments to someone else."

On cue, all three kids got up from the table, threw their breakfast dishes into the sink and hurried out of the room—a bad look from Jillian being left behind.

Jen sighed, halting Mac's spiel. "Joe also understands that the kids have a father," she countered, her words dripping with sarcasm.

Mac was beside himself. "I have work too!" he yelled.

Jen continued to write. "Then you'll need to work something out, won't you? They're your kids, too, Mac." As he struggled to maintain his composure, she added. "They can take the bus this morning, but you'll need to pick them up from school." She slid the paper toward him. "I've written the times down here."

Mac gritted his teeth, but before he could speak Jen rattled off a list of places to transport the kids. "Jill is staying after for basketball practice. Bella has to be at dance by four and Brady usually gets a snack as soon as he gets home."

You can't be friggin' serious, he thought.

"He likes those animal crackers," she finished.

"Are you sure that's everything, Jen," he barked, "'cause God knows I don't have any work of my own to get done."

"Welcome to parenthood, Mac," she said, minus the venom he'd injected into his words. "I'll bring home take-out, so the kids will have something to eat for dinner." She left the kitchen, said goodbye to the kids in the living room and shut the front door behind her.

"Damn it!" Mac moaned, snatching the paper off the table and looking at it. "You've got to be fuckin' kidding me." For a moment, he stared at the door, feeling dizzy on the toxic cocktail of emotions that fizzed inside him.

Mac entered the living room to find Jillian, Bella and Brady already dressed for school and watching TV.

"Did you guys eat breakfast?" he asked, at a loss over their normal routine.

They all nodded, never looking away from the TV.

"Yup," Jillian said, "you saw us eat breakfast."

"Everybody have a snack," he asked, ignoring her disrespectful tone, "or whatever you need for school?"

They all nodded, still hypnotized.

"Yup," Jillian said.

Clueless, he continued his line of questioning. "Everybody's homework's done?"

"We don't have homework yet, Dad," Bella said, her eyes glued to the TV. "We just started school."

Mac stepped in front of the television.

"We still have five minutes, Dad," Brady groaned.

"But I have work to get done," Mac said, "that is, if you don't mind." He looked at Jillian. "Can you walk them to the bus stop?"

"Sure, but Mom usually..."

"Good," he said, cutting her off. "Then I'll pick you up after school."

"Do you know the times?" Jillian asked, skeptically.

Mac nodded, displaying his instructions. "Mom was nice enough to write them down for me."

Picking up on the sarcasm, Jillian rolled her eyes.

After Bella and Brady kissed their dad, the kids left the house for school.

Mac looked at Jen's instructions one more time and, shaking his head, threw it onto the end table. He picked up his cell phone and dialed. "Hi Barbara, it's Mac. Please tell Ross I'll be working from home again today." He nodded. "Thanks."

With a pad of paper in his lap, he tried to do some work—but struggled terribly with it. *This is pathetic,* he thought. As he started to fidget, he grabbed the remote control. The TV was a nice distraction and he watched for a few minutes before nodding off.

Mac watched as Jen and the kids sat parked in an abandoned lot, laughing over something Mac couldn't make out. Out of nowhere, a speeding car slammed into the side of their van, nearly tipping it onto its side. Mac screamed out, but there was no sound. He tried to run to his family but his legs wouldn't cooperate. He saw Jillian's face in the passenger window; it was dripping in blood. He screamed again. There was silence. And then Jillian turned to look at him, only it wasn't Jillian's face any more. It was a boy, a teenage boy, begging for Mac's help.

Glistening in sweat, Mac awakened. Trying to recapture his stolen breath, he sat up straight and waited for reality to take hold. He glanced down at his wristwatch. "Oh shit," he said, jumping to his feet. He began searching frantically for the paper detailing the kids' pick-up times. He found it on the end table. After a quick glance, even more panic flooded him. *Damn it,* he thought before sprinting out of the house to get the kids. *The entire day's gone without a lick of work to show for it*, he realized. *I'm so screwed.*

Jillian, Bella and Brady stampeded into the house, with Mac behind them. "Guys, I still need to finish up some work," he told them, "so I'll be in the kitchen. Do you have homework to get done?"

"Not yet, Dad," Bella answered. "We just started the new school year."

Mac nodded. "That's right, you told me that already. Then watch TV or go upstairs and play...whatever. Just keep it down so I can get my work done."

"I'm hungry, Dad," Brady said.

"Then go grab a snack, Brady. Mom said she's bringing home take-out for dinner."

While the kids headed for their bedrooms, Mac grabbed his papers and moved to the kitchen to work alone on a new project. *Scott bailed me out on the Woodpine deal,* he thought, *but it isn't going to go that way again.* He pondered the recent weeks of failure at work and felt disappointed in himself for letting everyone down, especially himself. *And this new project is already threatening to make or break my career.*

As Mac paced the floor, one creative block after the other triggered the start of another anxiety attack. He couldn't concentrate and was pouring a drink to relax when Brady and Sophie barged in.

"Dad, can I..."

"Get out!" Mac screamed at his son. "I told you I'm trying to get some work done in here. Get out now!"

The young boy stood frozen in shock, while Sophie bared her tiny teeth and growled.

Jillian burst into the room, grabbed Brady and shot her dad a look that made a panic attack seem like a giggle fit. "He was only looking for a snack, Dad," she said disgustedly before pushing Brady out of the room, with Sophie on their heels.

"Damn it," Mac roared, tossing a ream of papers into the air. As they floated to the floor, he stood and finished pouring his drink. He tipped the glass to his lips and drank hard, savoring the slow burn. Shaking his head, he grabbed a box of animal crackers and headed for the living room.

He found that his children were now timid—even fearful—in his presence. *Shit,* he thought. "I'm sorry, Brady," he said, "Daddy didn't mean to snap at you like that. It's just that..." He stopped and took a seat on the floor. "How 'bout we just watch some TV together?"

Jillian and Brady looked at their father like he had three heads, while Bella clicked on the remote control. "It's my turn to pick," she announced.

They each took a seat on the couch where they ate animal crackers and watched TV.

"Dad?" Jillian said, tentatively.

"What is it?"

"We can't just have animal crackers for dinner."

Mac looked at the front door and nodded, angrily. "Mom's supposed to be bringing home dinner."

"But it's already past dinner time," Jillian reminded him.

"Then order a pizza."

Jillian stood. "Fine."

While she headed for the kitchen to make the call, Mac climbed up on the couch with his two youngest children.

"Dad," Bella said, "there's this terrible girl at school."

"What girl?" Mac managed, still preoccupied with staring at the front door.

"Her name's Ali."

"What's wrong with Ali?" he asked, still distracted.

"What's not wrong with Ali?" Bella said. "She's always in everybody's business and sometimes she even bullies people."

Mac looked at his daughter. "There's no such thing as a bully if you don't allow it, right?"

"I know that, Dad. She's not dumb enough to mess with me."

Grinning, Mac turned to Brady and shrugged. "I know I wouldn't mess with Beans," he teased.

Bella laughed.

"And I'm having trouble with math, Dad," Brady said, joining in the conversation. "It's stupid and I can't do it."

"It's not stupid, Brady," Mac told him, "and we never use the word *can't* in this house. You know that."

As Jillian returned from the kitchen, Jen walked through the front door, holding two pizza boxes. She cautiously approached Mac.

"You're late," he said; it sounded like a growl.

"Sorry, but there was a staff meeting that went over and I couldn't..."

"We've already ordered pizza," he snapped.

"You're already learning how to improvise with the kids," she muttered under her breath. "Not so easy, is it?"

He opened his mouth but nothing came out. *Bitch*, he thought, the throbbing vein in his forehead threatening to burst open and bleed him out. He gritted his teeth, preparing to do battle.

The kids looked up at him, their frightened eyes halting them both.

Not knowing what else to do, Mac stormed off to his bedroom.

Chapter 8

A week of dark nights passed. Mac was sitting in his recliner when he heard Jen laughing with one of his children in the kitchen. He muted the television to listen in.

"Mrs. Brown said that you didn't mean to hurt the class turtle," Jen said, laughing, "but that she'd like you not to turn him on his back anymore."

Mac pushed down the lever on his recliner and started for the kitchen.

"He looked tired to me, Mom," Brady said, "so I tried to put him to sleep."

"But that's not how turtles sleep," Jen said, laughing more.

Mac opened the door—and the two went silent. "What's so funny?" he asked.

Jen took a deep breath and sighed. Brady smiled. "Mrs. Brown told Mom that I was playing with the class turtle when I shouldn't have been."

Mac looked at Jen. "When did she tell you that?"

"At the parent / teacher conference," Brady reported.

Mac's rising blood pressure threatened to pop his head clean off his shoulders. "Are you friggin' kidding me?" he said through gritted teeth. "You're still keeping shit from me?"

Brady made a beeline for the door and disappeared from the room.

"You're erratic now, Mac, unpredictable," Jen replied, her flaring nostrils matching his rage. "There's no way I was going to let you humiliate our children again."

"Humiliate our children?"

She nodded, confidently. "After your insane reaction to Jillian's bullying situation, I wasn't going to risk..."

"My insane reaction worked though, didn't it?" he roared. "Jillian hasn't been bullied since, has she?"

"No, she hasn't, Mac," Jen hissed, "and you did such a good job protecting her that a lot of her classmates won't even talk to her anymore."

His eyebrows rose in surprise.

"That's right," Jen said, "but you wouldn't know that because you're so consumed with your own world that you have no idea what's going on in your children's lives." Jen glared at him. "Not that Jillian would ever share anything like that with you again."

Mac was taken aback, watching helplessly as his wife brushed past him and left the kitchen.

The following morning, Mac had just endured an intense anxiety attack and was slouched in the corner of his park bench when Brandt took a seat beside him.

"How did you know I was here?" Mac asked, sitting up and discreetly wiping his eyes.

"I had a hunch."

"I just called out sick from work," Mac confessed.

"I figured," Brandt said, looking at the flask. "It's a little early for a drink, don't you think?"

Mac shrugged. "I don't know what to think anymore, Brandt."

Brandt studied Mac's face. "You know, I've seen that face before."

"Oh yeah? And where's that, the gutter?"

"No," Brandt said, shaking his head, "the mirror."

Mac stared at his friend but said nothing.

"Do you want to talk about it?" Brandt asked. "Maybe we can figure it out together."

Mac felt insulted. "Why don't we just have a drink together instead?"

"We both know that's not going to help anything, Mac," Brandt said before leaning in closer. "Come on, you can talk to me. What's really eating at you?"

"It's just...I don't know," Mac said. "I'm going through a rough patch and the only thing my wife can think about is her own career. I need her to be there for me."

Brandt looked surprised. "Are you crazy, man? Your wife sacrificed everything to raise your kids."

"I know that, but...but I just feel off most of the time, Brandt," Mac said, his voice cracking. "I've struggled to understand why, but I just can't figure it. Nothing's really changed, not that I know of anyway. But I'm in the dumps all the time now, and that's when I'm not worried about having a stroke or expecting my heart to explode."

"Does Jen know?"

"She knows I've had panic attacks and that I went to speak to a therapist about them," Mac said.

"So you're in therapy," Brandt said, "that's a good thing."

"Not anymore," Mac admitted. "The shrink I was seeing was a complete buffoon. I'd ramble on and on, and she never once offered any advice to help me get past the attacks."

"There are definitely some bad therapists out there. But they're not all bad. Sometimes you have to try out a few until you find the one that fits," Brandt said, grinning at his clever wording.

Mac's face remained stoic.

"So, Jen knows you're suffering and that you're not in therapy?" Brandt tried to clarify.

Mac half-shrugged. "She still tries to talk to me about it, but I do everything I can to avoid the topic."

"Why?"

"To protect her from it, I guess," Mac said.

"Protect her?" Brandt repeated, surprised. "Listen Mac, you're not going to protect *anyone* by trying to hide any of this." He took a deep breath, exhaling slowly. "Trust me, you're not alone, my friend. Few people know this, but I've been suffering from anxiety and depression for years."

"Anxiety and depression," Mac repeated, adding a snicker. "It just doesn't make sense. You've seen my kids, my beautiful wife. I have a great job, a nice home."

Brandt grabbed a pen from his jacket pocket, as well as a folded white envelope. Tearing off a piece, he jotted down a telephone number and handed it to Mac. "His name's Faust Fiore. He's one of the best therapists out there. Give him a call, Mac." He stood to leave. "And you should let Jen know what's going on. She's your wife, for God's sake." He patted Mac's shoulder. "There's no reason to go through this alone, buddy. Believe me, it'll only make things worse."

Mac nodded. "Thanks Brandt."

As Brandt left, Mac looked at the piece of paper before sliding it into his pants pocket. "It'll only make things worse," he said under his breath, adding a snicker. "How in the hell can things get any worse than this, Brandt?" He took a long drink.

Avoiding a visit to the Progressive Club, Mac went home to see if he could get some actual work done. He was at the kitchen table, his head buried in a ream of blank papers when Jillian walked in. "What do you want?" he asked her.

She looked sideways at him, her face painted with disgust. She didn't reply.

"I just asked you a question," he said, his voice louder.

"I came to get a drink. Don't worry, I won't bother you."

"Then make it quick," he said.

"Whatever," she mumbled.

Mac detested the word, as it either served as a term of surrender or a disrespectful dismissal. Instinctively getting to his feet, the hair on the back of his neck stood erect like the hackles of an attack dog. "What did you just say to me?" he hissed.

In an instant, Jillian's face changed from cocky to frightened. "I'm...I'm sorry," she stuttered, her voice thick with emotion. She hurried out of the room, never getting her drink.

Mac swallowed hard. "Damn it," he said, giving it some thought. *If I live a hundred years, I doubt I'll ever be able to erase that scared look on Jill's face from my memory.* He shook his sorrowful head. *And I caused that.*

He walked over to the window to see Jillian out in the backyard. Tipping the vodka glass to his lips, he gulped until his throat was set on fire. With one last swallow, he slammed down the glass and slid on his shoes.

Beneath a shedding tree, Mac approached Jillian. "Sorry about yelling at you like that," he said.

The teenager shrugged. "What..." She stopped before completing her favorite word. "It's fine," she said, obviously fibbing.

"No, it's not fine," Mac said. "I'm sorry. I am." He looked up at the sky. "I've just been really tired lately and stressed from work..." He shook his head. "Can you forgive me?"

She half-shrugged, still avoiding any sustained eye contact.

"Wanna have a game of catch?" Mac asked. But before she could answer, he ran off to the shed and grabbed two mitts.

Although Jillian tried to conceal her excitement, from the moment the first ball was thrown neither could stop smiling.

Mac punched his fist into the old catcher's mitt, while Jillian bit on her bottom lip in a display of intense concentration. "Come on, Jill," Mac encouraged, "right down the pipe. Let's see what you've got."

The girl let one fly. The slap of leather caused Mac to stand and pump his arm. "Strike!"

Jillian nodded.

"That's what I'm talking about," Mac said proudly. "You keep throwing the ball like that and you'll be in the playoffs next season for sure."

Sharing the late autumn sunshine, the two continued to play catch. Sophie was just happy to run back and forth between them, doing her best not to get stepped on.

When they finally came in from their much-needed one-on-one time, Mac found Jen and Brady seated at a cluttered kitchen table. Jen was helping their youngest boy with a fundamental math problem: six plus seven. Brady struggled as much with the reasons for learning the math as with the problems themselves.

"It's stupid," Brady claimed. "I can't."

Jen began to answer. "Brady, I already told you..."

Without thinking, Mac took a seat. "It's not stupid, Brady," he interrupted, taking over without meaning to, "and I've told you, we never use the word *can't* around here." Mac smiled. "Son, math is just another way to open your mind and flex your brain." He lifted his arm to flex his bicep. In spite of himself, Brady giggled. Mac ruffled the small boy's hair.

Jen stood. "My God, Mac, when did we stop working as a team all together?"

Mac felt confused. "Huh?"

She walked away, shaking her head.

Instinctively, Mac stood and started after her—but he stopped. Though he felt bad, he chose to take care of his son. Even as he reclaimed his seat at the table, he knew it was the wrong choice.

"Thirteen," Brady answered.

"What?" Mac asked, looking back at his son.

"The answer is thirteen," said the young boy.

Mac looked down at the paper. One eyebrow rose in a display of confirmation. "You're absolutely right. Thirteen it is." He then looked toward the living room where Jen had disappeared. *I didn't mean to interfere and one-up her*, he thought.

Brady patiently awaited his father's attention.

Mac caught his son's blank face and smiled. "I'm telling you, Brady, all you have to do is apply yourself and someday you'll be flying the space shuttle for NASA."

Brady's dancing eyebrows considered the possibility before his innocent eyes showed belief.

Mac and Brady became consumed in the remaining problems of addition and subtraction, completing the homework assignment in record time.

Once Jillian and Brady had been tended to, Mac ventured off to Bella's bedroom. He knelt beside his little girl in a room awash in pink. Together, they spoke to

God. "Now I lay me down to sleep," Bella prayed, "I pray the Lord my soul to keep. If I should die before I wake, I pray the Lord my soul to take."

There was a pause. Mac nodded for her to continue.

"Father," she said, "please bless my mom, my dad, my brother and sister, and Sophie—our dog. Amen." As an afterthought, she added, "Oh, and God, please make Mommy and Daddy stop fighting."

"Amen," Mac agreed before tucking his innocent child into bed and pulling the covers under her chin. He finished the nightly ritual with a kiss. "Sweet dreams, princess," he whispered.

"Sweet dreams, Daddy."

He paused at the door to catch one last glimpse of his yawning angel. *From the mouth of babes,* he thought, sadly turning off the light.

Jen stepped into her bedroom a few hours later, finding it in complete darkness—and Mac asleep. *He's probably just faking,* she thought, considering her own survival strategies as of late. *At least I'm not the one who has to pretend tonight.* She stared at him for a long while. *One second he's barking at Jillian,* she thought, *and the next, he's playing catch with her.* She inhaled deeply. *How did we ever end up here?* she wondered, still unable to understand how things had turned so bad so quickly. *And wherever we're heading, it doesn't feel like the same place.* Something had recently snapped in her—like a switch being thrown—and she knew it. She was now more concerned with being a protective mother than a supportive wife—*who continues to be neglected and abused by her husband.*

No matter how many times it occurred, Mac was no match for the instant startle sensation. Struggling for oxygen, he sat up straight in bed. As if in imminent danger, his body froze while his mind sensed the primal need to flee. But two invisible chains had tethered his legs. The symptoms came on fast and furious: heavy sweating, hyperventilation, spiraling thoughts of impending doom, nausea, twitching and tightness of the body—even a thumping heart that felt like it randomly skipped a beat.

As quietly as possible, he got up, grabbed his pillow and headed for the living room.

Shutting off the lights, he collapsed onto the couch, trying desperately to ride out the macabre wave.

To his surprise, Jen entered the room several minutes later. "You're going to stay out here again tonight?" she asked.

"What difference does it make?" he asked in a wounded voice, his forearms draped over his eyes.

"Maybe you should start looking for another..." she started to say under her breath before stopping and leaving the room.

Mac sat up straight, continuing to suffer through the full blown attack. The symptoms quickly evolved into tingling extremities. Sitting white faced and alone, the attack's intensity lasted no more than five excruciating minutes. *My life's become a living hell,* he thought. But to the credit of his unbending will, he'd stayed away from doctors—even as the attacks were becoming more frequent.

Streetlights strobed in and out of the tinted windows. A soft ballad played on the van's radio, while the windshield wipers kept perfect beat to it all. Bella and Brady were dressed in Halloween costumes, while Jillian stayed home to hand out candy.

As the rain continued to fall, Mac rubbed the back of his neck, trying to work out the knots. Looking to his right, he found Jen dozing off. He released an agitated breath before his eyes began dotting between the road ahead of him and the rear-view mirror. Bella and Brady were asleep, their eyes shut and mouths agape. Mac continued to search behind them, while a cloak of worry was draped over him.

"Now what's bothering you?" Jen asked, breaking the thick silence and startling Mac.

He exhaled heavy, his wide eyes never leaving the rear-view mirror.

Jen turned her head to look behind them.

"Now what's bothering me?" he roared, spit covering his mouth. "What do you think's bothering me?"

Jen gritted her teeth, ready to do battle. There was some shuffling from the backseat, halting her and sending her into an obvious state of frustration. "Who do you think you are," she hissed, "talking to me like that? I really have had it with you."

Mac glared at her, feeling a complete lack of love for his spouse. "You've had it with me?" he said, continuing at a hush. "What a joke. I bet you haven't had it with Joel, though, have you?"

The two stared at each other with disgust.

"Maybe your new boyfriend's the reason you're late coming home from work all the time?" he suggested.

Jen's face burned red, while she clearly choked on her indignation.

"As a matter of fact," Mac added, "I think your boyfriend's right behind us. Maybe he's going to follow us home to do some trick-or-treating?"

Jen turned to look out the rear window again, but snapped back when she realized there was no one behind them. "You are such a child, Mac," she said. "I told you weeks ago that Joel is gay. More importantly, he's my colleague and my friend and, if you can't handle that, then too bad."

"Too bad?" he screeched.

"Yeah, too bad. If you weren't so busy at work, so preoccupied with everyone but me, then I wouldn't need Joel or anyone else to confide in." She started to cry. "If you remembered how to be a husband, then..."

Mac slammed his fist on the steering wheel, causing Jen to shut up. Whimpers from the back seat traveled toward the front of the car.

"That's nice, Mac," she growled. "Keep acting like an animal. The kids don't have enough to be afraid of."

Mac scanned the rear-view mirror again before quieting his tone. "What do the kids have to be afraid of, Jen," he hissed, "having their mother trade in their father for a newspaper photographer?"

"No," she retorted at a scream, "having their mother find a real man who..."

"No more, please!" Bella yelled out. "I can't take it anymore." Her weeping was contagious, rubbing off on Brady.

Mac peered into the rear-view mirror and cringed. His two frightened children were sobbing.

"See what your insane jealousies have done to this family?" Jen managed through gritted teeth. "It's going to end, Mac. I swear it. You'll be living alone before I allow these kids to live in fear."

Mac cracked the window to let in a blast of fresh air. His flushed face felt ready to burst. *Jen's blaming the family problems on me*, he thought, illogically, *and not the affair she's trying to keep secret.*

While he shook with fury, Jen comforted her children. "You have no right to accuse me of something I'd never do," she whispered over her shoulder to Mac. "It's your fault we've grown apart, not mine."

Sobs and sniffles played back up to the rain that pelted the windows. The entire family returned home in a state of utter despair, sharing their grief with Jillian at the front door.

∞

Once the children were put to bed—Jillian slamming her bedroom door shut—Jen took her shower. Mac stepped into the children's rooms to say his goodnights. From the girls' rooms to Brady's bedroom, he shouldered the brunt of their fears.

"Dad?" Brady asked.

"What is it, buddy?"

"Are you and Mom gonna split up?"

Mac took a seat on the foot of the boy's twin-sized bed. "I want you to know that Mom and I owe you kids an apology. We shouldn't be fighting in front of you. It's wrong and I'm sorry."

There was silence, the little guy still awaiting his answer.

Mac spoke softly. "I don't want you worrying about anybody splitting up. Mom and I are dealing with some adult issues right now...things that you and your sisters shouldn't be concerned with."

"But are you gonna be livin' alone like Ma said?" Brady asked.

"No son, I'm not going anywhere and neither is Mom." In response to his son's doubtful eyes, Mac concluded, "You have my word."

A tiny grin replaced the young boy's anxious frown. He snuggled beneath his spaceship covers, satisfied with his father's solemn promise. Mac kissed Brady's forehead before heading off to the girls' rooms.

∞

Bella was sitting up, waiting for her father. "Daddy," she began tearfully, "I was wonderin'..."

Mac hurried to her bed and placed his finger to her trembling lips. "Don't wonder about anything, princess. Just because Mom and I fight, that doesn't mean that anything's going to change around here, okay?" He kissed her cheek and ran his fingers through her hair. "I love you and your sister and brother more than you could ever imagine. Mom and I just have to find a way to stop fighting." He kissed her. "For now, just know that Mommy and I love each other. Now get some sleep."

His innocent daughter looked up at him.

"What is it?" he asked his little girl.

"Can you say my prayers with me?"

He and Bella got on their knees and clasped their hands together.

"Now I lay me down to sleep," Bella recited, "I pray the Lord my soul to keep. If I should die before I wake, I pray the Lord my soul to take."

There was a pause. As always, Mac nodded for her to continue.

"Father, please bless my mom, my dad, Jillian, Brady and Sophie. And God, I know I keep asking but can you *please* make Mommy and Daddy stop fighting?"

"Amen," they both said.

Mac stood and hugged her again. "I love you, princess. Sweet dreams."

"Love you more, Daddy," she whispered before closing her eyes.

∞

Mac caught Jillian coming out of the bathroom. "Goodnight, Dad," she mumbled, starting for her bedroom door.

"Whoa," Mac said, "no kiss goodnight?"

Jillian reluctantly went to him.

Mac kissed her cold cheek. "I want you to know that Mom and I owe you an apology. We shouldn't be fighting in front of you. It's wrong...and I'm sorry."

Nodding, Jillian turned to walk away.

"You don't accept my apology?" he asked.

She shrugged. "Sure, if you don't fight again tomorrow." She reached her bedroom door. "But you will," she said before stepping into her room.

In the master bedroom, Mac discovered that Jen had already gone to bed. She was obviously pretending to be asleep. "Jen?" he whispered, feeling emotional over the conversations with his three worried children.

There was silence. He placed his hand on her shoulder.

"Don't touch me," she hissed.

He didn't expect the contempt in her voice; it startled him.

"And I wasn't kidding," she said. "If you can't control your adolescent paranoia or your emotional outbursts in front of the kids, then maybe you should start looking for another place to live."

He grabbed for her, but she violently shook off his attempt at tenderness.

"Come on now, Jen," he pleaded. "You're being ridiculous. I know we've been going through a really rough stretch, but..."

Jen turned to face him; there was great pain in her eyes. Grabbing his pillow, she threw it in his face. "Get away from me," she hissed. "I don't want you near me."

"But Jen, the kids."

"Get out of my bed!" she said with even more conviction.

Mac sat at the edge of the bed, his mouth hung open and his head spinning. Physically, he and Jen were only a few feet apart. In reality, they were worlds removed from each other. Reality was frightening. *I think I made a mistake by not letting her in all the way—by not sharing my personal little hell,* he thought, his eyes welling with regretful tears. *I think I made a terrible mistake.*

As she stepped out of the room, the merciless symptoms of a brand-new panic attack took hold.

Chapter 9

Mac sat on his park bench, a half-empty vodka bottle propped up beside him. Heavy bags hung under his eyes from a full week's loss of sleep. He was physically tired, but the exhaustion he felt went so much deeper. It was a need—even a yearning—for peace. His shoulders drooped from the weight of sorrow. Except for his heavy breathing, the world was silent and the park deserted.

Without even noticing his boss arrive, Ross Panchley was suddenly sitting beside him. "Brandt told me I'd find you here," he said, his tone and body language anything but friendly.

Mac looked up at the man, the lump in his throat muting him for an awkward moment. "I'm...I'm sorry, Ross," he finally managed, "but I..."

"What's the status on the Brighams's Auto World project?" Ross asked, cutting him off.

Mac felt tormented, a new level of desperation filling his soul. He couldn't speak.

Ross looked down at the pint of vodka beside Mac. "I just asked you a question," he said, shaking his head.

"I...I..."

"Have you gone to see a doctor yet?" Ross asked.

"Yeah, I did," Mac mumbled. "He said everything looks good. My cholesterol is a little high, but everything else is fine." Although Mac tried to play stupid, he knew he wasn't pulling it off.

"That's not the type of doctor I'm talking about."

"Ross, please," Mac snapped back. "I don't need you telling me how to conduct my personal business."

"Yeah Mac," Ross quickly interrupted, "you do need me telling you how to conduct your personal business. You've been to work three times in the last two weeks. And when you do show, you're either drunk or pawning off your work to one of our junior people." He exhaled deeply. "It's unacceptable."

Mac was speechless, again.

"You don't think I've been in this business long enough to recognize the difference between a rookie's work and that of a seasoned veteran?" Ross asked, his face two or three creases away from wrath.

Mac never answered. Part of him couldn't have cared less. *My failing marriage is more im...*

"We were lucky to save the account," Ross said, interrupting Mac's thoughts, "but it's unacceptable, Mac." He shook his disgusted head again.

Mac never batted an eye.

Ross looked up at the sky before sighing once—and then dropping the hammer. "Mac, I was going to talk to you this morning anyway." He took a deep breath. "I've been in touch with Human Resources. The company's prepared to assist you in any way possible...therapy, rehab, whatever you need. But for the time being, consider yourself..."

"Fired?"

"On vacation, Mac. Consider yourself on vacation until you can pull yourself together."

Mac stood. "Un-fucking-real!" he barked, thinking, *What else could possibly go wrong?* He stormed off, leaving Ross alone on the bench like some frowning bobble head.

∞

The yellow school bus was just pulling away from the curb when Joel Ward swung his van into the Anderson's driveway. Jen was standing at her front door. She forced a smile.

Oh no, the photographer thought, his happy mood taking a dive, *something's wrong*. He rolled down the van's window. "Don't you look like crap," he teased. "Didn't want to take off the Halloween mask just yet?"

She smirked. "Thanks. I really needed one of your compliments this morning." With a wave of her hand, she beckoned him into the house to join her. "Come on in, I just need to shut off the iron."

But we're already late for work, he thought. With a shrug, he shut off the ignition and grabbed the two hot coffees.

Joel handed Jen one of the Styrofoam cups before following her in. In the kitchen, he took notice of the wall clock and looked at his wristwatch. Placing his timepiece to his ear, he shook his head. *Cheap-ass gift*, he thought. While Jen unplugged the iron, he removed the timepiece and wound it. "Hey, what's up," he asked, looking at Jen, "more trouble in paradise?"

She shrugged once but, when she opened her mouth to speak, the tears started to flow.

Oh no, Joel repeated in his head, placing his watch onto the kitchen counter. Gently approaching her, he put his arm around her and led her to the door. "Come on, Jen. You can tell me on the way."

Trembling, she fumbled with her pocketbook and a handful of notepads. Suddenly, her face bleached white. "The interview," she blurted, sounding desperate.

"The world won't stop turning if we're late," Joel assured her with a smile. "Well, maybe not Joe's world, but Joe's world is due to take a break anyway."

Jen grinned and stepped into the photographer's van. Joel started it, turned off the radio and backed out of the driveway.

Mac struggled for air, as his wife and her photographer rolled past him. *This cannot be fuckin' happening...* His knuckles, now white, were wrapped around the steering wheel, which threatened to crack under the pressure. He tried to scream, but only a squeak would escape. *Son-of-a-bitch,* he thought, his heart aching with a pain he'd never known. *Please God, not this...* The first few tears broke free.

A mile away, Jen turned to Joel. "I'm so sorry to put this on you," she said.

Joel placed his hand on hers. "Now you're insulting me. I thought we were friends?"

She nodded. After retrieving a tissue from her purse, she began to ramble. "I just don't know anymore, Joel. Things haven't been great with Mac for quite a while now, but recently it's gotten so that it's unbearable to be around him. He yells at me in front of the kids and then snaps at them for the stupidest reasons—which has never been like him. When I ask him to talk to me, to share what's troubling him, he usually turns on me and starts screaming. And I've just about had enough of that crap." She stopped to slow her angry breathing. "He won't tell me anything, Joel. He constantly accuses me of cheating and..."

"Cheating?"

Through the sniffles, a subtle grin appeared. "Yeah," she said, "and of all people—with you."

In spite of the heavy situation, Joel released a hearty laugh. "No offense, sweetheart, but did you tell him that you're not my type?"

"I did, but your sexual preference shouldn't dictate whether he trusts me or not." She shook her head. "I would never mess around on Mac. And I've never given him reason to mistrust me. It's infuriating." She took a deep breath. "I gave up my career to raise our kids, for Pete's sake. Now that I'm trying to get some of it back..."

"I don't get it," Joel said. "When did all of this start?"

She took in a lung full of air. "Over the summer, he began having anxiety attacks."

"Oh, no..."

She nodded. "He started to get help, but stopped seeing his therapist after a few sessions."

"Because the attacks stopped?"

She shook her head. "I don't think so, though I couldn't really tell you because he keeps everything to himself."

Joel sighed. "That's not good."

"Things got even worse when the kids started school and I decided to go back to work. I haven't been able to communicate with him since. Everything turns into a fight."

"If you ask me, Jen, you guys should get into family counseling. At the very least, you could both learn not to fight in front of those beautiful children."

Jen nodded. "I suggested it a while back, but he said things would get better, that he was just going through a tough time and that I should understand—be more patient." She became more upset. "I really think there's something more, something he's not telling me." She drifted off in agonizing thought. "Something's really wrong, Joel. Mac hasn't been himself in a long time." She half-shrugged. "Maybe he's the one who's been screwing around?"

"Easy with the accusations, detective," Joel teased. "You know how that feels. If you ask me, you guys just need to reopen the love lines. You know—a little wine, a little sweet talk, and then..." Joel made some vulgar suggestions.

Jen slapped his arm in fun. "Stop it, you goof. This is serious."

"I'm just teasing." He laughed. "And I know it's serious. But maybe that's half the problem? If you and Mac didn't take everything so serious, then maybe life wouldn't be so miserable all the time."

The van pulled in front of City Hall where the interview was scheduled. Joel checked the time. "Shit, I forgot my watch at your house. What time do you have?"

She checked her cell phone and smiled. "We're just in time." Regaining her composure, she reapplied her makeup while Joel parked. With a nod, she opened the door and got out. "I can't thank you enough," she said. "I feel better already. I only wish Mac knew how innocent our friendship is, and how much I miss being able to talk to him like this."

"I don't suppose he ever will unless you tell him," Joel said with a wink.

"You're probably right," she said. "I need to get past my own anger and resentment and talk to him again." She nodded. "I may even try tonight." Her eyes filled with tears again. "I honestly can't tell you how much I've missed him, Joel, the old him, anyway."

Joel raised an eyebrow. "Then you should tell him that, too."

Buttoning her coat, Jen looked back at her partner— and then put on her game face.

Without even remembering how he got there, Mac was parked in his driveway. As reality registered, he jumped out of the car and slammed the door.

As he proceeded through the kitchen to grab a beer, he stopped. There was an unfamiliar wristwatch sitting on the counter. He picked it up and turned it over. It read: *To Joel. All My Love, Mickey.*

A murderous venom bubbled in his veins. With a single war cry, he heaved the watch onto the floor where it shattered; there was a loud pop, the air being released from the crystal. *No! No! No!* he screamed in his throbbing head. Then, in a fit of blinding fury, he began demolishing everything that wasn't bolted down.

At the end of the destructive meltdown, he fell to his knees where he began to weep mournfully. "How could you do this to me, Jen?" he whimpered, the feeling of despair stronger than the will to get off his knees. "Why Jen," he screamed, "why?"

While Joel watched on, Jen picked up the phone and dialed New Dimensions Advertising. Mac's secretary answered.

"Hi Barbara, can I speak with Mac, please?"

There was an awkward moment of silence. "I'm...I'm sorry, Mrs. Anderson," Barbara muttered, clearing her throat, "Mr. Anderson didn't tell you?"

"Tell me what?"

There was a pause. "That he's on a leave of absence."

Jen's jaw touched her chest. "I'm sorry. Did you just say that Mac's taken a leave of absence?"

Joel placed his hand on Jen's arm.

"No, not exactly," Barbara explained. "Mr. Anderson didn't have a choice."

Jen nearly dropped the phone. "Well now, isn't that just wonderful."

She hung up and, while Joel tried telling her to remain calm, she immediately called home. The answering machine picked up, the kids greeting her in chorus. "Hi, you've reached the Andersons. Please leave a message and we'll get right back to ya. Have a great day."

"Unbelievable," she muttered before the machine beeped to receive the message. She looked at Joel. "Mac got canned at work," she explained.

"I'm sure he has a reasonable explanation," Joel said, "and you need to give him a chance to..."

"Why am I not surprised by this?" Jen interrupted, talking more to herself than to her colleague. "Un-fuck-ing real!" she squealed.

∞

When Jen returned home with the kids, she couldn't have been more furious. And then she stepped into her kitchen. Shock stopped her and the kids in their tracks. Jen's wide eyes took in the damage. *My kitchen's destroyed*, she thought, spotting her husband sitting on the floor with his knees to his chest. He smelled of booze. She turned to Jillian. "Take them upstairs," she said, gesturing toward Bella and Brady.

No sooner had the kids—visibly horrified—left the room when Jen went off like a roman candle. "What the hell did you do to my kitchen?" she yelled, angrier than she'd ever imagined being.

"How long has it been going on?" Mac asked in a hoarse whisper.

"What?" she asked, as though she were whispering in a saw mill. "I just asked you a question and I want an answer!"

Mac leapt to his feet. There was madness in his eyes. "And I just asked you how long you've been cheating on me?"

This is the last friggin' straw, Jen thought, her emotions seesawing between disgust and rage. "Get out," she screamed, hurrying for the living room. "Get out now!"

He grabbed her arm, pulling her to him. He stuffed a broken wrist watch into her face.

Her fury was instantly consumed by fear. *He's...he's crazy,* she thought, her mind scrambling at a dizzying pace.

"Right in our own home?" he screamed, even louder.

"Stop it, Mac, you're hurting me," she cried. "Let go of my arm." The tears began to build.

As Mac let her go, he fired the watch directly at the TV, causing the screen to crack; a giant spider instantly appeared. "I swear to God," he slurred. "I'll fuckin' kill somebody before this family's taken from me." He walked to the fireplace, grabbed a framed photo of the family from the cluttered mantle and threw it against the wall where it shattered into pieces.

Jen took the opportunity to run into the bathroom. *We need help,* she realized. Hyperventilating, she locked the door behind her. *Oh no,* she thought, scolding herself, *I should have grabbed the kids.* She picked up the phone and, as she punched in the numbers 911, she heard glass smash against the living room wall again. *The kids,* she thought again, panic welling up inside her.

"What is the nature of your emergency?" the monotone voice inquired on the other end of the line.

"My husband's tearing our house apart and...and he's...he's made threats to... Oh God, my...my kids are upstairs," she stuttered. "Oh, dear God..."

"Ma'am, you need to calm down and tell me the address."

"It's 19 Thornton Street...in...in...Dighton. Please hurry. I've never seen him like this." By now, she was panting. "Oh God, my kids are upstairs listening to this."

Mac stood outside the door, banging away. "Open this door now, Jen. We're not done talking!" he roared, punching the wood. "Open this fuckin' door before I break it down!"

With one hand on the knob, Jen stood on the other side of the door. *Stop, Mac*, she begged him in her head. *Please stop*. She started for the lock when Mac pounded his fist wildly against the wood again.

"Open this door before I break it down," he screeched.

Every cell in Jen's body swelled with panic. "Mac, I just called the cops and they're on the way," she warned. "Please stop. Please think of the kids and stop this insanity right now."

The pounding immediately stopped, followed by one loud thud. *His back against the door*, she surmised, picturing him collapsing to the floor. She could hear him crying uncontrollably. "I lost my job today, Jen," he babbled in a drunken daze, "and then I lost my wife." She could hear him hyperventilating. "Oh God," he moaned, "please, dear God, not my kids too."

Jen cried along with him, but for different reasons. *I just want him out of this house.*

There was a loud knock at the front door before a deep voice called out. "Open up, it's the police."

Jen unlocked her door and, rushing past her weeping husband, answered the front door.

Two police officers entered the house; a silver-haired veteran and his muscle-bound partner who looked like he recently graduated from high school. While they surveyed the damage of the violent outburst, the younger cop intentionally stood between Mac and Jen—who spotted the kids peeking through the banisters of the staircase that led upstairs. Each was trembling, sobbing to each twitch. *Oh God*, she repeated amidst the surreal nightmare. She looked at her husband. *You bastard*, she thought, *putting our children through this.*

"Ma'am, can you tell me what happened here?" the veteran officer inquired.

Mac tried to answer. "Officer, I..."

The younger cop was quick. "He wasn't talking to you, pal. You'll speak when he asks you to." He looked back at Jen. "Go ahead, Ma'am."

"When I came home, my kitchen was destroyed," she said, her voice shaky. "I sent the kids upstairs and asked my husband what had happened. He started ranting and raving about me cheating on him with another man." The sobbing began.

Through his staggering drunkenness, Mac tried again. "Officer, please, it's just a misunderstanding between me and my wife. There's no need..."

"You open your mouth again and I'll slap the cuffs on you right here," the muscular cop roared. "Understand?"

Even more terrified by this, the kids emerged from the shadows.

Mac instantly straightened up, nodding that he understood.

Unable to even look at him, Jen struggled to go on. "He grabbed me by the arm, showed me some wrist watch and then threw it at the TV. He started smashing things and making threats and..." She couldn't finish.

The older police officer grabbed his portable radio and pushed the button. There was one squelch before he spoke. "Central, be advised, we'll be transporting one on domestic assault charges."

In one swift motion, the man's younger partner removed a set of handcuffs from his belt while grabbing Mac by the arm.

Mac freaked. "Jen, please," he yelped, pulling away from the aggressive cop. "Tell them this is a mistake."

"Sir, please," she pleaded, "not here, not in front of our children." Although she shared her husband's anxiety, hers was for her children.

Mac scowled at her once before yanking his arm out of the officer's grasp in a rush of panic.

The muscle head, however, wouldn't have any of it. Like a cornered badger, he pounced on Mac and began wrestling with him until they fell to the floor in one massive thud.

Jillian ran to her father's side. "Stop hurting my dad," she screamed. "Mom, make him stop!"

"Please officer, not here," Jen repeated.

Mac's thrashing body was rolled until he was face down. As the younger police officer knelt on his back, the other forced Mac's arms behind his back.

Mac bucked and convulsed, groaning like a wounded animal. "This is my home," he panted.

"You need to comply," the older officer said, already winded, "before you get hurt."

Finally surrendering to the officers' manhandling, Mac's body went limp. "Come on," he whimpered, "not in front of my kids." As the handcuffs were applied, he looked up at his children. "I'm sorry, guys," he whimpered. "I'm so sorry." Mac was jerked to his feet. "I love you guys more than anything in the world," he told them, his grimacing face betraying his physical discomfort.

By now, everyone was crying.

"I'm sorry, Ma'am," the silver-haired officer claimed. "Under these circumstances, we have no choice but to arrest."

Jen was in shock. "I...I understand."

As Mac winced from the pain in his wrists, each officer grabbed an arm and began walking him out of the house. He was looking at Jen with contempt and hatred before he refocused on his children's horrified eyes. Everyone froze and, to their surprise, the officers allowed him a moment to speak. He could barely get the words out; they were clearly stuck behind the lump in his throat. "Guys, I'm so sorry you had to see this. But don't you worry about Dad, okay? It's all just a big mistake. Mom and I will clear this whole thing up."

While Jillian kept her distance, the two smaller kids ran to him, wrapping their arms around his quivering legs. Two sets of wide eyes looked up, searching for their father's comfort.

"I love you guys more than anything in the world," he vowed, "always remember that." Looking over at Jillian, he fought back the tears. "And I'll be home soon. I promise."

As the officers escorted Mac out the front door, Jen dropped to her knees, spreading her arms to her frightened children. Bella and Brady immediately went to her. Jillian, however, refused her mother's comfort. They all grieved—violently.

Between sobs, the echo of a deep voice traveled back into the house. "You have the right to remain silent, tough guy. You have the right to an attorney. If you cannot afford..."

His fingers stained black, Mac's belt and shoes had already been removed from him when he used the station's desk phone to dial home. The kids sounded happy. "Hi, you've reached the Andersons. Please leave a message and we'll get right back to ya. Have a great day."

As his eyes filled with tears, the booking officers took notice. A young police officer grabbed him by the arm and laughed. "Well pal," he said, "that's your one and only phone call. Looks like you'll be spending the whole night here at the roach motel."

The older officer—understanding more compassion—pulled his inexperienced partner's arm off of Mac, lifted the telephone out of its cradle again and handed it to their prisoner.

Mac was still in a state of shock. "Oh, that's okay. Thanks anyway," he mumbled, "but I have no one else to call." He hung up the black handset.

The officer looked confused. "What about your attorney? Don't you want to make bail and get out of here?"

Mac shook his head. "I don't want to bother him at home. I'll call him in the morning." He shrugged. "If it's just the same, I'll stay here tonight."

The older officer offered a solemn nod and escorted his pathetic prisoner into one of the grimy cells.

At the door, Mac turned to him. "Maybe I could try to call my house again in a little while?" he suggested.

The man nodded. "I'll come get you in a bit when we don't have any company." He looked up the short corridor. "It's easy to mistake kindness for weakness around here and I don't need to get my balls busted over it."

Mac nodded. "I understand. And I appreciate it." He took a seat on the bunk. Within seconds, he rolled himself into the fetal position where a whole new feeling tapped him on the shoulder; it was depression.

There was an evil force that pulled at Mac and, though he didn't want to go, his tired mind gave in. The tunnel was dark and he saw no end. Carrying a tremendous weight upon his shoulders, he only wished to rest—perhaps sleep forever—but the fear of staying in this tunnel of hell made him want to forge ahead. He sensed there were others in the tunnel, but a vicious loneliness tore at his soul. Each step was agonizing, as he went nowhere.

Finally collapsing onto the cold floor, he wondered, *Does anyone even know that I'm lost? Does anyone know how to pull me out?* While one last tear tumbled down his twisted face, a tormenting fear welled up inside of him. He'd reached despair, perhaps, for him—*the end.*

Life at the Anderson house was no less bleak. Jen was an emotional wreck, as she tried to straighten up her kitchen in the aftermath of Hurricane Mac—a swath of devastation left in his bizarre wake. "You had to see him, Diane," she said, resting the phone in the crook of her shoulder. "He was a madman. I really didn't know if he was going to hurt me."

"That son-of-a..." Diane squawked, "putting his hands on you like that. You're going to press charges, right?"

"The police told me that it's out of my hands," Jen explained between sniffles. "They said they're charging Mac with domestic assault."

"Good enough," Diane said.

Jen shook her head. "I know Diane, but it's just..." She couldn't believe it, but she still felt the need to defend her husband. *Focus on the kids*, she told herself.

"It's just nothing! The kids don't need to see that crap, Jen. And you certainly don't need to live like that either. No woman does."

"I know, Di, I know," Jen said. "I didn't think it would come to this, but I realize now that Mac needs professional help."

"And he'll get it," Diane snickered, "right where he belongs."

Jen continued to shake her head. "The kids are a mess, Diane, and I really need your help. Can we come over?"

"Of course. Come over."

"Thank you," Jen said. "We'll be there in a few minutes."

While Bella and Brady wept in their bedrooms, Jillian sat on the couch—appearing more angry and confused than ever.

Jen entered the room and extended her hand. "Let's go to Auntie Diane's. We can talk about all of this over there."

The teenage girl refused her mother's trembling hand. Instead, she got up and marched out the front door.

"Bella and Brady, come downstairs," Jen called out. "We're going to Auntie Diane's."

Within seconds, they appeared—coats in hand.

Taking them by their hands, Jen hurried out of the house, leaving the lights on.

It was late when Mac punched in the last number and waited.

"Hi, you've reached the Andersons," Jillian, Bella and Brady said in chorus. "Please leave a message and we'll get right back to ya. Have a great day."

A tear broke loose and traveled the length of his cheek. The old police officer looked away.

The machine beeped to take the message.

"I love you guys so much..." Mac said, his voice cracking. "...and I'm so sorry."

One beep later, there was silence.

Chapter 10

Wearing handcuffs, Mac was escorted into the court for his arraignment. Jen gasped at the sight of it. Although his eyes quickly found her, he immediately looked away. *He looks numb*, she decided, unable to truly read him. *Not like the animal that wrecked my kitchen.*

Ray Howard, the Assistant District Attorney, stood before her, breaking any future eye contact between Jen and Mac. "Mrs. Anderson," he said, "even though the state is charging your husband, we're going to require that you testify."

I need to testify? Jen thought, suddenly feeling nauseous. Before she could respond, Attorney Howard added, "And unfortunately, the only way we can guarantee your family's safety is for you to request a restraining order."

As the first tears gathered in the corners of her eyes, Jen stared blankly. "I don't..."

"I've seen hundreds of these cases, Mrs. Anderson," the A.D.A. quickly interrupted, "and many end up..." He stopped to search her face. "Why don't we just impose a temporary order, until your husband gets help for his anger?"

"Ummm, I...I suppose," she said, hesitantly nodding.

Attorney Howard broke a smile just as the judge entered. "Everyone rise," Court Officer Beaupre ordered, "the honorable Judge Marge Tremblay presiding."

"Please be seated," the judge said.

Everyone did as they were instructed before the charges were read: *One count, domestic assault. One count, resisting arrest.*

"Mr. Anderson, how do you plead to the charge of assault and battery?" the judge asked.

Roland Dube, the family attorney and friend, clasped his hands together. "Not guilty, your Honor."

Attorney Howard winked at Jen, and then turned to offer his manipulative spiel. "Your Honor," the A.D.A. said, "Mrs. Anderson is requesting an immediate 209A, restraining order. Due to the circumstances, I believe this would be most prudent at this time."

Jen felt ill at the request, but told herself, *I need to protect the kids.* Through her peripheral vision, she saw Mac flinch. The judge's hand motioned to begin the proceedings.

Attorney Howard recited the details of the horrible night's events, while Judge Tremblay quickly skimmed through the report. "Your Honor," the A.D.A. said, "please note that the officer described the terrible condition of the Anderson's kitchen, the angry state Mr. Anderson was in and the bruises that began forming on Mrs. Anderson's arm."

As if she'd already made her judgment, the judge glared down at Mac.

Mac had his head down; he appeared removed from the scene until Jen was called to take the witness stand. Slowly, she stepped up. After being sworn in, Attorney Howard began his vigorous line of questioning. "Mrs. Anderson, on the evening in question, did your husband physically damage property within your home?"

Jen nodded.

"Is that a yes, Mrs. Anderson?"

"Yes," she said, choking out the word.

"Did he make threats of inflicting bodily harm upon anyone?"

"Ummm...yes, he did," she replied, painfully.

The A.D.A. quickened his pace. "Did he also place his hands upon you, causing bruises?"

Jen felt like she might actually vomit. "Yes," she answered, "but..."

"A yes or no answer will suffice, Mrs. Anderson."

Jen realized that Attorney Howard was clearly not a compassionate man. "No, it won't!" she said, turning to the judge. "Your Honor," she pleaded, "this is my family's future we're talking about here. I believe I should have the right to speak freely."

The judge looked over at Mac and then back at Jen. "Please just answer the questions, Mrs. Anderson," she said, devoid of any emotion.

"My husband did do everything you've said," she told Attorney Howard, "but he was drunk." Torn between her roles as wife and mother, she shook her head. "Mac has never been a violent man. He's always been a good husband and a wonderful father." She was hyperventilating now. "Things have gotten out of hand lately and he's shown signs of violence, but until last night he never physically acted on them. I suppose everything's been building for weeks now and came to a head yesterday. He..."

"Mrs. Anderson, is your husband employed?" the A.D.A. asked, cutting her off.

"Yes...I mean, no."

"Which is it, Mrs. Anderson?"

"He lost his job yesterday before everything came to a head."

"A yes or no, please," the Attorney Howard said.

Judge Tremblay shifted uneasily at the discovery that Mac was currently unemployed.

"And I know alcohol isn't a defense," Jen added defiantly, "or even an excuse for his actions, but Mac..."

"Mrs. Anderson," the A.D.A. barked, cutting her off again, "I would appreciate it if you wouldn't…"

"He came home and found a male watch belonging to a colleague of mine," Jen blurted. "Even though I've been true to him, he believes I've been unfaithful." The first tear tumbled down her burning cheek. "All I'm saying is…my husband is not a criminal. He's a man who's been in pain for a long time now and…and can no longer contain his temper. He's a man who needs help." The sobbing became worse. "I've…I've…tried to be there for him." She looked at the judge. "I'm begging you, please get him the help he needs."

Although the A.D.A. was clearly frustrated with Jen, the judge straightened herself before she spoke. "Mrs. Anderson. I appreciate your candidness. However, in all good conscience, this court must consider the welfare of your children above all else."

"Yes, of course," Jen blurted.

"So I must ask you now," the judge continued, "after yesterday's ordeal, do you believe that your children will be completely safe in the presence of their father?"

Jen looked at Mac and more tears broke free.

Mac leaned forward, panic filling his face.

"No, not until Mac gets some help for his anger." She trembled at the truth of it. "No, I don't think that our children are completely safe around him right now."

Attorney Dube leapt to his feet. "Your Honor, I object! I haven't even had…had the opportunity to…to defend Mr. Anderson." He was talking so fast that he began to stutter. "We…we haven't come to a finding on the charges. How can we even entertain the notion of a…of a restraining order?"

The judge peered down her long nose. "Mr. Dube, let me be frank. This is my court and I have been granted great discretion in my rulings on family matters. So let me fill you in—your client has no past criminal record and until yesterday, he was gainfully employed. Therefore, this court does not view him as someone who needs to serve jail time. However, it is quite evident that something is going on with Mr. Anderson that is not in the best interest of his wife and young children." Scanning over the piece of paper before her, the frigid woman's eyes returned to the shocked lawyer. "This court will impose a temporary 209A restraining order on behalf of Mrs. Anderson and her children. However, as there is no prior record, I am willing to dispose of the case this morning, Mr. Dube. If your client is so willing, I'd be inclined to impose a three-year pre-trial sentence of probation."

"But your Honor," was all Attorney Dube had left.

"There are no buts here, Mr. Dube," the snarling judge advised. She pointed at Mac. "Mr. Anderson, shame on you for putting your children through such trauma. You need to find yourself some help, sir."

"Please, your Honor," Mac whimpered. "Please don't take my kids away from me."

The judge broke eye contact, confirming that Mac's plea had fallen upon deaf ears. The court clearly felt it was working in the best interest of the children. Mac folded himself in half, awaiting his formal punishment.

Attorney Dube addressed the court. "May I have a moment with my client, your Honor?"

"Granted," the judge said.

Attorney Dube pulled Mac aside. There was urgency in both his movements and tone. "Mac, listen to me now. Based on what I've heard here today, this is the best deal we're going to get."

Mac's entire body was buzzing with panic. "The best?" he repeated, his mind spinning out of control. "What about my kids, Roland?"

"Pre-trial probation has nothing to do with the restraining order," Dube said.

"Roland, please!" Mac's body was trembling near the brink of convulsion.

"Mac, you need to accept that you're not going to be able to see the kids for a while," Dube advised. "The judge *will* impose the restraining order." He patted Mac's shoulder. "As far as the criminal charges go, as long as you comply with the terms of the probation the case will get dismissed after three years."

Mac glared at Roland. His long-time friend was missing the real punishment. "Fine," Mac muttered in despair, adding a term of surrender he'd never imagined saying, "whatever."

∞

Dube addressed the court. "Your Honor, my client is willing to accept your recommendation on the assault and battery charge."

The judge nodded and noted this in her documentation. Seconds later, she looked back at Mac. "Mr. Anderson, I'm sorry, but..."

To Mac, the rest sounded like *blah...blah...blah...* He collapsed back into his chair. To him, being separated from his children—for any period of time—was equivalent to receiving the death sentence. The remainder of the hearing passed as some cruel haze. In the end, Mac was found guilty of domestic assault. Probation was imposed for a period of three years, along with a mandate to attend domestic violence classes for a period of two months. "Upon graduating from the program, visitation with your children will be further entertained by this court," Judge Tremblay concluded.

The black-robed lady left the bench long before Mac emerged from his fog. It took a few nudges from Attorney Dube to bring him back. "Mac, are you even listening to me?" Dube asked.

"What? What's that, Roland?" Everything was so blurry.

"There was nothing more I could do," the sad-looking lawyer confessed. "These proceedings are a crapshoot at best and we drew the wrong judge today. She's a tough one and she doesn't screw around when it comes to domestic violence." He shook his head. "I don't think I've ever seen her rule in the favor of..." He stopped.

Mac remained catatonic.

Dube grabbed his arm. "Listen to me, Mac. The judge has imposed some stiff sanctions here. We have a court date scheduled in two months. I know it hurts, but in the meantime you have to stay clear of Jen and the kids. The restraining order is only temporary, but it's still *no contact*." He finally slowed down. "It's also imperative that you attend every domestic violence class. And I promise you, Mac, if you violate the restraining order, this judge will revoke your probation and send you straight to jail. Do you understand?"

Mac shrugged. "I don't understand anything anymore, Roland." *I can't see my children for two months*, he thought. *What else matters?* In a room full of people, he felt completely alone. And then it happened—a panic attack to beat all panic attacks. Mac felt like his entire central nervous system had been hacked, making his body—inside and out—involuntarily convulse.

On her way out of the courtroom, Jen wiped her eyes and stopped before her shattered husband.

Expending every ounce of energy just to breathe and stay conscious, Mac couldn't look at her. It didn't matter. Even if his body wasn't shutting down, his despair would not have allowed it. *You fuckin' bitch*, he screamed somewhere inside his spinning head.

Feeling like he'd just experienced surgery without anesthesia, Mac went down to the abandoned lake to where he and the kids had sailed on many sunny days. The moored boat rocked back and forth, beckoning him to board. He contemplated it. *But without the kids...* he thought, his heart heavy with grief. *I lost my babies today*, he thought and, without notice or permission, his mind returned directly the birth of his last child.

For the fourth time in his life—the first being with Jen—Mac fell head-over-heels in love.

"Congratulations," the doctor exclaimed, "You have a healthy baby boy!" Overwhelmed, Mac took his son Brady into his arms and carefully inspected the fragile, squirming gift. Ten fingers, ten toes and the wail of a siren that made his eyes fill with tears. The boy was beautiful, absolutely perfect, and—for the third time—the endless possibilities for the future washed over Mac like a magical tidal wave. He cried for the dreams they'd share together and the lessons he was anxious to impart: baiting a hook, hitting a curve ball, being a gentleman without being a weak man—*all of it*. Mac was sure that this boy was his reward for every good intention he'd ever had.

Mac opened his eyes in the present. *What I didn't realize*, he thought, *was that all of those dreams were contingent upon the success of my marriage.*

Without another thought, he walked into the icy water—clothes and all—and waded up to his waist. Numb from the shock of it all, he collapsed backwards, surrendering to the lake and his natural buoyancy. The water was bitterly cold, enveloping him and threatening to swallow him whole. He could feel the chill but it was more like his body's afterthought. As his ears submerged, all sounds became muffled. Only his feet and face floated above the water line. The sound of other people had mercifully been removed. He could only hear his breathing now, shallow and labored. *Fuckin' bitch,* he thought, picturing his traitor wife testifying on the witness stand. *How could she do this to me? She screws around on me and I lose my kids? Yeah, that's real fair. What a crock of shit! So, what happens if the bitch suddenly dies? The kids would go with their father, right? They'd have to, unless the authorities could prove I had something to do with it.* His mind continued to spin like an internal gyroscope that was out of control.

A rippling wake bucked his flaccid body, rocking him up and down, threatening to yank him under. He didn't care. In fact, at this point it made no real difference whether he stayed afloat or sank to the very bottom. *Might be best for everyone if I went down,* he thought. He looked up toward the sky and felt like he was floating face down in it. The water had completely removed any sense of gravity, making him feel like he was suspended in time and space. It would have been relaxing, even peaceful, if his heart wasn't sending pain signals to his brain, pleading for some sort of relief. He prayed hard, his tearful eyes lifted toward the heavens; his soul, raw and open to his creator. *Please God, I need your help—now more than ever.* But he did not feel God's presence with him, not a hint that the Divine cared enough to even listen. Right away, he knew this was not Jen's fault. *I can't blame her for this*, he thought. This feeling of abandonment and isolation was of his own doing. He'd spent years drifting away from his faith, with no real need—or so he thought—for the Lord in his life. Now, on his back and in desperate need for any sign of mercy or comfort, he felt completely alone. His once-stoic faith was now an empty vessel, incapable of holding a single drop of water to soothe the fire that burned in his soul. "I'm so sorry," he cried out, "so, so sorry." He closed his eyes and mourned deeply. *At least show me a sign that everything will be okay,* he begged, *anything...please.* But there was no sign. Instead, he simply floated above the water like some abandoned fishing bobber, irrelevant and adrift.

When Mac opened his eyes, the blue sky had vanished, suddenly replaced by a bank of dark gray clouds. *Of course*, he thought. The first drops of rain pelted his face and splashed the water around him. *Not the sign I was looking for, though.* He just lay there. *Screw it*, he thought and closed his eyes again, as the bleak skies opened up and stung his skin with a hard driving rain. *Screw it all!* For the first time in his life, he felt pain while being on the water.

It was late when—soaked and shivering—Mac picked up the motel room's phone. He'd spent hours going through every detail of the nightmare in his tired mind; all of the blame continued to circle back to Jen. At the risk of violating the restraining order and going to jail, he called her.

"Hello?" Jen answered, sounding exhausted.

"You have no right to take my kids from me," he said, louder and angrier than he'd intended.

"I have every right, Mac," she answered, calmly. "A big part of my job as their mom is to protect them."

"From me," he screamed, "protect them from me?"

"Look Mac, you left me no choice—acting like a lunatic, destroying the house...making those threats. The kids shouldn't have to live like that. I shouldn't have to..."

"Jen, please," he cried, cutting her off. "I love the kids. I would never hurt them. You know that."

"But I don't know that, Mac," she whimpered. "I don't know anything about you anymore. You're angry and you're violent." There was a cruel pause. "Look, God only knows what's going to happen to our marriage, but as far as the kids—the last thing I want in this world is to keep them from you. They need you." She took a deep breath, sounding strong again. "But until you get help, I don't feel comfortable with them being around you."

Mac was so enraged that he actually began to froth at the mouth. He couldn't hold back any longer. "You fuckin' bitch," he roared, berating her, "you betrayed me! I needed you and you betrayed me, so let's forget about our failed marriage, okay? As far as the kids, I'm their father. I helped bring them into this world. I have every right..."

"Just hang up and call the cops," he could hear Diane yell in the background.

"Mac," Jen interrupted. "I'm not going to be victimized by your malicious outbursts anymore. Go get help and then we can talk. But if you call here again, I'm contacting the police." She sounded firm in her decision.

Mac slammed down the phone. *She's dead wrong,* he thought, *The kids aren't in any danger around me.* He collapsed onto the lumpy motel bed. *In one single fucked-up day, I lost everything that means anything to me.* Sitting up, he grabbed his vodka bottle, put it to his lips and tipped it to the ceiling. He pictured Jen's smug face and coughed on the fire water that trickled down his throat. *Fuckin' bitch!* he repeated in his aching head.

He took another long draw. *There's always an accident,* he thought, his mind returning to the darkness, *Jen could have an accident. Accidents happen all the time. I remember when I was in college, my professor was going through a nasty divorce. Then, his wife just up and drowned. That guy didn't lose anything—not his kids, his house, or his dog. And if I remember right, he collected enough insurance money to retire early.* Mac nodded. *Now that's what you call justice! Lucky bastard.* He stared off into space. *But if I kill Jen or hire a professional to do it, the kids won't have a mother.* Tears streamed down his face. *And I know what that's like.* He took the breaths his body kept forgetting to take in. *There's always the possibility of an accident,* he finally told himself, *and I'm due to catch a break at some point.*

An entire world away, Jen was stunned from the call. She turned to find her sister, Diane, shaking her head.

"I told you," Diane said, "just call the cops and let them deal with him."

"Thinking back now," Jen said, taking a more careful account, "I was so consumed with getting the newspaper job and with…" She shook her head. "Mac lost his job…he found Joel's watch on the kitchen table…" She slowed her breathing to avoid hyperventilation. "My husband needed me and I wasn't there for him, Diane."

"Whoa Jen," Diane jumped in. "I understand the whole marriage bond and all, but how were you supposed to be there for him—as a punching bag?"

"He'd been drinking, Diane," Jen snapped back.

"Yeah, and the selfish asshole's been drunk for months. The judge was right to impose the restraining order and you know it."

"Our family's ruined, Di. Do you understand that? The kids can't sleep. They're already asking for their father. What do I tell them, huh?"

"Tell them the truth. Tell them that their father couldn't keep his hands to himself."

Bella stormed into the kitchen and glared at her aunt, then at her mother. "You don't have to tell us anything!" she screamed, tears glistening on her face. "We already know it's your fault that Daddy's not here."

Mortified, Jen stood and took a step toward her daughter, her arms opened wide.

Bella stepped back, recoiling from her mother.

"But Beans, I didn't..."

Bella refused her touch. "You're the one who made Daddy go away," she whimpered, "and you're the reason he won't come back." Jen could see the little girl was overwhelmed with emotion. "You don't have to tell us anything," Bella wept. "We know."

Jen took another step toward her young daughter.

Bella hurried out of the room to be with her sobbing brother, whose muffled cries could be heard in the distance.

"My God, what have we done?" Jen asked, looking at her self-righteous sister.

For once, Diane was at a loss for words.

Jillian stepped into the room. "I'm glad he's gone," she said, her tone and face both even, "and I hope he doesn't come back."

"Oh Jill," Jen gasped, and began to cry.

The light from an obnoxious neon sign pulsated through the old, yellowed curtains. The cramped motel room included all the luxuries that forty-seven dollars a night could buy. The short shag carpet—drab green and pep-pered with cigarette burns—offset the pumpkin-colored bedsheet, which undoubtedly concealed a horror show that any black light could easily illuminate.

Plastered drunk, Mac lay with an empty vodka bottle at his side. "No more home," he slurred, counting on his fingers. "No more wife." He hiccupped. "No more kids..." He choked on the last three words and began weeping mournfully. "It's all gone," he sobbed, "everything..." He hiccupped. "...all of it." His body convulsed from the excruciating pain in his heart. "My children..." He hic-cupped. "...my life."

Mac took one last breath when his cell phone rang. Hiccupping, he looked at the number on the phone and quickly answered. "Hello?"

"Dad, it's me, Bella," his daughter whispered.

"Oh Beans," Mac whimpered.

"Mom doesn't know I'm calling," the young girl whispered, "but I couldn't go to sleep without telling you I love you. We all do."

"I love you too, princess," he cried, stifling another hiccup, "all of you."

"We love you more, Daddy. Goodnight." The line went dead.

Mac collapsed face down on the bed, his body rock-ing to a mix of hiccups and heavy sobs. *What have we done?*

Chapter 11

Without much warning, Christmas arrived. Four stockings hung over the Anderson mantle, the house decorated like it was located in the North Pole itself. Music played in the background, while the smells of a home cooked dinner filled the air. Still, something was missing. Even Bella, faithfully standing sentry at her window, couldn't find it.

"So, is everybody ready for Santa Claus to come?" Sue asked her grandchildren, calling them over to help trim the Christmas tree with her and their mom.

Jillian rolled her eyes, while Bella and Brady began cheering. "Yes...yes!"

Jen chuckled.

"Have you guys been good this year," Sue asked, "and listened to your mom and..." She stopped. "You've behaved in school and eaten everything on your plates, right?" she added, quickly recovering.

Brady nodded.

"Everything but ham," Bella said. "I don't like ham."

"I noticed that at dinner tonight," Jen interjected, struggling to untangle a ball of Christmas lights that Mac normally wrestled with.

"And we have ham every year for Christmas," the girl said. "Why?"

"Because that's our traditional holiday dinner," Jen said, her tongue hanging out of her mouth in frustration.

"I really love Santa," Brady said, preferring to return to the original topic of conversation.

"Me too," Jillian whispered, unclear about her sincerity.

"Yeah," Bella agreed.

"I hope he leaves lots of presents under the tree this year," Brady added.

"A tree inside the house," Sue said. "Now there's a peculiar holiday tradition, don't you think?"

Jillian sighed heavily, garnering a few bad looks.

Bella and Brady agreed.

"After America won its independence in 1776," Sue explained, "many Germans came to the United States and began sharing their traditions. One of them was the Christmas tree, which they decorated with small dolls and ornaments made from sugar."

"Wow," Brady said, impressed.

"That's right, and the reason they placed trees inside their homes was to show their hope for the forthcoming spring," their grandmother added.

"They made ornaments from sugar?" Bella asked, hanging a plastic Disney ornament on the tree.

"Yes, and they also decorated their trees with apples, roses, candies and colored paper."

"Mmmmm," Brady moaned, "what kind of candies?"

"The kind that didn't last long on a tree, I'd guess," Sue teased.

Everyone but Jillian laughed.

"Years later," Sue continued, "a man named Martin Luther was walking home one December night when the beauty of the stars shining through the branches of a pine tree inspired him. He hurried home and placed candles on the branches of the Christmas tree in his living room."

"That sounds dangerous," Bella said.

"It sure is," Jen said, abandoning any hope for the ball of lights she'd been tackling, "and that's why we don't play with candles or matches, right?"

Bella and Brady nodded.

"But stringing electric lights on a Christmas tree ended up being a pretty neat idea that stuck," Sue said.

"Can I have a candy cane from the tree, Mom?" Brady asked, impatiently.

"Yeah, me too," Bella said.

"You guys sure you don't want an apple instead?" Jen teased.

"No," they groaned.

"Do you like candy canes, Grandma?" Brady asked.

"Actually, I love them," she said. "In fact, I haven't met a candy yet that I couldn't get along with."

Jen and the two little ones laughed. By now, Jillian was sitting alone in the corner, wearing her usual scowl.

"Okay," Jen said, "you can each have one, but..."

"...but only if one of you can tell me where candy canes came from," Sue interrupted, smiling.

The kids groaned again.

"Oh, here we go," Jillian mumbled under her breath.

Jen shot her a look that nearly guaranteed her silence.

Sue handed a candy cane to both Bella and Brady. "As you guys now know," she said, "once folks began using Christmas trees, they decorated them with everything from cookies to candies. At first, straight white peppermint sticks were used as one of the confections. But legend has it that the choirmaster at Germany's Cologne Cathedral asked local craftsmen to bend the white sticks into the shape of shepherds' crooks."

"Mmmmm..." Brady moaned, enjoying his sweet treat.

"Can you guys guess why?" Sue asked.

As they both shrugged, Jillian sighed even louder from the corner.

"The treats were given to children to keep them quiet during ceremonies at the living Nativity scene,"

Sue explained, ignoring her eldest granddaughter again, "and the tradition of passing out the candy canes soon spread throughout the world." She smiled. "So, what does that teach us?" she asked.

Bella shrugged. "That kids can't talk and eat candy at the same time?" she suggested.

Sue clasped her hands together. "You got it," she said, "candy canes help you listen better."

While the family enjoyed their sweet treats, Jillian snickered loudly. "I think I'm going to be sick," she said, no longer concerned about her volume.

Jen took a break from the tree trimming and went to her disgruntled daughter. "You okay?" she quietly asked.

The pouting teenager shook her head. "Grandma thinks she's Dad now, trying to teach us everything."

Jen looked at her.

"She's nothing like Dad," Jillian said.

"Jill," Jen said, "I know it's been tough with your dad gone, but I think we need to get used to it. I'm not sure..."

"I know that, Mom," Jillian interrupted, "and I don't care. It's more peaceful in the house now." She sighed heavily. "I just can't take Grandma pretending to be him."

"Be nice," Jen whispered. "Grandma's trying to help."

"I think I like her better when she's drinking spiked egg nog," Jillian whispered back, getting up and stomping out of the room before she could be scolded for being disrespectful.

"God bless us, everyone," Sue said, heading toward the kitchen. "I'm making myself a stiff drink," she told Jen. "Do you want one?"

Jen nodded. "Oh, I think I need one," she said.

∞

Within the chaos of the bustling newsroom, Jen finished another article and sat back in her chair to proofread it. The office was decorated in red and green, garlands hanging everywhere. Joel pulled a chair up to her desk and threw her a package of snack cakes. "Here," he said, "Merry Christmas."

"Oh, you shouldn't have," she said, throwing the draft onto her desk. "You're much too kind."

Joel giggled. "It's the least I could do."

Jen didn't counter. She felt troubled.

"So, how's life on the home front?" Joel asked, picking up on her melancholy.

She shrugged. "The same. It's been a little bit easier since my mother moved in, but you know..." The mounting tears were already fighting to break free. "The kids are just devastated, Joel. Jillian blames me. And even though they've been afraid of him for months, Bella and Brady don't understand why Daddy doesn't come home." She shook her head. "And I'm supposed to play Santa Claus in four days."

"So, what do you tell them about Daddy?"

"What can I tell them?" she asked. "I don't even understand what happened myself. One minute, life was fantastic and the next, Mac was stomping around the house and screaming at everyone, ramping up for his epic meltdown."

"And how is Mac these days?"

"There's a restraining order in place, so I have no real idea. But I'm guessing he's not good." The tears finally broke free and gravity took over. She searched for a tissue from her purse. "He refuses to talk to anyone. I'm sure he thinks I'm trying to destroy him by keeping the kids from him." She looked up at her friend. "But Joel, my kids are priority one. They have to be."

He grabbed her arm. "Jen, you're doing the right thing. You really are. It's obvious that something pretty dark is going on in Mac's head." He leaned in to stare her in the eyes. "And until he decides to deal with it, you don't need the kids seeing things that kids don't need to see. Besides, it's in the hands of the court now."

"But I'm worried about him," Jen said. "He's still my husband, Joel, and he's so alone right now. He's not working. He won't talk to any of our family or friends. He hasn't gone to counseling." She reached for another tissue. "We go to court tomorrow on the temporary restraining order and, from what I understand, he hasn't even attended one of the anger management classes that the judge mandated. The court will never allow him to see the kids until he finishes those." She had to stop to collect herself. "Mac's spiraling, Joel, and I don't know how..." She became hysterical and couldn't finish.

Joel stood and began rubbing her back. "It's not up to you anymore, Jen. Just take care of your kids and we'll all pray that Mac finds the strength to get the help he needs." He shrugged. "The rest is up to Mac and the judge."

Amongst the wreaths and Christmas music, Jen arrived at court—a place where the truth is as rare as a lawyer willing to tell it. She was early in the hopes of talking to Mac before the proceedings began.

Seconds after Jen approached Attorney Dube to discuss her husband's grave state, Mac arrived, looking disheveled and in ruin. *Oh my God*, she thought, mortified. He took a seat near his lawyer, avoiding eye contact with his estranged wife, who stood right in front of him.

"Mac, please," Jen pleaded, "we need to talk before things get so out of control that we can't..."

"Roland, would you please ask her to leave," Mac said, facing his lawyer. "I don't need to go to jail for violating her restraining order."

"Mac, I didn't want this," she cried, her heart walking the sharp picket fence between spousal love and maternal protection once again. "I really didn't."

Roland looked at her. "Please, Jen," he whispered, gesturing that she step away.

Court Officer Beaupre approached Jen, asking that she be seated. A moment later, the judge entered. "Everyone rise," Officer Beaupre ordered. "The honorable Judge Marge Tremblay presiding."

"Be seated," the judge instructed.

Everyone did as they were told, just in time for the nightmare to unfold.

Judge Tremblay opened a folder, fingered through several reports and looked down at Mac, disapprovingly.

Daniel Aguiar, Jen's attorney, broke the silence. "Your Honor, Mr. Anderson has failed to complete the domestic abuse program mandated by this court and has also..."

"Take a seat, counselor," the judge barked. "I can read."

The judge turned to Mac and waved her finger for the defendant to rise. Mac stood. "Mr. Anderson," the judge said, "two months ago, when you appeared before me, was I unclear with my instructions?"

"Pardon me, your Honor?" Mac said, his voice no more than a squeak.

"Do not try my patience, Mr. Anderson," the judge roared. Reclaiming her composure, she quieted her tone. "I'll ask again. Did I not instruct you to attend domestic abuse counseling for your explosive temper?"

Mac nodded. "You did, your Honor, but I've been sick and..."

"...and not truly concerned with seeing your children?" the judge finished, sarcastically.

"No, your Honor, not at all. If you'll please allow me to explain."

The judge wouldn't hear it. "I think I've just about had it with your explanations, Mr. Anderson," she said. "Why don't you take a seat, get comfortable and allow me to explain a few things to you."

As if he were pushed, Mac collapsed into his wooden chair. The judge fingered through the folder, wrote down something and cleared her throat. "Mr. Anderson, you were ordered by this court to attend domestic abuse counseling. Attorney Aguiar was kind enough to point out that you did not complete the program. However, even he has failed to report that you did not attend so much as one. I can only perceive this as a blatant act of defiance on your part."

Feeling ready to vomit, Jen looked over at her husband, who now sat paralyzed.

"I...I tried," he mumbled, "I really did." It was as if he were talking to himself. "I tried to attend the classes," he added in a whisper, "even made it to the front steps a few times, but..."

While everyone shifted in his or her seats, Dube drummed up the courage to speak. "Your Honor, if I may speak on behalf of my client."

"Take a seat, counselor, or find yourself in contempt," the judge bellowed. "Which will it be?"

Dube sat, throwing his pencil onto the mahogany table in a show of frustration. "There's nothing more I can do," he whispered to Mac.

The judge directed her next words at Mac as well. "Although Mrs. Anderson has never contacted the authorities, I'd say it's also a safe bet that you've violated the restraining order, am I right?"

While everyone in the courtroom took a deep breath, Jen stole another look at her husband. He never flinched. *His eyes look dead*, she thought.

The judge was hardly concerned with a response. "Mr. Anderson, let me cut to the chase," she said. "For the time being, your probation will remain intact and you will be spared incarceration. The temporary restraining order protecting your wife and children, however, will be extended to a period of one year."

There was a sudden wave of chaos, causing the judge to raise her voice. "Or until you can convincingly prove to this court that you are not a threat to yourself or anyone around you." She looked directly at Mac. "Am I clear this time, Mr. Anderson?"

Mac stood. "A year?" he screamed. "I'd never hurt my kids. They're everything to me. How could you..."

Jen could feel her husband's extreme pain; it was as though the walls were closing in all around them and the room was starting to spin.

Attorney Dube grabbed Mac and forcefully placed him into his seat, preventing a certain jail term. Mac was wheezing, struggling to take in oxygen.

The judge's harsh ruling was exactly what Jen had feared. Her heart ached. And the pain—which was now completely in control of everything around them—was gaining momentum. Yet, she could do nothing but sit back and mourn.

Once the room quieted, the judge softened her cruel demeanor. "Mr. Anderson, contrary to your beliefs right now, I am not an unreasonable woman," she explained. "You need professional help. It's also clear to me that this is something you must choose to accept in order for your family to be reunited someday. In the meantime, I have no choice but to protect your children and insure that they are kept out of harm's way." There was a thoughtful pause. "I don't expect that you'll ever thank me for this, but hopefully, you'll understand someday. Until then, as a parent myself, I implore you to search your heart and commit yourself to a hospital that can treat whatever ails your mind and make you well again." Without another word, she stood and exited the court.

There was silence. Mac, Jen and their respective attorneys each sat in shock.

"I can't see my kids for an entire year," Mac confirmed aloud, crying whatever inconsolable tears remained.

At the next table, only twenty feet away, Jen struggled to breathe. *Can this really be it?* she wondered, confused about a deep love they once shared and enduring the abuse of a man she no longer recognized. *Is it really over?*

For several weeks after the dismal New Year passed, Mac cycled through the first four stages of grief—denial, anger, depression, bargaining—like he was on a cross-country trek. But maintaining a constant drunken stupor made it difficult to separate fantasy from reality.

One night—as he did on many nights—he staggered aimlessly for hours, until he spotted a couple holding a whining golden-haired puppy wearing a tiny red collar. He lost his breath, nearly vomiting over the precious scene. *Enjoy it while you can*, he thought, his mind returning to the not so distant past.

Bella had begged for months before Mac and Jen finally relented and decided to adopt a four-legged friend for her. For many reasons, their family situation was best suited for a small breed: a lap dog. They looked around for a while before ending up at a local breeder that specialized in tea cup poodles. "There's no way," Mac told Jen in the gravel driveway. "I love dogs, big dogs, not guinea pigs with wagging tails." They went in to meet the puppies anyway. There were two new litters to meet and consider.

From the moment Bella saw the little balls of fur, hopping around like hyperactive bunny rabbits, Mac realized the decision had already been made. "How big do they get?" he asked the breeder.

"Some can get up to four and a half pounds," the grinning man said.

Oh my God, Mac thought. *I just ate a bigger breakfast than that.*

Weeks later, Santa Claus delivered a female tea-cup poodle that Bella named Sophie. The tiny creature whined so much that first night that Mac actually slept on the living room floor with her. In the days that followed, Sophie relieved herself in a litter box—like a cat—before she was fully house trained. And Mac quickly learned that he'd never be able to take her for a walk. Sophie's legs were so short that she'd become hypoglycemic and collapse due to exhaustion. To overcome this challenge, Jen purchased a baby stroller—in Bella's favorite Cheetah print—so the dog could explore the world outside of their backyard.

Even full-grown, Sophie weighed just under four pounds. And looking like a puppy, she was treated as such. When she barked to protect their family, she sounded more like a squeak toy than a dog. Preferring to snuggle than play fetch, she played with cat toys. *She's nothing like those big mutts I've adored my whole life,* he thought.

Mac was a fairly big guy in physical stature, so his self-esteem had been tested multiple times because of Sophie. At the veterinarian's as well as the groomers, while other guys walked out with their bulldogs and German Shepherds, Mac walked in with a dog that weighed half of what most house cats weigh. But he couldn't have cared less. *I don't think I've ever loved a dog more than Sophie.* They loved each other, completely and unconditionally. *And as an added bonus, she's reminded me not to take myself too seriously.*

When push came to shove, he would have done anything for the dog—except push a Cheetah-print baby stroller. *Every man has his limits,* he told himself.

∞

And now Sophie's been taken from me, too, he thought, returning to his world of pain. His eyes welled with tears. *Everything's gone.*

Returning to his cell-like room, he sat on the edge of the bed and stared at a TV screen of gray static. An intense flurry of anxiety ripped through him, one debilitating punch after the next. While country music drifted in from the bustling street, flickering, holiday lights, yet to be taken down, joined the roach motel's neon sign in penetrating the dingy draperies. *It's over,* he finally decided, *done.* He reached for the nightstand, opened the top drawer and removed a pistol. He spun the revolver's barrel once before staring at the cold blue steel. *There's no coming back from this,* he told himself, his eyes beginning to leak. As he spun the pistol's barrel again, slowly placing the muzzle against his throbbing temple, he took notice of the telephone. Reluctantly, he put the pistol down, lifted the telephone receiver and dialed.

All three kids answered. "Hi, you've reached the Andersons. Please leave a message and we'll get right back to ya. Have a great day."

He hung up and bawled. Reaching into his wallet, he removed a picture of the kids and dialed the phone again. Jillian, Bella and Brady repeated the same. "Hi, you've reached the Andersons. Please leave a message and we'll get right back to ya. Have a great day."

Mac stared at the photo—and dialed again.

"Hi, you've reached the Andersons. Please leave a message and we'll get right back to ya. Have a great day."

"How did this happen?" he groaned, sobbing like a baby. "How did I get here?"

Suddenly, his own words of wisdom returned to him. *There are people, very sad people,* he'd told his children, *who go through life blaming everyone but themselves. They complain about their troubles and all the things they want and don't have. The problem with that is—as soon as you consider yourself a victim in this world, you've lost control of your own life.* He'd peered into his kids' eyes. *We're given one life,* he'd said, *so take accountability for it and make it a great one.*

Mac looked down at pistol. "It's me," he whimpered, nodding at the anguished truth of it. "It's always been me and I need to own it." Swiping the pistol onto the floor, he looked at the photo of his kids and dialed home again.

"Hi, you've reached the Andersons. Please leave a message and we'll get right back to ya. Have a great day."

The sound of his children's voices made him dry-heave. *I can't friggin' do this to them,* he realized. *I won't. They're what's most important: their feelings, their well-being, their lives.* Anger welled up inside him. "I have to stop playing the victim," he grumbled. "I'm the only one who can fix this." Immediately, he decided that anger was a much better place than despair.

He dialed one last time and listened. "Hi, you've reached the Andersons. Please leave a message and we'll get right back to ya. Have a great day."

He hung up and walked to the mirror. Wiping his swollen eyes, he stared hard into them. "You're going to let everything just slip away, you stupid bastard?" He shook his head. "I don't think so." Hope had arrived and not a moment too soon.

Mac finally understood why he hadn't allowed himself to reach the final stage of grief. *There will be no acceptance*, he vowed in his mind, *not in this lifetime*.

Quickly rummaging through his wallet, he slid out the wrinkled piece of paper that Brandt had given him. He picked up the phone again and punched in the numbers. *Wherever this call takes me*, he decided on the first ring, *whatever it takes, I need to get back to my kids*.

Jen had always loved shopping, but these days she only left the house out of necessity. *The little ones need new shoes*, she realized, but the moment she stepped into the store, her heart sank. An unexpected memory—once happy—backhanded her across the face.

It was early autumn. Mac and Jen were enjoying one of their overnight getaways. Hand-in-hand, they strolled the cobble-stone street, sipping flavored coffees and window shopping. Mac hated to actually shop, so when Jen dragged him into a shoe store he marched straight up to the register and asked the girl, "Do you carry men's clogs?"

"Clogs?" the girl repeated, while Jen watched from the safety of a tall shoe rack.

Mac nodded, clearly struggling to keep a straight face.

The young clerk called out to her manager. "Do we have men's clogs?"

"I'm looking for wooden clogs in a size twelve," Mac added, as the manager made her way to the counter. "I'm a professional Irish step dancer and I never stop dancing until I can smell smoke."

Jen laughed from the shadows, drawing several curious looks.

The girl behind the register studied Mac's face for a moment before cracking a smile. "You're joking, right?"

He started laughing. "I am," he admitted before heading for the door. "I'll be outside waiting," he yelled to Jen, who shook her head over his sick sense of humor.

He's so crazy, she thought, still laughing.

Jen looked around the same shoe store, now empty of her husband's joyful spirit. *I miss that craziness,* she thought, a heavy cloak of grief draped over her slumping shoulders. She took a deep breath to help her refocus. *Just get the damn shoes,* she told herself, *and get the hell out of here.*

Officially checked in to the puzzle factory, Mac sat on his new bed dressed in a Presbyterian Hospital robe and slippers. While a howling Nor'easter piled up snow outside his window, there was a knock on the door. "Come in," Mac said, surprised that his voice sounded so shallow and broken.

Dr. Fiore, a kind-looking cleric, entered. He extended his hand for a shake. "Mr. Anderson, I'm Dr. Fiore. Do you mind if I take a seat?"

Although Mac nodded, he felt confused. "Sure," he said, "but I'm not sure I need a priest."

The doctor chuckled. "Actually, I'm a clinical psychologist, who also happens to be a cleric." The man sat in the corner chair and opened Mac's folder. "Mr. Anderson, by signing yourself into our care, I truly believe you've made a wise step in the right direction. It may not seem that way today, but I can assure you that before you know it life will return…"

Although Mac tried to pay attention, not even the rumble strips carved into the side of the road could have kept him in the present. His mind was already drifting off.

It was morning. Mac and the kids were at the sailboat slip. He could picture them, each donning their bright orange life vests. *It was a calm, sunny day*, he recalled, *with a few clouds bringing about slight winds—a perfect day for Brady to break into sailing*. He envisioned the three children seated at the rear of the boat, listening attentively as he worked the sails and gave a lesson on safety. He looked up to see the animals foraging on the shore, the birds gliding in the sky—all that was natural and good in the world. He then looked back to discover Brady entranced in the freedom of it all. "It's the feeling of freedom," he told the boy, "that's what you feel." Searching all three faces, he added, "But guys, you don't need to feel happy or peaceful to feel free. Like everything worth living for, freedom lives right in here." He pointed to his chest, inhaling deeply to drive his point home. The kids followed suit. Grinning, he began to work the main sail. The kids looked at each other and smiled. *What a glorious day…*

"Mr. Anderson?" Dr. Fiore said, waiting for Mac to return to reality.

"Huh? What?" Mac said. "Oh yeah, I'm sorry."

The doctor smiled. "Looks like you were quite a ways from here. Where'd you go?"

"To where my kids are...or were anyway."

The doctor picked up on the melancholy. "Can't wait to get back to them, right?"

"I wish," Mac said, sadly. "The judge took them from me and I'm not sure I'll ever be able..."

"Whoa there," Dr. Fiore said, cutting him off. "Where's your faith?"

"Faith?"

"Yeah, *faith*. You don't honestly think this is the end of the line for you, do you?" He shook his head. "Oh no, this is just another starting point, Mr. Anderson, that's all." He nodded. "You'll be with your kids again. Just by the look in your eyes, I can guarantee it."

"You must know something I don't, doc," Mac said gratefully, "but I hope you're right."

"Sure I'm right," the man confirmed, smiling. "Besides, how can anyone take something from you when it lives right in here?" Dr. Fiore slapped his chest.

Mac's heart skipped a beat, while goose bumps covered his body and every hair stood on end. Dr. Fiore continued smiling like an angel sent from heaven— an angel who knew Mac well. *It can't be a coincidence,* Mac thought. *Is this the sign I asked for?* In one random moment in time, his faith had been challenged and left bare for further examination.

Forty miles away, Jen and Jillian were having a difficult conversation about why Jillian had been suspended from school for three days.

"Are you hurt anywhere?" Jen asked.

"*I'm* not, but Amy's probably not feeling too good right now," Jillian said defiantly.

"What on earth were you thinking, Jill? Now I have to worry about you getting into fist fights too?"

"Are you going to let me explain?" the teenager asked, her resentment apparent.

Jen took a seat at the kitchen table, gesturing for Jillian to do the same. "Go ahead. I'm listening."

Jillian took a seat. "I confided in Katie about Dad going away and the blabbermouth started telling everyone. Next thing I know, Amy Case, you remember her, the nasty girl from elementary school?"

Jen nodded.

"Anyway, we were at lunch and everyone was sitting at the table when Amy walks up and says, 'So your dad's been locked up, huh?'" Tears glassed over Jillian's eyes. "So I stood up and got right in her face."

"Oh Jill," Jen whispered, shaking her head.

"And I punched her as hard as I could right on the nose." Jillian became more upset. "I've never seen so much blood," she said, starting to cry.

"Oh Jillian," Jen repeated, torn between anger and feeling bad for her daughter. "I know you were defending your father, but he wouldn't want you fighting either."

"You know what?" Jillian said, nearly convulsing. "I wasn't defending my father. I was defending myself." She shook her head, a mix of pain and anger betrayed in her eyes.

Mac's always been Jill's hero, Jen considered, *and she's been so filled with bitterness and resentment since he's fallen off her pedestal.*

"I don't give a damn what my father wants," Jillian added. "If he really cared about me, he'd be here with…" She stopped, trying to gather herself. It was no use. Now hysterical, she ran out of the room.

"Sweetheart," Jen said, hurrying after her, "that's just not true."

Chapter 12

The distinct scent of apple pipe tobacco wafting on a warm breeze competed with the smell of freshly cut grass. Mac straddled the seat of a weathered picnic bench beneath the shade of a weeping willow tree. He took in a deep breath and then another. A giant clam boil was being prepared in an oval, copper pot, fish steaming in wax paper on top. While the Boston Red Sox played ball on a small transistor radio, empty quart bottles of beer helped to raise voices and inspire laughter. Mac looked left to see his grandpa stepping out of his pigeon coop. Removing his cap, the old-timer wiped his brow with a red handkerchief retrieved from his worn denim overalls. There was a dog, Buttons, at his heels, awaiting the old man's next command. Mac headed for the willow tree, past the circle of women gossiping in lawn chairs. He was deep into the tree's thick limbs—his Army Base Camp—when he looked out onto the yard. *I bet Grampa would let me drive the red tractor if I wanted*, he thought, *or maybe even let me win another arm wrestling match.* He considered jumping down, as the changing light of dusk always made him feel like he could run faster than he could, chasing fireflies with an empty mayonnaise jar. Instead, he lay on his belly in that tree and watched as the night crept in and the faces of those he loved became unrecognizable shadows until they completely disappeared.

∞

Mac opened his eyes, awakening from a brief afternoon siesta. *I'm not in heaven*, he suddenly realized, a wave of thick sorrow rolling over him. *I'm still here,* he thought, *still alive.* Through squinted eyes, he surveyed his small, white hospital room. *Well, that really sucks,* he thought— until he remembered his kids.

∞

Joel stepped up to Jen's desk wearing a plaid blazer. He spun twice like a male model, working it hard on a New York City runway.

"Well, don't you look sharp today," Jen told him.

He smirked. "As opposed to any other day?" he teased.

"I didn't say that. You always look nice." She shook her head. "I never could get Mac to wear bold prints like that."

"So you're suggesting that I'm a gay stereotype then?"

She slapped his arm. "Listen, I've got enough to worry about. I don't need to start walking on egg shells around you too."

He started laughing. "Relax, boo," he said. "I'm just playing with you."

"Please find another play thing," she said, grinning.

"Nope, I happen to like the one I got," he said, spinning again to show off his new blazer.

She laughed.

"So have you decided whether you're going to Lauren's winter wonderland wedding?" Joel asked.

Without having to give it much thought, Jen shook her head. "I doubt it," she said sadly. "I love Lauren but I can't bear the thought of…" She paused. "I don't think so," she added, trying to clear the emotion lodged in her throat.

Joel quickly placed his hand on her arm. "I get it, girl," he said. "I didn't mean to upset you."

"It's not you, Joel," she told him, "trust me."

∞

Dressed in his faded hospital pajamas, the scratchy sound of slippers dragging the floor led Mac into one of the many offices off the main corridor. Dr. Fiore gestured that he take a seat. Mac did. He opened Mac's pea-green folder and wasted no time in getting down to business. "Mr. Anderson…"

"It's Mac."

"What's that?" Dr. Fiore inquired.

"Please call me Mac. I won't be able to confide in you if you call me by my grandfather's name."

Dr. Fiore smiled. "Very well, Mac," he said, looking up from the folder. "Tell me about yourself."

Mac took a deep breath. "Well, let's see, I recently destroyed my career and dozens of professional relationships that took me years to build," he confessed. "I lost my marriage and my…" He stopped, unable to say it. "I'm such a…"

"…a good man who needs help," Dr. Fiore interrupted. "I think we need to concentrate on…"

Mac tried to stay focused, but he was already slipping back into the past.

Beneath a shedding tree in their back yard, Mac and Jillian shared a game of catch, both smiling contentedly to be in each other's company. "You keep throwing the ball like that," he told his eldest daughter, "and you'll definitely be in the playoffs next season for sure."

Returning into the house, he found his son at the kitchen table, struggling with a math problem. In time, they worked it out together. "I'm telling you, Brady," he told the young boy, "all you have to do is apply yourself and someday, you'll be flying the space shuttle for NASA." The boy believed.

Mac then knelt beside Bella in her pink bedroom. Together, they spoke to God. He tucked his little girl into bed, pulled the covers under her chin and finished the nightly ritual with a kiss. "Sweet dreams, princess," he said.

"Sweet dreams, Daddy," she answered.

Everything in the world is exactly how it should be, he thought.

"Mac, are you still with me?" Dr. Fiore asked.

Mac's mind stumbled into the present, where he found Dr. Fiore sitting beside him. The man's hand was actually resting on Mac's shoulder.

"Mac?" the doctor asked, softly.

Mac peered up from his fog. "What? Oh yeah, I'm sorry. I don't mean to be rude. I was just thinking about my kids."

"Listen, I'm sure there's no happier place than being with your children," Dr. Fiore said, "but for right now, we need to concentrate on what's going on with you so we can get you back to them, okay?"

"I'm sorry, Dr. Fiore. I..."

"It's Faust."

Mac looked up, puzzled.

Dr. Fiore smiled. "If we're going to cut out the formalities, then let's do it all the way around." Faust Fiore extended his hand. Mac took it. "The name's Faust." After a firm handshake, the therapist said, "Listen, we need to get you into our rehab program right away to address your alcohol abuse. It's imperative for you to get healthy again before we can..."

"Rehab program?" Mac interrupted, his internal alarm clock going off.

Faust nodded. "That's correct. We need to deal with the past before you can tackle the future, Mac, and all the pressures of life that come with it. But we can't do any of it until we wean your body off the chemicals you've grown addicted to."

Mac thought for a minute. "Okay Dr. Fiore," Mac said, "I mean, Faust."

"Good man," Faust said, nodding. "As I'm sure you've learned, drugs and alcohol are nothing more than Band-Aids that'll eventually drag you deeper into your own hell."

Mac nodded vigorously in agreement. "But how long will it take?" he asked. "Rehab?"

The doctor shrugged. "It varies for everyone, but what I can tell you is that it's taken you some time to get where you are right now, so it's going to take you some time to make your way back." He smiled. "It'll take as long as it takes, Mac. The only thing that matters is that you commit yourself to the process, one hundred percent, no matter how long it takes."

Mac sighed heavily. "I...I will," he reluctantly stuttered, surrendering. "I can't keep going on like this." He nodded. "I'll do whatever I need to do."

"Good," Faust said, nodding. "If you give me a signed commitment to work through a rigorous treatment plan, I guarantee the worse of it will be over for you." He looked down at Mac's pea green folder. "Besides treating your addiction, we can also cover off the domestic abuse classes that the court has ordered."

On the outside, Mac remained calm, nodding that he understood. Internally, he was crawling out of his skin. *But how long will all of this take?* he screamed in his head. Panic worked its way back into his heart and mind. *What about my kids?* he wondered, considering so much time being separated from them. Tears began to build. Then, as if he reached a place called acceptance, he softly muttered, "And if I commit to the program, then what?"

"Then I'll go to court myself, if I need to, and testify that you're one of the most loving fathers I've ever met," the doctor said, "and that it would be an absolute injustice to your children that they spend another day without you in their lives."

Mac nodded, agreeing to the inpatient treatment plan. Although he began to cry, his tears were filled with hope.

Faust broke out the contract. "Mac, let me be clear. Once you sign this contract, you'll be mandated to stay on the hospital's premises until I deem that you're healthy enough to be released. If you leave for any reason before then, I will not be able to help you or testify on your behalf." He slid the contract toward Mac and offered his pen. "It's important that you understand."

I have no choice, Mac thought, knowing that without the doctor's testimony the court would tear him to pieces. "I understand." He grabbed the pen and, with a trembling hang, signed himself into the mercy of this smiling stranger.

Tucking the signed contract into the green folder, Faust sat back in his chair. "So let's get started." He raised one eyebrow. "Tell me how you feel."

"Right now?" Mac asked.

The doctor nodded. "Yes, and how you usually feel."

At last, Mac was given the chance to hit the release valve on his pressure cooker. "Most of the time, it starts with cotton mouth. Then I can't swallow and it feels like a pillow's been lodged in my throat. My heart starts pounding and my chest becomes tight, like there's an elephant standing on it." He shook his head. "You name it—I get sweaty palms, trembling hands. Even my fingers and toes start tingling. My breathing gets quick and shallow. And although I do my best to stop it, I usually start hyperventilating. Then, the worse happens, and it feels like it comes right from my..." He stopped.

"From your?" Faust prodded.

"I'm not sure. What I do know is that I get this sense of doom that becomes so intense that it's unbearable. I feel like my friggin' heart's going to explode, or worse, like I might actually lose my mind. I get lightheaded, drunk on fear, making me feel like a man who's lost all control." He shook his head again. "The adrenaline rush is so intense, I can't even explain it." He took a few deep breaths. "But when I search out a reason for it, there's never anything there—nothing for me to defend myself or run from. And that makes things even more confusing." He paused again. "And afterwards, when the rush is over, I always feel off, you know?"

The doctor jotted this down in his notes. "That's very helpful. Anything else?"

"Even when I'm in the middle of one of these God-awful episodes, I'm more afraid of the next one that I know is coming right behind it. It's...it's friggin' torture. I've begun to avoid most people and places, which just makes me feel depressed. It's a horror show. I feel like something invisible is always chasing me." His voice became desperate. "I really can't take it anymore. I'm so tired and I need it to stop," he whimpered, "...for me and my kids."

Faust remained silent, watching him. But Mac couldn't manage another word. "The shortness of breath, the pounding heart," the medicine man explained, "those are called anxiety or panic attacks."

Mac shook his head like he was trying to ward off the man's words. The term *panic* had been used often in the past few months, but Mac was still having trouble accepting the label. *I'm no coward*, he told himself. *I've never panicked about anything in my life.* His grandfather had taught him to be a man, to handle whatever situation he was confronted with. *Am I really so much weaker than I thought?*

With a gentle, logical voice, Faust explained. "In some strange sense, your problem is physical. Although we need to identify and understand the root cause, what you're experiencing is a chemical imbalance that takes place in the brain. Sometimes, it's hereditary. Does anyone in your family have a history of anxiety or depression?"

Mac shrugged, filling his lungs with enough air to speak. "I don't know. I didn't really know my parents," he said, his head spinning. "I was basically orphaned when I was young." He shook his head, his mind going off on another tangent. "I was young when my mom passed away. My memories of her are more like a set of feelings than actual pictures in my mind. I vaguely remember how our relationship ended." He stared into space. "A black dress hanging on my parent's bedroom door, my dad's awful sobs, a table covered in casserole dishes and then finally, my grandparents showing up to take me away. I was too young back then to realize the permanence of my mom's premature death and that it was the perfect opportunity for my father to disappear." He shrugged. "I suppose that's why being a good, dependable dad has always been so important to me." *My father was never there*, he thought, horrified to have his children endure the same painful fate.

Faust smiled. "I'm sure we'll get into it."

Mac nodded, trying to return completely to the present. It wasn't easy.

Faust stood. "I'll order your meds. Nurse Costa will be in shortly to administer them." He peered into Mac's eyes. "Make sure you take them, okay?"

"Okay," Mac answered, no longer feeling in control of his own life.

"Very good," the doctor said, patting Mac's shoulder and leaving the room.

Mac sat alone and afraid, again. If he understood anything now, he knew there was a very long road ahead. *A panic attack is what happens to other people,* he told himself again...*until it began happening to me.*

An older woman with graying, wavy hair entered the room. Mac could tell right away, *This lady's all business.*

Marching straight toward him, she extended a small plastic cup, containing two pills. "Here, take these," she ordered before handing him a paper cup of water.

"Thank you, Nurse Costa," he said, reading her faded name tag.

"Call me Mal," she said. "I don't go for all that formal bullshit." She studied him for a moment. "You good for now?" she asked.

No-nonsense with a hint of compassion, he thought, adjusting his profile of her. "As good as can be expected, I guess," he said.

She peered into his eyes once more. "You're good," she said, as if reporting her initial assessment, and then marched out of the room the same way she'd barged in.

That's what you think, Mac told her somewhere within his skull-splitting migraine.

The house phone rang. Jen stretched past her mother on the couch to pick it up. "Hello?"

"Hi Jen, it's Roland Dube. How are you?"

At the man's first word, her heart began to race. "What's wrong, Roland?" she asked, expecting to hear the worst about her husband.

Sue leaned in toward her for an update. Jen raised her index finger for the woman to wait.

"I shouldn't even be talking to you, Jen. But given the awful circumstances and me being a family friend and all..."

"What is it, Roland?"

"I thought you should know that Mac has signed himself into inpatient treatment," Roland said. "It's an intense program that will take months to..."

"Months?" she repeated.

Sue tapped Jen's leg. Again, the index finger went up.

"I thought you should know," Roland said before lowering his tone. "At this point, the restraining order is probably in the best interest of everyone. From what I'm told, it's best that Mac has no interaction with outside influences while he's undergoing treatment and working through things."

"Oh...okay," she said, not knowing how else to respond. She looked at her mother and shook her head.

Sue looked ready to burst from curiosity.

"Listen Jen," Roland said, "I could get into some hot water if..."

"I get it, Roland," she said. "Mums the word. I promise."

"Okay," he said, "thanks."

"Thank you for calling. I really appreciate it."

"Sure. I'll keep you in the loop as much as I can," he said before hanging up.

Jen placed the telephone into its cradle.

"Well?" Sue asked, sitting on the edge of her seat.

"It was Roland Dube. He said that Mac's finally signed himself into treatment."

"Thank God," Sue said.

"Yeah, it's a good thing," Jen said, nodding. "Roland said it's an intense program that could take him months to complete."

Sue sighed heavily. "Whatever it takes for him to get well again, right?"

Jen was riddled with confusion. Although she felt a tremendous amount of pain—as she'd loved this man deeply—she also felt there was no choice but to move forward without him in their lives.

"What is it?" Sue asked, studying her daughter's face.

"There's a very real chance that Mac's not coming back from this and..." She stopped, feeling the shock of this sudden realization.

"And?"

"And I may need to build a life for me and the kids that doesn't include him." The tears began to fall. "I've loved him from the moment I met him, Mom, but..."

Sue wrapped her in a tight hug. "I know," she whispered. "I know."

"I have to think of the kids," she whimpered.

"And yourself," her mom added.

Bella knelt by her bed, her hands clasped together. Tears peppered her beautiful, little face. "Dear God," she prayed aloud, "I know I probably don't talk to you as much as I should, but I really need to talk to you right now. God, I'm so sorry for being bad sometimes. My mom has to yell at me and my brother and sister because we don't listen, or we don't finish our chores. But God, I promise, if you let my daddy come back home—my good daddy, not my angry daddy—I'll never be bad again. And I'll make sure that Jillian and Brady will be good too." Tears filled her eyes. "We'll eat everything on our plates. We'll go to bed on time. And we won't ever talk back again." She shrugged. "And I won't even hide Brady's sneakers before school anymore, so Mom can yell at him. Please

God, all we want is our old daddy back." She nodded. "That's all we want. If you do that for us, then we'll be the best kids you ever saw—honest."

She blessed herself, stood and walked to the window to watch for her dad's return. As she peered out the dark window, she whispered, "God, please let my daddy come home. We miss him so much."

Just then, Brady's scream traveled across the hall. When Bella entered his bedroom, she found her mom hovered over her little brother. Brady was hugging their mom and crying. Jillian was also there, her face cherry red.

"Tell Mamma, baby," their mom told Brady, "what is it?"

Brady hyperventilated. "It's Daddy. I...I keep dreaming about him." The boy's heavy sniffles forced him to stop.

"I know, Brady," his mom said, "I know it hurts. Go ahead, get it out. There's nothing wrong with crying."

"I keep dreaming that Dad's not coming back. I keep seeing him running far away from us. It's dark and he keeps running and running..."

"No, Brady. Dad didn't run away from us. He'd never do that. It's just that he's sick and he needs time to get better." She paused, clearly at a loss for more words. "Everything will be okay," Jen finally said, "I promise." Her last two words sounded less than convincing.

"But Daddy promised, too," Bella said, starting to cry. "Daddy promised that he wouldn't leave—that he'd never leave!" The little girl cried harder.

"Maybe you should watch what you wish for," Jillian mumbled, appearing in the doorway.

Everyone looked up at her.

"Have you guys already forgotten how scary it was when Dad was here?" she asked.

"He wasn't always like that," Bella screamed, defensively.

"Yeah," Brady said, "he was only like that at the end."

Jillian shook her head. "We're better off without him," she mumbled under her breath.

"Jill, don't say..." Jen stopped.

Jillian disappeared from the doorway.

While Brady clung to his mom, Bella shook her head over-and-over.

"It's going to be okay," Jen repeated at a whisper.

To help console her little brother, Bella lay down beside him, trying to provide any comfort she could. As Brady's eyes grew heavy, their mom tip-toed out of the room. Bella, however, never budged. Lying beside her baby brother, she whispered, "I'll never leave you, buddy."

Jen collapsed onto the living room couch, where she grieved her uncertain future so deeply that it shot pains across her constricted chest. Rolling herself into the fetal position, she tried giving herself the hug that she desperately missed. *Where do I go from here?* she wondered, feeling as though the weeks of overwhelming emotion had suddenly caught up to her. *What do I...* She dozed off.

Jen was sitting at her friend Lauren's winter wonderland-themed wedding—alone. *It's now or never,* she thought, *and I need some alone time.* The time seemed right, so she slipped away from the wedding reception and headed straight past the coat check to the ladies room.

Jen checked her look in the mirror. Even though she was all dolled up, her nose cringed at the sight of herself. She shook her head and started for one of the empty stalls. She locked the door behind her and, without any intentions of relieving herself, took a seat. She opened her clutch, retrieved a single razor blade from her sunglass case and pulled up her left sleeve. Surveying the twisted map of old scar tissue and recent cuts, she located a fresh patch of skin. Positioning her arm between her legs, she made the first incision. It was a deep cut that stung and throbbed at the same time, making her feel alive. *At least I can feel this*, she thought, knowing it was the only pain in her world she could control. While blood dripped into the toilet from the first cut, she made the second incision. *Stop!* a small voice screamed in her head, but the voice was too small. She made a third cut, but with all the blood covering her forearm she'd crossed over some deep scar tissue. The blood flowed heavily now. *Shit*, she thought. *I went too deep*. She placed the sharp blade back into the glass case. Just then, the bathroom door opened and two women entered. Instinctively, Jen lifted her legs to conceal her presence. While the two women lingered at the mirror, touching up their make-up and gossiping about "how ugly those bridesmaids' dresses are," Jen quietly grabbed a roll of toilet paper and spun it in her right hand until she held a thick wad. She placed it over her left forearm and watched as the white paper became saturated in crimson red. The pain was mind-numbing, alternating between a harsh burn and aching throb. It made her smile. She dumped the paper between her legs into the toilet and rolled up another wad. This one she held to her forearm to help with the clotting. In the meantime, women came and went; some used the toilets, but most freshened up their faces while verbally bashing other wedding guests. Three wads and two flushes later, Jenn applied sterile gauze over the new wounds and quickly taped them up like a veteran field medic. She rolled down her sleeve, flushed the toilet one last time and unlocked the stall door. Her forearm felt like it was on fire. *Oh, sweet release...*

As she stood in front of the mirror this time, she was even more repulsed. *Beast*, she thought, throwing her small fist into the mirror. It barely rattled. Shaking her head, she checked her dress sleeve to ensure the thick gauze was keeping her secret at bay. *Good.*

Lauren was finishing her table-to-table rounds when she caught up to Jen. "Where have you been?" she asked.

Jen shrugged, her face turning pink from embarrassment. "The ladies room," she whispered. "I've been having some issues."

"Oh no," Lauren said, giving her a hug. "You're not feeling well and you still came to share this day with us?" She looked into Jen's eyes. "Thank you so much, Jen."

Jen put on her best fake smile. "Are you kidding me, Lau? I wouldn't have missed your wedding for the world." As the lovely bride walked away, Jen looked down at her arm; her sleeve was still dry but her knuckles were red and swollen. *Beast*, she repeated in her head.

Jen awakened from her dream and lay still. Her body felt weak from convulsing and her throat was sore from all the wailing. She reached up to wipe her eyes, surprised that she'd run out of tears. The dream was so vivid, so real. *Self-mutilation*, she thought. *Is this what I've done?* She looked down at her forearms, expecting to find ladders of pain that climbed up each of her arms. There wasn't a scratch. *No physical scars anyway*, she thought.

"Mom?" Bella asked.

Startled, Jen discreetly wiped her face before looking up. "Yeah babe." She patted the seat cushion beside her.

Bella took a seat. "I love Daddy and I miss him, but I'm also afraid..."

"Afraid of what?" Jen asked, enveloping the little girl in her arms.

"That Daddy will come back and be angry at us again."

She looked into the child's puffy eyes. "Sweetheart, Mommy would never let him come back like that." She squeezed Bella tight. "Daddy's sick, babe, and he needs to get better." She took a deep breath, exhaling slowly. "Daddy needs to get back to who he was before he got sick, or he'll never step foot back into this house. I promise."

Although Bella nodded, her eyes were filled with confusion.

"There'll no more yelling in this house, babe. Mommy won't allow it."

Bella nodded again and stood. "Is it okay if Sarah sleeps over this weekend?"

"I think that's a great idea," Jen said, never hesitating with the answer. *We could use some laughter in this house again*, she thought.

Bella kissed Jen's cheek. "Goodnight, Mommy."

"Goodnight baby." She patted her daughter's backside. "Sweet dreams."

While the world continued to spin, without Mac taking any active part in it, he wrote a short letter to his children.

> *Dear Jillian, Bella and Brady, I hope this letter finds you all well. I've been working really hard to get back to you. According to my doctor, his name's Faust, I'm already*

making some progress. The three of you are the only thing I think about. I love you with all my heart. Every day, I imagine how wonderful it will be on the day we're all reunited. Please take good care of your-selves. And Jillian, please look after the two little ones for me while I'm away. Know that I'm thinking of all of you. You Live in My heart—Always, Dad.

Peering through the fog of sedation, Mac folded it up and placed it into the unsealed envelope. He then knelt beside his bed and prayed, "Dear Lord, please give me the strength and courage to get well and return to my children as soon as possible. Bless Jillian, Bella and Brady. Shroud them in your angels and keep them safe. In Jesus' name, Amen." He blessed himself, grabbed the framed photo of his children from his metal nightstand and kissed it.

There was a knock just before Faust peeked his head into the room. "Are you ready for our session, Mac?"

Mac nodded. "Come in, Faust, please." He sat on his bed, while Dr. Fiore took a seat on the chair and reviewed his notepad. "It's been more than a week and my kids haven't responded to one of my letters, Faust," Mac said. "I'm afraid to call, but..."

"And you shouldn't," Faust said. "That would defi-nitely be a bad idea. Even as far as the letters, Mac, they're not the best idea." He raised an eyebrow. "You do realize that any contact is a direct violation of the court's..."

"I know...I know..." Mac interrupted.

Faust opened the folder that contained his notes. "So tell me when the symptoms started. Even a ballpark timeframe."

"Oh, I can do better than that," Mac said. "If I lived a thousand years, I'd never forget the day it started."

Faust waited.

"It was late August at my son's birthday party. I was blowing up a balloon when all of a sudden, I couldn't breathe."

"From inflating a balloon?"

Mac shook his head. "I don't think that was the actual cause. I mean, I'm not in the best physical shape I've ever been in, but..."

"So what was going on at that time?" Faust asked. "Do you remember anything out of the ordinary?"

Mac inhaled deeply. "No, not that I can remember." He gave it some thought. "Let's see, my creative team and I were working on the Woodpine Project at the time, which carried a pretty rigid deadline. But that's nothing unusual." He shook his head. "It can't be that."

"What else?"

"Hmmm, my sister-in-law was around a lot at that time and she's a real pain in the ass." He shook his head again. "Nah, she's always been a small price I've had to pay to be married to the woman I..." He stopped again.

Faust allowed it. "Okay, let's try to pinpoint it a little better." The man leaned in. "I want you to picture that first panic attack you had—blowing up that balloon."

"Okay," Mac said, nodding.

"And then I want you to back in or rewind everything that transpired just before that attack." He nodded. "Go back minutes, hours, days—until something clicks."

"Well, as much as I'd rather not, I can definitely remember that first panic attack. Before that..." He stared off into space, allowing his mind to travel back. "It was a busy weekend. My wife and I were celebrating our fifteenth wedding anniversary and enjoyed a wonderful dinner at D'Avios in the city. We were driving home and..." Suddenly, Mac felt like he'd been kissed on the temple with a sledge hammer; all the air in his lungs left him. "Shit...shit...shit..."

Faust leaned forward in his chair. "What is it, Mac?" he asked. "Tell me."

It was that accident we passed, Mac realized. *That's what kicked off this friggin' nightmare I've been living through...*

"Mac?" Faust repeated.

In a state of shock, Mac looked at the man. "On our way home from the restaurant," he said, still unsure why he hadn't put the puzzle together until now, "Jen and I passed a pretty bad car accident. We slowed to help, but..." He stopped.

Faust waited, studying Mac's face.

"But I..." Mac stopped again.

"Go on," Faust said.

Mac shook his head.

"Was someone hurt in the accident? Did you know them?"

"I didn't know the people in the crash," Mac said, "but...but there was a lot of blood and..."

Faust continued to study him before jotting down some notes. "I think we may have found your trigger," he said quietly. "Have you ever been in a motor vehicle accident?" Faust asked.

Like a violent stalker who'd just been exposed, the first glimmer of truth rushed back to Mac, nearly knocking him off the bed.

Mac had been half-asleep in the passenger seat. His friend, Sam, was driving much too fast for the slippery conditions. And that's when Mac looked up and saw them. Two teenage kids—a few years younger than him—in a beat-up Chevy Camaro pulled out from a poorly lit parking lot. "Shit!" Sam yelled out, hitting the brakes hard. Just as Sam and Mac's car struck the Camaro, the boy in the passenger seat stared straight into Mac's eyes. Mac couldn't imagine a more dreadful sight. The boy's expression was the definition of pure fear.

The sounds of broken glass and twisted steel preceded the horrid screams of human pain. In an instant, the world lay still again. Mac felt a dull throb travel the length of his body. He was hurt. Looking left, he saw that Sam had already fled the wreck. Mac struggled and struggled, trying desperately to free himself. At one point, he heard one of the teenagers moaning. Wondering why the other remained silent, he fought harder to get out of his own crushed vehicle. *I have to save them*, he'd thought. *I have to...*

Panting the same way he had on that awful night all those years ago, Mac returned to the present. He looked up to find Faust staring at him.

"Talk to me, Mac," the doctor said, his voice nearly a whisper.

"I...I can't talk about it, Faust," Mac stuttered, an overwhelming amount of terror filling him. He sprung off the bed, gasping for air. As he paced, he embarked on another full blown panic attack and struggled to breathe.

"Repressed memories," Faust muttered, writing the two simple words into his notes. "Here, take this," Faust said, handing Mac a pill. "Your anxiety will subside in a few minutes."

Mac swallowed the pill and collapsed onto his bed, still struggling against the onslaught of the most horrendous feelings.

"Just breathe, Mac," Faust said in his soothing voice. "You're okay. The only thing you have to do right now is breathe."

Mac struggled to catch his breath, finally composing himself. "I'm...I'm sorry," he said in a wounded voice.

Faust shook his head. "Sorry? Sorry for what? There's nothing to be sorry for, Mac. You're in a lot of pain and I'm here to help you. You know that, right?"

Mac nodded.

"I would never hurt you, Mac," Faust said, "I'm here to help you heal. You need to trust that."

"I do," Mac muttered, nodding, "I do, Faust. It's just that I...I can't..."

Faust nodded. "Be patient, Mac. We'll get there. I promise." He stood to leave. At the door, he asked, "How are you feeling now?"

"Better, thank you."

"Patience, okay?" Faust said before closing the door behind him. "We'll get there."

Mac grabbed the framed photo of the kids again. "Patience?" he whispered, shaking his head, "I don't have time for patience." He sat on the edge of his bed and placed his head into his hands. "A car accident," he said aloud, "all of this pain and torment because of a car accident that happened a lifetime ago?"

He pulled out the letter he'd written to his kids and added a post script: *PS—Guys, I just made a major breakthrough and think I finally understand where my suffering originates from. Although I have a way to go, I'm confident this will speed up the days before we see each other again.*

Nurse Mal stuck her head in. "You doing okay for now?"

Mac shrugged, unsure of how to answer the stern-faced woman.

She lingered for a moment before offering a nod. "You're doing okay for now," she answered and left.

Where the hell did they find Nurse Ratchet? Mac wondered, still happy for any distraction he could get.

Chapter 13

Jen sat slouched over, the weight of the world resting on her shoulders. Joel approached her messy desk and grabbed her by the hand. "Okay, okay, the doctor's here," he said, "Want to go for a cup of coffee?"

As they walked, Jen filled him in. "I honestly don't know what to do, Joel."

"About what?"

"Mac finally got himself into therapy. He's at Presbyterian."

"Good for him," Joel said. "It's about time."

"The problem is, I got a letter from him yesterday and it's addressed to the kids."

Joel cringed. "Uh, oh."

"Exactly. If the court finds out about it, Mac will get sent to jail for violating the no contact order."

"What did the letter say?" Joel asked.

"I couldn't even bring myself to open it," she said sadly.

"So what's the big deal?"

As if he were insane, Jen stopped and glared at him. "The big deal is that I honestly don't know what to do with it." She shrugged. "Joel, I have no idea how long Mac is going to be there. If I let the kids read it and..."

"You can't let the kids read it," Joel blurted.

"Yeah, that's what my mother says."

"And she's right. Hey, I know it sounds cruel, Jen, but if I were you I wouldn't get the kids' hopes up."

Jen's heart skipped a beat. "That's what I was thinking," she reluctantly admitted. "They've just gotten to the point where they can function somewhat normally again. I'm not sure it would be all that smart to jeopardize that."

Joel nodded in agreement. "I know it stinks, but you have to keep the letter from them. I'd hold on to it and give it to them when all of this craziness blows over."

"See, I'm not sure I should do that either. They'd hate me for keeping their father from them. They already feel..." She stopped, feeling so torn and overwhelmed.

Joel grabbed her hand. "Hey, you're not keeping their father from them, Jen. You're protecting them from more pain, that's all. I'm sure they'll understand when they get older."

Jen nodded her gratitude, feeling a tinge of relief. "I just hope Mac doesn't send any more letters. It's tearing my heart out."

Dressed in a hooded sweatshirt, worn jeans and a new pair of running shoes, Mac sat in a circle of recovering alcoholics and addicts, each one sharing details of the nightmares that had landed them there.

"Every day I waste away in this shit hole," an angry patient named Andrew said, "is another day I'm not with my kids, teaching them everything they need to learn."

Mac's stomach flopped sideways. He couldn't have chosen better words himself. As one of the counselors spoke of the glory found along the Twelve Steps, Mac's mind drifted off.

I have three wonderfully different children, Mac thought, *and each one of them needs me to be home.* A different version of panic filled his heart. *There's no way I can teach them that dreams come true unless I'm there to show them. There's so much I need them to believe...to know.* He felt dizzy from the bombardment of examples that saturated his brain. His eyes filled, as he longed to offer his kids the lessons they needed to get from him. *Luck is the place where opportunity meets preparation,* he told them in his head, *and opportunity often disguises itself as a mix of hard work and perseverance.* In the midst of his daydream, he pictured his kids' wide eyes as they absorbed his carefully chosen words. *We can make even the wildest dream come true, guys, but we have to work very hard for it.*

∞

Butch Belanger, a fellow alcoholic, tapped Mac on the shoulder, jerking him back into a cruel reality. "Are you all right, man?" he asked in a hoarse whisper.

"Yeah, thanks," Mac answered, returning the whisper. "Did I miss anything?"

"Nothing you won't hear a thousand more times in the next few months." He grinned.

Dorothy Cabeceiras, the group therapist, spotted Butch talking. "Would you like to share with us, Mr. Belanger?" she asked.

Butch smirked. "I was just telling my new friend here that I used to be a real go-getter back in the day," he said, pausing for effect. "I'd drop my wife off at work and then I'd go get her." He laughed.

Shaking her silver head, Mrs. Cabeceiras scanned the room. "Perhaps someone who can be a little more serious would like to share?"

There were no takers.

"It's no joke," Butch said, trying to contain his smile, "I'm talking about the same woman who maxed out my credit card at the Dollar Store."

Retaining her professional demeanor, Mrs. Cabeceiras turned to George Saber—the patient on Mac's left—and asked, "Would you like to share with us today, George?"

George snickered. "Well, I know I wouldn't be here if it wasn't for my bitch ex-wife," he started.

"Without cursing, please," Dorothy said.

George paused, clearly considering whether he wanted to share. One deep breath later, he kicked off the most intelligent and terrifying rant Mac had ever heard. "My marriage was done long before we ended it," George explained. "My wife and I decided to act like real adults and do what was in the best interest of our children." He shook his head. "This, I learned, was impossible because the best interest of our children was as different in our minds as our ideas for saving the marriage. Right away, my newly estranged wife considered our kids her closest allies and decided that she and the kids were a package deal. She couldn't see the separation. My kids were hers and if I wasn't with her, then I was an outsider." He took another breath. "Basically, if she and I were going to be separated, then so were the kids and I."

Mac's blood turned to ice water, sending an awful shiver down his spine. His right knee began to bounce from nervous energy.

"With our youngest just a few years out of diapers," George said, "irreconcilable differences dragged me into a world of hell." He swallowed hard. "While my kids watched cartoons, the wife and I went to court, an intimidating place that should bring justice to criminals, not tear fathers away from their children."

Mac recalled his own nightmare in court and felt a bolt of lightning rip through his chest. *I figured I was punching way above my weight class*, he thought, look-ing sideways at George, *but now I can see that I wasn't even allowed in the ring.* There was never any question about the value of a mother's love. *But at what point did a father's love become less valued?* he wondered.

"At nearly two hundred dollars an hour, both law-yers told half-truths, while some stranger dressed in a black robe spent ten whole minutes deciding my fami-ly's future." George stopped to collect himself. "Before it started, it was over. Society's views of our parental roles had dictated the outcome long before we'd stepped into that courtroom. With nothing for me to do but watch, my entire world was slowly dismembered, piece-by-piece." George's words were now choked with emotion. "Of course I started drinking," he said, his voice becom-ing louder and angrier. "That fuckin' judge issued a punishment harsher than any prison term I could have ever received."

Dorothy squirmed in her chair. "Language, please," she reminded him.

But George was fired up now and never broke stride. "With one crack of the gavel, the deal was sealed. I could now take my own children on loan two nights a week and every other weekend. I was in shock," he said, his eyes glassing over. "I'd heard the brutal rumors, read the one-sided stories, but I still couldn't believe it. Yet, there I stood, a man who was being criminalized for committing no crime..." He became choked up. "...a father who was no more than one-half of a relationship that no longer worked."

By this point, Mac had stopped breathing. He was either feeling the man's pain, his own or both.

"I never imagined that the person who hated me most," George said, his eyes glassed over with restrained tears, "would be given complete control over the people I love the most." He gritted his teeth. "It's so damn unfair—the inequity between mothers' rights and fathers' rights. And most men are only one decision, one single choice away from being where I am and this decision probably won't be theirs to make."

No more, Mac yelled in his head, feeling wracked with pain over this poor man's familiar story. Surprised that he even had the strength, Mac stood and hurried for the door.

"Mac," Dorothy called after him. "Mac…"

But he never stopped. As if the room were engulfed in flames, Mac picked up the pace and shuffled out of there.

Mac returned to his tiny room. Pulling the ear buds from his neck, he threw them onto the small wooden desk that sat in the corner of the room. As he prepared to collapse onto the bed, he spotted a letter. Right away, he recognized Brandt's handwriting. He sat on his bed, tore open the envelope and read:

Dear Mac,

I hope this letter finds you well. I've considered coming to visit you a few times, but decided that you'd probably value your privacy rather than having company at this point. I'm sure I would, if I were in your shoes.

Anyway, I wanted to write to let you know how much I admire you.

Mac cleared his throat, sitting up straighter. *Admire?* he thought, not expecting this.

It takes great courage to tackle anxiety and depression head on. You should be very proud of that. I know your kids will be.

Mac stopped reading; the tears in his eyes would not allow it. When he finally continued on, he could hear Brandt's compassionate voice in his head.

It's true, Mac. Your children are very lucky to have you as their dad.

Mac wept so hard he began to shake.

What you're doing to get back to them is nothing shy of inspirational. And I think you have to take whatever time you need to get well, so you can take control of your life again, no matter how long that takes. You getting healthy has to be priority one.

Wiping his tear-soaked cheeks, Mac nodded in agreement.

In the meantime, please go easy on yourself. We're all human, my friend. We all make mistakes. The real tragedy would be not returning to who you've always been.

Mac put the letter down, wiped his running nose and took a couple deep breaths in order to finish it.

Keep up the good work, Mac. I'm here for you—no matter what you need. And remember, you're not alone. Your friend, Brandt.

Mac dropped the letter onto his bed and wept. Brandt had always been a friend, but Mac didn't realize just how good of a friend until this very moment. He read the last line several more times until it became his mantra. *You're not alone,* he repeated in his head, feeling the words re-energize him and steel his resolve. *You're not alone.* Mac thought, *Brandt has no idea what this means to me; there's no way he ever could.* He wiped his eyes. "You're not alone," he whispered aloud. "Thank you, Brandt."

Mac picked up the letter to read it again, confirming just how profound and impactful the written word could be.

Upon returning home from work, Jen closed the door to her bedroom and began a letter to Mac.

Mac, I should have written this letter a long time ago. If I'm being honest, I've written it a thousand times in my head. *So where do I start? I suppose at the beginning. I love you, Mac. I've always loved you. And I realize now that I always will. And I miss you more than I've ever imagined being able to miss anyone or anything. I'm not the same person without you in my life, not even close. I finally realize what the term "better half" means. I am lost and alone and I'm not sure I'll ever recover from whatever actually happened to us. I grieve, I mourn for what we were and all that we've lost. And I'm terrified that we'll never have the opportunity to get it back. I didn't want this, Mac. I knew you were hurting and I tried desperately to participate, but you kept me in the dark. The last thing I ever wanted was to keep the kids from you. You may never believe this, but it's hurt me as much as it's hurt you. We're not a whole family without you. I fear we may never be again. I'm sorry. I'm so sorry for all of it. I pray for you night and day. I pray for our family.* She signed it, *my love—your wife, Jen.*

After proofreading it, she crumpled it up and threw it onto the floor. Collapsing onto the bed, she grabbed Mac's pillow and hugged it tight. *I do miss you*, she told him in her mind, the tears rolling fast, *but I need to get past that if I'm ever going to survive this nightmare.*

Sitting alone in the corner of the hospital day room, Mac awaited his next round of medication. He looked up to find Nurse Mal standing in front of him, her hands rested on her thick hips.

"Are you going to waste another day of your life sulking in the corner?" she asked.

"Sulking?" he repeated, his heart rate on the rise. "You have no idea what I'm going..."

"You really need to stop feeling sorry for yourself," she said, interrupting him. "You might find the healing process a lot quicker, if you do."

"Excuse me?"

"Trust me, there are people out there who are facing much tougher roads than you are."

"Is that right?" he asked, a ferocity rising within him.

"That's right," she said, offering a disarming smile. "My husband and I are going to a fundraiser this weekend for a kid who sustained a complete spinal cord injury, leaving him a quadriplegic."

"Oh no," Mac said, momentarily forgetting his own troubles. "What happened?" he asked, leaning in to hear more.

Nurse Mal took a seat beside him. "His name's D.J. Bishop and this past summer, he dove into some shallow water at a local lake."

"Oh no," Mac repeated.

She nodded sadly. "He hit his head on a rock and fractured his C4, C5 and C6 vertebrae. He was rushed to Rhode Island Hospital where he underwent emergency surgery." She shook her head. "His burst C5 was replaced and his spine was fused. After eighteen days in the medical ICU, he was moved to Spaulding Rehabilitation Hospital in Boston to begin his rehabilitation."

"How's that going?"

"He's made progress but the insurance company's decided that his time at Spaulding will be coming to an end."

"That's terrible," Mac said.

"It is, but his therapy will continue, at least on an outpatient basis." She shook her head again. "It's private pay for the family which is why some friends are raising money. D.J. will be supplementing his occupational and physical therapy with an intensive exercise regimen at Journey Forward out in Canton."

"Wow," Mac said, at a loss for more words.

Nurse Mal grinned again; it was the type of smile that betrayed wisdom. "D.J. has already overcome many unexpected hurdles throughout his recovery and he's certain to face more. But the one constant that's remained is his positive attitude and will to fight."

Mac nodded, unable to find any words.

She placed her warm hand on Mac's forearm. "D.J.'s a gladiator, Mr. Anderson, and you could learn a lot from him." She removed her hand and stood to walk away. "We all could."

Jen had just completed her fourth and final interview at the City Hall, gathering all the quotes she needed to complete her article on the Highway Department's wasteful spending. Her head was buried in the work; it had quickly become her happy place where she could focus on something other than her suffering family.

The tiny hairs on the nape of her neck tingled, signaling that someone might be staring at her. She looked up. Across the room, she spotted Philip, a much younger colleague with the physique of an Olympic swimmer, looking in her direction.

Not likely, she thought, snickering to herself. *He would have been too pretty for me on my hottest day.* She returned to her work.

The hairs tingled again, sending a shiver down her back. She looked up again.

Philip was still looking at her.

He's gawking, she thought before looking behind her. There was no one there.

Philip smiled wide and stood. Without breaking eye contact, he started walking straight toward her.

There's no way, she was thinking when her mouth went dry, all of the moisture reappearing on the palms of her hands.

"Hi there," Philip said, a few feet from her desk.

"Hi there," she repeated, feeling like a giddy school girl.

"We've never formally met," he said, extending his beautiful hand. "I'm Philip."

Aware that her hand was clammy, Jen had no choice but to give his a shake. "I'm Jen," she said, "and it's nice to formally meet you."

As if he'd picked up on her nervousness, he grinned. "So, what are you working on?" he asked, clearly more interested in keeping the conversation going than the mountain of paperwork on her desk.

He's flirting with me, she confirmed, but still looked down at her project. "It's a piece on the Highway Department that I've been investigating for three weeks." She looked up to find him staring at her left hand. *He's checking for a wedding ring*, she thought, and was immediately brought back down to earth. "Well, it was nice to meet you," she said in a polite but dismissive tone.

"Absolutely," Philip said. "I look forward to seeing you around." Before he turned to leave, he shot her a wink.

She didn't know whether to swoon or laugh. *He winked at me*, she thought. *He probably hasn't been legal drinking age for more than a year, but he winked at me.* She laughed for the first time since she could remember. But the brief reprieve from misery made her feel guilty. She looked down at her wedding band and could feel her smile completely dissolve.

While sheets of heavy rain washed Mac's small hospital window, he tossed and turned in his sleep, dreaming about his teenage daughter with the same vivid detail he'd experienced when the memories had actually occurred.

∞

Jillian entered the world with an umbilical cord wrapped around her neck. Mac still cringed, remembering it. She was blue—not bluish or kind of blue; she was blue. Mac's knees had buckled and nearly pulled him to the hospital floor. The room immediately filled with medical personnel, causing the worse wave of panic he'd ever felt. But it was their quick response that led to the prognosis, "Your daughter will be just fine, Mr. Anderson." The truth of it suddenly hit him and he began to cry. As he started to breathe again, he also realized there was nothing they could do to recover the time that had just been erased from his life.

He also remembered surprising her on Jillian's thirteenth birthday, picking her up early from school.

His healthy daughter—for which he still thanked God—had turned thirteen. Mac asked how she wanted to celebrate the coveted passage into her teenage years. She shrugged. "Whatever," she replied. Although Mac usually despised this term of indifference, Jillian was being honest. She really didn't care how they celebrated the day.

After handing her a mushy greeting card—containing a gift card that confirmed this birthday was just as special as any other—they ended up at a restaurant that served breakfast food for lunch; it was a favorite they both shared.

As they accepted the giant menus, Mac's only request was that Jillian put away her cell phone while they were there. "No texting or tweeting, just a normal face-to-face conversation." She respectfully honored the request.

While Jillian began with her usual update—how school was going, what her friends were up to, how she was dreading all the schoolwork she faced in the coming weeks—Mac sat back, sipped his coffee and took an inventory. While she talked, he found himself taking an account of the most precious task he'd ever been blessed with—raising this girl and her siblings.

Physically, Jillian was tall and lanky, weighing much less than she should. As such, Mac ordered extra pancakes. A few years earlier, she had discovered that she was best suited as a softball player, which she trained and competed hard at, filling Mac with pride.

Jillian was a smart kid. In fact, she thought she knew much more than she did. Fortunately, Mac wasn't too old to forget that he wasn't all that different at her age. The good news was, coming from her technology-savvy generation, she'd proven resourceful enough to find answers she didn't actually know. This trait had always been important to Mac.

As they ate and one topic led to the next, Jillian informed Mac, "It's not considered disrespectful to return a phone call with a text message." Although this remained a hotly debated topic between them, she was being truthful; communicating online was precisely how her smartphone generation communicated—period.

Mac sopped up the yellow yolk with an English muffin and smiled at his daughter, realizing, *Jillian's a work in progress, requiring a few more coats of polish.* But he also knew that a solid foundation had been poured—*a base strong enough to frame a good human being.*

Nearly an hour and a half had passed before Mac paid the bill, left a tip and they started for the door.

"Thanks for everything, Dad," Jillian told him.

He shook his head. "Thank you, Jill," he told her and meant it. He'd always believed—from that awesome and terrifying day thirteen years earlier—that the true success of his life would be measured against the woman his daughter would become.

They got back in the car and Mac had to smile. *The doctors were right*, he thought, *Jill turned out just fine.* "Where to next?" he asked her. There was silence. He looked into the rear view mirror.

Jillian was already back on her cell phone, both thumbs tapping away at an impressive rate—getting caught up on all that she'd missed during her birthday lunch.

Maybe I should just text her? he thought, before heading off to their next adventure together.

Emerging from his restless slumber, Mac scrambled to find a pen and paper, needing to capture his thoughts and feelings for his first-born.

Dear Jillian,

I hope all is well with you. Well, let's be honest, I'm sure you're very angry with me right now. I know I would be. As you know, I was raised by your great-grandparents so I understand only too well what it's like to be without a parent. Believe me, it's the last thing I wanted for you—for us. I only hope you'll come to understand that when I have the chance to explain, and that you'll find it in your heart to forgive me. I need that from you and your sister and brother more than anything in this world.

Jillian, I'm so sorry that I'm not there for you right now. Believe it or not, I remember being a teenager and I can honestly tell you they were some of the toughest years of my life...as well as some of the best. At your age, you think you know everything. You don't. I know that for a fact because even at my age, I don't know everything... not even close. But if you need to know anything at this point in your life, it's this: You are an amazing girl who will become an even more amazing woman. You are smart and beautiful, both inside and out. You are a protector, a natural leader—someone who I couldn't be more proud to call my daughter. And you're also kind without being frail.

It was something Mac liked to think Jillian had learned by example. He paused to get the rest of the letter just right.

You care more about people than things and, for the most part, you're polite—at least you've always been polite in my company. You're not afraid to stand up for your beliefs and can even get loud when you feel passionate enough about the topic at hand. But you're equally thoughtful and considerate—as much as you can be for your age.

Mac was not delusional. He knew his daughter wasn't perfect. But he never expected perfection; he expected effort.

Sooner than later, I hope you realize just how special you are, Jill, because I realize it and have from the second you opened your eyes in this world.

I need to sign off for now, but remember that spring training will be here before you know it. I hope you've been practicing. You're going to have an unforgettable season. I just know you are.

You Live in My Heart—Always,
Dad

Chapter 14

Jen held the telephone receiver close to her ear, listening attentively.

"From what Mac tells me," Roland Dube reported, "he's doing better." He coughed once. "He's making some real progress dealing with his alcohol abuse. And he's finally gotten on a consistent medication regimen to manage the anxiety and depression."

"Is he still having the panic attacks?" she asked, her voice uneven.

"He is," Roland said, "but he's working through them with one of the best doctors in the business."

"Oh good," she said, at a loss for more words..

There was a pause. "Well, I guess that's it for now, Jen," Roland said, lowering his tone. "Again, this is a bit of a conflict for me, so…"

"I appreciate the update," Jen said, "and I won't share it with anyone."

"Good. Thanks." He coughed again before clearing his throat. "You haven't heard from Mac, right?"

"He hasn't tried contacting me, no, but he has sent a few letters to the kids."

"Shit," Roland blurted.

"Don't worry," Jen said, "I'm not looking to hurt him, Roland."

There was another pause. "Right," he said, "good. We'll talk soon then." The line went dead.

Jen hung up the receiver, *Not too soon, I hope,* she thought, recognizing just how difficult it was to live in two worlds at one time—*or impossible to move on.*

Overwhelmed with another panic attack, Mac sat like a frightened child in the corner of his hospital bed. He looked at his nightstand. "I need a pill," he gasped and, after swallowing it, he stood and paced—eventually calming himself down.

Faust entered. "Another attack?"

Mac nodded. "Yeah, but I think I was able to get out in front of this one. It should be on its way down now."

"Did you take a pill?"

Mac nodded.

"Good, that's progress," Faust said, taking a seat across from his patient. "If you had diabetes, you'd take your insulin, right?"

"I would," Mac admitted, "but the meds make me feel apathetic, Faust, almost unable to function." He shook his head, thinking, *Sometimes I feel like I'm suspended in a sea of thick syrup where life becomes surreal.*

Faust nodded, waiting for him to go on.

"I feel increasingly more detached from reality and everyone around me," Mac explained. "Every pill I pop, I only want to sleep." *Maybe even escape forever,* he added in his head.

"Well, until we address the root cause of the anxiety," the doctor said, "it's better than the panic attacks, right?"

Mac nodded. *Hell yeah,* he thought. *It's not even close.*

Faust returned the nod. "Listen, Mac, I think we're very close to a breakthrough."

"We are?" Mac asked tentatively.

"We are, but..."

"But?" Mac repeated, scared.

"...but you need to make peace with the past, Mac, before you can even consider stepping into the future."

"Faust, if you're asking me to..."

"Mac, you have to tell me about your car accident, every detail you can remember."

Mac shook his head, feeling another wave of panic crash over him.

"I know it's not easy," Faust said, "but you have to trust me. It's necessary for you to get past the anxiety and depression...for you to truly heal." He paused. "I also believe it's the only path that'll get you back to your children."

"I...I don't know."

"Do you feel relaxed right now?" Faust asked.

"Well, not relaxed but..." Mac stared at Faust for a few moments until surrendering with a nod.

"Let's try it again, Mac. Just make yourself comfortable and take your time. You know you're safe here, right?"

"I do." Mac said before lying down on his bed and closing his eyes. For the first time in a very long time, he allowed his mind to return to that dreadful night, where each detail was as vivid as when it actually occurred. "It happened years ago, a year before I'd met my wife, I think. My friend Sam and I had worked late and were rushing home to get a few hours of sleep before our first class. He was driving and I was half-asleep in the passenger seat. The rain had stopped earlier, but the streets were still wet. I remember thinking that Sam should slow down when I saw them." He took a deep breath. "A beat-up Chevy Camaro pulled out of a dark parking lot. Sam hit the brakes hard, but our car barely slowed." He paused. "Just as we struck the side of the Camaro, the teenage boy in the passenger seat—he was maybe two or three years younger than me at the time—he stared me straight in the eyes." Mac started crying. "No matter how hard I've tried, I can't get that kid's terrified face out of my head."

"Go on, Mac," Faust said, encouraging him, "you're doing great."

Mac took a deep breath. "The rest seemed to happen in slow motion—the sounds of broken glass and crumpling steel and then..." He paused. "I heard one of the teenagers scream. It was the most horrible sound I've ever heard." He stopped and wept, mournfully.

Faust didn't say a word, but waited patiently for him to continue.

Mac composed himself a bit. "I noticed right away that Sam was no longer sitting behind the wheel." He shook his head in disgust. "I thought he'd been thrown from the car, but found out later that the asshole fled the scene, leaving the rest of us for dead." He stopped.

"And you?" Faust asked. "What happened to you?"

"I couldn't get out," Mac said, recalling every painful detail. "I tried. I really did. And then I heard one of the kids moaning. I don't know how, but I finally squeezed out of my car and started for the Camaro. The driver was still moaning, but the kid in the passenger's seat was quiet...and he wasn't moving. That scared me even more, so I hurried to them." Mac began sobbing again.

Faust remained silent, waiting.

"I...I remember fighting back the urge to puke up my guts. The Camaro was a heap of junk with both boys trapped inside. I grabbed the passenger's side door handle and...and although I'd never seen a dead body before, I knew right away that this kid was gone. There was so much blood and his body was contorted..." He stopped, sobbing so hard that he dry-heaved twice. "My God, he was only a couple years younger than..." Convulsing and struggling to breathe, Mac took a break from the story.

In a show of support, Faust reached over and placed his hand on Mac's arm. "Take your time. This is poison, Mac, old poison and you need to get it all out."

Between sobs, Mac forged on. "The kid behind the wheel was screaming for his life, so I hurried to the driver's side door and pulled as hard as I could. It was no use. No matter how hard I pulled, the door wouldn't budge. So I reached in through the window, grabbed him by the shoulders and started pulling. He was halfway out the window when he looked up at me and..." Mac wailed. "Oh, dear God..."

Faust squeezed Mac's arm. "You're almost there, Mac," he said quietly. "This is it. Go on."

"...and he looked like he wanted to say something," Mac sobbed. "For a second, I even stopped pulling on him to listen. But he could only gurgle...and I've never seen so much panic in someone's eyes until...until they became distant and..." Through his heavy grief, Mac shook his head violently, pushing through to finish. "That's when I heard the sound of sirens, but...but I knew they were too late. The kid went limp. I pulled once more, maybe twice, before we both collapsed to the street. I...I looked into his face. His eyes were still staring at me, but there was nothing behind them. That's when I stopped breathing."

"And for years, you've been able to repress this memory, right? Just push it down so deep that it's disappeared from your mind."

Mac nodded. "Anytime I thought about it, I just pushed it out of my head. But now..."

"But you haven't been able to do that since the accident that you and Jen witnessed on the night of your anniversary," Faust finished.

Mac nodded.

"And it's been hard to breathe ever since, right?" Faust whispered.

"Yes," Mac said, "If Sam had only..." He stopped.

"What happened to your friend?"

"He's hardly my friend," Mac snapped. "When they finally found him, they locked him up. I was questioned as a witness and cleared of any wrongdoing. I saw a therapist a few times, but I quit the weekly sessions just as soon as I could sleep again." He half-shrugged. "I've never talked to anyone about it since."

Nodding, Faust jotted down another note. "Do you remember how you felt when help finally arrived on scene?"

"I remember grabbing for my chest when the ambulance arrived for the boys we killed. I actually thought I was having a heart attack right then and there."

"Killed?" Faust asked, a puzzled look on his face.

Overwhelmed with the same guilt he'd felt on that hideous day, Mac couldn't speak.

"You didn't *kill* anyone, Mac," the doctor said. "You weren't the driver and, more importantly, it was an accident—something that could have just as easily happened to me."

Mac hung his head in shame.

Faust leaned forward and patted his patient's arm. "This is huge, Mac. We've finally shined some light on the demon that's been chasing you all these months."

Mac nodded, unable to verbally respond.

"The car accident you witnessed when returning from dinner with your wife was enough to light the wick on the time bomb you've been carrying around inside of you for nearly two decades," Faust said. "From that point on, your anxiety level became so heightened that the panic attacks took over and then became so severe that it was nearly impossible for your body to ignore the repressed trauma any longer."

Mac nodded again.

"And the rest played out like it normally does."

Mac's sorrowful eyes pleaded for him to explain further.

"At first, the symptoms frightened you to the point where you acted rashly," Faust said, "and then it consumed you to the point where you lost the ability to manage your actions. From there, you railed against the world for putting you in this position. And finally, you arrived at the understanding that only you could get yourself out of it."

"Exactly," Mac said; the word sounded like a distorted grunt.

"As a consequence of Post-Traumatic Stress Disorder," Faust added, "you also started suffering from depression."

"P.T.S.D.," Mac murmured, feeling disheartened.

"Mac, listen to me: Two teenage boys died in an accident that you were also the victim of. Nothing can ever change that. But it was an accident, an accident that could have happened to anyone." Faust leaned in to hammer his point home. "And the only way you're going to heal is to forgive yourself."

"Forgive myself?" Mac interrupted in disbelief.

"Mac, I have no doubt that you did everything in your power to save those boys. And I'm sure you would have given anything for a different outcome. But that was not to be. Trying to accept fault or blame for their premature deaths is nothing more than self-mutilation. What you need to do is accept that it was an accident. And you need to forgive yourself for not being able to change how it turned out. Although you never realized it, you've been walking around poisoned with guilt and shame for years. And it is poison, Mac, poison that doesn't do anything but destroy everything it touches. So we need to get rid of it, once and for all."

Mac shook his head, both his heart and mind riddled with this newly-exposed guilt. He began to cry.

Faust leaned in closer. "I need you to do something for me." He cleared his throat. "Actually, I need you do something for you."

"What is it?"

"I need you to write a letter to those two boys who died in the accident."

"What?" Mac asked, thinking he'd heard wrong.

"Write them a letter, Mac," the doctor confirmed with a nod, standing to leave, "and tell them how you feel. Once you ask for their forgiveness, I promise you'll find it easier to ask yourself for the same."

After Faust left, Mac sat on his bed, gathering himself with more than a few deep breaths. Grabbing a pen and paper, he began to write his letter to the dead boys. As Mac wrote the letter, he dictated it aloud. "Dear boys, forgive me for not knowing your names, though I can promise that I'll never forget your faces." It seemed strange calling them boys given that they weren't much younger than him at the time. "I'm so sorry for that night," Mac continued, "I'm sorry it rained and the streets were wet. I'm sorry Sam didn't see you sooner. And I could never begin to explain just how sorry I am that we weren't able to stop in time." He paused, crying. "I tried to save you, I swear I did. You were so young, with your whole lives ahead of you. I'm so sorry that was taken from you. Please forgive me, boys." He wept freely. "Oh God, please forgive me..." He wept harder. "Forgive me...*Mac.*" He dropped the pen onto his bed. *Please Mac,* he told himself.

Jen sat at the kitchen table, trying not to cry. She'd found an old family photo album—covered in gaudy gold foil—in the hall closet. *Should I even look at this?* she wondered. *For all intents and purposes, I've lost my husband.* Slowly, she flipped open the front cover.

The Anderson family photo album was one of life's wonderful treasures, but Jen was hesitant about taking the trip down memory lane. Even more slowly, she began flipping through its bent pages. Each picture was like rediscovering their family's lives together.

The album began with baby pictures of Jillian, Bella and Brady. *The three miracles I begged God for,* Jen thought. Jillian, the first born, was actually the smallest, weighing in at six pounds, eleven ounces. The pink knitted cap covered her cone head. She lay in her dad's arms and Mac couldn't have looked prouder. Bella came next, cradled in her dad's arms right there in the same hospital chair, with Mac beaming just as brightly. Brady followed suit. *He was such a porker,* she thought, and laughed. *Nine pounds even.* As she recalled, *At the maternity ward window, some people said, 'He's such a big boy and so handsome.' And Mac had agreed with every one of them.* She was already getting choked up.

Jen stared at the photo and felt conflicted to see her husband's smiling face again.

Tiny bums in bathtub shots were almost as cute as those of all three kids sleeping on Mac's chest. *I can still remember walking into the living room to find my babies snuggled against their dad,* she thought. *That's when I knew, if only for a moment, life could be perfect.* She paused to collect herself. *Mac had always insisted on catching everything on film. At one point, we took so many photos that I decided to rearrange them according to event and not chronological order.* She chuckled. *I don't think he liked it, but I did.*

Jen quickly returned to the book. She could see her children growing up on each page she turned.

After capturing the three trips home from the hospital, Jen caught the grubby faces of people learning to eat on their own. She snapped their first steps, with Mac waiting with his arms spread wide. There was even one that was supposed to show Jillian speaking her first word. *Jill grunted Dada,* she thought, grinning, *and Mac never let me live it down that he came first.* Jillian's tiny eyes were bright red in the picture, evidence of the crying that must have taken place before the shot.

The next series of pictures was devoted to Christmas. There were brilliant glossies of Mac stringing lights on some sad-looking trees with some little people at his feet. The kids were covered in tinsel, their eyes beaming in anticipation of a fat man in a red suit. Christmas mornings began with a mountain of unwrapped gifts neatly stacked beneath decorated evergreens, followed by the squinted eyes of children still half asleep. They were dressed in different-colored feet pajamas and, though they looked innocent, Jen now held evidence that proved differently. The once orderly living room had become overrun with balls of red and green wrapping paper, with hints of children jumping from one toy to the next. "Oh God," Jen said aloud. There were even a few surprise shots of Mac. He always looked the same— dead tired. *Looks like he enjoyed too much eggnog,* Jen thought, and sighed. *Those were the days.*

Jen dove back into the thick photo album discovering that birthdays were obviously her next theme. Glowing chocolate cakes shimmered from the pages and, behind each one, the pucker of a child. Homemade chocolate cakes were all Jillian, Bella and Brady ever blew out. The presents that followed, year-after-year, showed their changing styles of fashion. Various haircuts were trapped in time. Jen shook her head. *I remember when Jillian feared a trip to the beautician more than going to see the dentist.* Jen laughed, thinking, *Amazing. Everyone looks so young. Even those who are no longer with us look like kids themselves.* She shook her head again.

Turning the page, the first pictures of the three kids heading off to school were priceless. Each waited at the bus stop in new clothes, holding their lunch boxes and willing themselves to be strong in the face of the unknown. *I remember it like it was yesterday,* Jen thought, *and for Brady, that's not so far from the truth.*

She turned the album's oversized page. Summer vacations began with day trips. There were poses taken in front of museums, amusement parks, zoos and the aquarium. One summer, Jen and Mac went all out and hit every highlight in New Hampshire. The photos revealed the Old Man in the Mountain, Clark's Trading Post, with its dancing bears, Santa's Village, Story Land, Six Gun City and the Polar Caves. In five long days, they saw it all and the pictures betrayed the incredible energy spent. Jen had captured each warm moment.

As the kids got older and money was easier to come by, Florida replaced New Hampshire, with Magic Mountain preferred over the White Mountains. Staring hard at the memories, Jen admitted to herself, *I still can't decide which was more fun. Sometimes, it really felt like we had more with less.* She shook her head. *There was more need for imagination and it was better appreciated.* The album proved a long-standing theory that Jen had always believed. *Summer vacations aren't relaxing. They're hard-fought missions.*

Softball pictures showed Jillian in her striped uniform. Bella's dance recitals were held during that same period of time. *Mac really loved those four-hour recitals,* she thought, chuckling.

Jen realized that she was already thinking in the past tense. Although it felt odd, there was a certain amount of relief that came with it.

She returned to the book. Next were the school plays. Brady never lived down his role as Peter Pan at summer camp—or the green tights that made him famous. Bella made a distinguished Betsy Ross and, for whatever reason, Jillian never made it beyond the roles of talking trees and walking snowflakes. Jen laughed.

Picture after picture, Jen decided that her favorites were not those that were posed for, but the ones that were unexpected. A photo of Brady smiling on the potty like he'd just learned the secret to world peace was invaluable. There were also shots taken at the beach. As she recalled, Jillian had carried the camera that day. From the sand dunes, the young girl had captured every inch of Jen buried from head-to-toe. *Mac kidded that if he could cook well enough to keep the kids alive, he would have left me for the buzzards,* Jen thought, chuckling. Her giant smile in the photo spoke volumes.

The Halloween costumes got cooler with each passing year, as super heroes were traded in for rock stars.

Jen turned the page again. *At summer cookouts, when water balloons soaked the camera, I'd scream while Mac chased me all around the yard,* she reminisced. *I used to be pretty quick.* She studied the shot. Through the pages, she could almost hear her husband's contagious laughter.

Photos of three grinning snow angels revealed glimpses of their playful dad in the background. Jen couldn't help it: tears were starting to build up behind her blinking eyelids. *Mac and I really did put together a portfolio of love,* she thought. The album was a growing and maturing book of life.

"Where did the time go?" Jen whimpered aloud. "It seems so unfair." She shook her head. *But I shouldn't complain,* she thought, *because we enjoyed every moment.* She shrugged to herself. *Well, at least most of them anyway.*

She closed the cover—on some magical childhoods in progress—and wiped her eyes. *Whether or not the world would agree, Mac and I have been the wealthiest people on earth.* She nodded. "Maybe I should share this with him the next time..." she said aloud, her voice barely audible from emotion.

"Share what?" Jillian asked, startling her mother.

"Oh, I didn't see you there," Jen said before pointing at the closed book. "I was just looking at an old photo album I found in the closet."

"Sounds like a waste of time to me," Jillian remarked sarcastically. "You should just throw it out."

"Never!" Jen said defensively. "Listen, just because things have changed doesn't erase everything we've shared."

"Whatever. It doesn't matter."

"Why doesn't it matter?"

"Do you really think Dad's ever coming back?" the tortured girl asked.

There was a long pause before Jen answered. "I really don't know, sweetheart," she finally said, needing to be truthful.

"Do you want him to?"

The simple question felt like a punch to the gut, emptying Jen's lungs of air. "I don't know that either," she whispered, shaking her sad head. She studied her teenage daughter's eyes. "Either way, there's nothing wrong with remembering all the good times, Jill," she said. "I'm sure you have many great memories of your dad."

"I don't," Jillian fibbed.

"I don't believe that for a minute," Jen countered.

"Whatever you do, don't share that photo album with the kids," Jillian said. "They've finally stopped whining about Dad coming back." She started to leave the room. "And I don't want to have to hear it again."

∞

Jillian returned to the safety of her bedroom. Although she didn't want to—and had spent months intentionally avoiding it—her mind travelled back in time to those glorious days with her dad.

∞

While the two little kids made a beeline for the swings, Mac and Jillian said hello to the other adults on supervision patrol. Most offered a grin, a nod, or a heavy sigh, and then quickly returned to the army of small children who attacked the jungle gym without mercy. Mac took a seat and shifted to get comfortable on the hard green bench, opting to do some people watching. "Why don't you go play," he told Jillian.

She shook her head. "I will when you do," she teased.

He smiled, watching as his younger children played nicely with other kids. "Sometimes I wonder whether you guys are paying attention when Mom and I are trying to teach you," he said, pointing at Bella and Brady, "and then I watch you guys out in the world and I realize that you are." He grabbed Jillian's hand. "All three of you are genuinely good people..." He nodded, his eyes misting over. "...selfless and kind."

While Jillian choked back some unexpected tears, Bella and Brady approached the bench. "Will you play with us, Dad?" Bella asked.

"You too, Jillian," Brady said.

Mac shook his head. "With all these other kids running around, you want me to play with you?"

Both kids nodded, grabbing for his hand.

He stood and allowed them to lead him. Jillian happily followed.

At first, they tackled the slides, but that was only a warm-up. From there, it was on to the real games. Like wild gorillas, they hit the jungle gym hard. Before long, the air turned hot. While playing hide-and-seek, Mac's big butt and Bella's giggles gave them both away. Jillian picked the game of tag next and it was complete, unadulterated fun. Each of them laughed, really laughed, and was loving every second of it. There were no real adults there to tell them what they couldn't do. They were royalty and knowing this, they quickly claimed their territory. They built a fort under the jungle gym.

Resting on a floor of dirt and wood chips, Bella made a birthday cake out of mud. While she, Jillian, and Brady sang out of tune, Mac blew out the candles. Then, to everyone's surprise, Brady found a bottle cap, reacting like it was the most valuable thing on earth. "It's a real treasure," the little guy squealed. "Let's bury it for some other lucky kids to find thousands of years from now."

"What a treasure," their dad agreed.

Quietly digging a hole, all four buried the bottle cap where nobody would ever find it. Mac marked the spot with a stick, while they promised each other, "We never tell anyone." It was their secret, something they could rediscover at a future visit to the park.

Jillian returned to the present, her cheeks soaked in tears. *I don't want to remember*, she thought, her body convulsing with heavy sobs, *not ever again.*

Chapter 15

The long weeks of separation were enough to shatter the coldest heart or test the strongest faith, as Mac learned the incredible effort it took to heal. From his confined cell at Presbyterian Hospital, he finished writing another letter.

Dear Bella, my beautiful princess,

Guess what? I was thinking about you today. And yesterday. And the day before that. And I'll be thinking about you tomorrow and every day after that. I miss everything about you, sweetheart. But the feelings that sometimes make me feel sad—like missing you and your sister and brother— also give me the strength and inspiration to fight even harder to get well and get home to you guys.

Do you know that it's impossible for me to think about you and not smile? It's true. You're such an wonderful girl. I hope you know that. You'd better.

Even being here in the hospital, I can still feel your love. From the moment you came into this world, I've felt a very strong connection to your spirit, like I knew you before you were born. That probably seems strange right now, but I have a feeling it'll make good sense to you when you get older.

I'm so excited to see what the future holds for a heart as big as yours. And I'll be there, Bella, I promise. Once I get home, I'm never going away again.

Be a good girl. Say your prayers. Most of all, be happy. Your dad loves you so, so much.

You Live in My Heart—Always,
Dad

After folding up the letter—addressed to *Ms. Bella Anderson*—Mac sealed the envelope and gave it a kiss. There was no stamp. He'd stopped mailing the letters weeks before.

For the third time that morning, Philip, Jen's not-so-secret admirer at the newspaper, walked by her desk and winked.

She grinned, involuntarily.

He stopped, turned and started back toward her, the look of a young hunter sparkled from his green eyes.

Oh boy, she thought, *here we go again.*

"Have dinner with me," he said, standing at the corner of her desk. It was more of a statement than a question.

Somebody's a little too confident, Jen thought, but said, "I can't."

"Because you don't eat dinner?" he asked, his grin aimed at tearing down whatever defenses she'd erected.

"I do, but I can't."

"Really?" he asked, more surprised than dejected.

"I'm flattered," Jen said, "I really am, but..."

"But you're married, right?" he said.

"I am that," she said, "though my husband is gone and I'm not sure he's ever coming back." Hearing the words aloud, she felt a jolt tear through her. "The reason I can't is because my children need me right now a lot more than I need to be going out on a date."

"Really?" he asked again, his emerald eyes betraying even more surprise.

Jen grinned. "Really," she confirmed.

"We could have some fun and your kids would never have to know," he whispered, maintaining his devilish smirk.

"But they'd know that I'm somewhere other than with them," she said, shaking her head. "It's not happening," she grinned, "at least not right now."

"Okay then," he said, starting to slink away.

"But I'm flattered," she repeated.

He looked over his shoulder and smiled.

But if the kids were a little older and didn't need me so much, she thought, watching him walk away, *oh, would you be fun...*

As the endless days ticked by, Mac struggled to adjust and overcome in his new world. With Butch on his heels, he grabbed a plastic tray and entered the cafeteria.

"Schools don't teach kids practical skills anymore," Butch said, "not even cursive so they can sign their own names." He shrugged. "Kids today can't balance a check book or write a resume and it's all intentional to fleece the masses."

"Okay, Mr. Conspiracy," Mac said.

"Whatever," Butch countered. "Back when we were kids, at least we received the basics."

Mac slid his tangerine-colored tray along the stainless steel rails like he was back in school. The shower-capped cafeteria lady looked at him, waiting to fill his order.

"Let's go," Butch teased the grimacing woman, "breakfast isn't going to serve itself."

After picking the watery scrambled eggs and under-cooked bacon, Mac and Butch looked for an empty table in the bustling cafeteria. As they scanned the room, Nurse Mal approached. "You boys doing okay?" she asked.

Mac smirked. *Two broken souls and a smart-ass nurse that does her best to look after them*, he thought.

Butch leaned in toward her, as if he were about to share a secret. "Poor guy," he whispered near her ear. "Mac is a bit on the slow side and it's really not his fault." He looked back at Mac and grinned. "He's here because he split his head open while drinking from the toilet and suffered some serious brain damage. It was so bad that they had to put a plate in his head."

"Oh really," Mal said, pausing to play along.

Butch shrugged. "He couldn't afford metal, so the doctors went with a paper plate." He shook his head. "I don't think it worked, though." He looked over at Mac again. "Every time Mac takes a shower, the plate gets wet and he starts talking with a lisp."

She obviously tried to hold it in, but looked at Mac and laughed.

Mac couldn't help himself and chuckled along with her.

"I'm glad to see you've finally found a friend, Butch," she said.

Butch shook his head. "Friend? We're business partners."

Her eyebrow rose.

"When we get out of this pit, we're going to raise hamsters together." He nodded. "They're a little tough to herd and they kind of freak me out..." Leaning in even closer, he lowered his tone. "Did you know that the harder you squeeze their bellies, the more their eyes bulge?"

She studied his face for a moment. "You really are nuts, huh?" she whispered.

Mac nodded in agreement. "You have no idea," he confirmed, releasing a hearty laugh that rocked his entire body.

Butch smiled. "A little, I guess."

It's been forever since I've laughed like that, Mac realized.

Shaking her head, Nurse Mal walked away.

"We should go buy that old witch a gift certificate to the local pet groomer's," Butch said, his face now serious, "so she can get her hooves filed down and polished."

Mac studied his friend's changed demeanor. *Nurse Mal definitely knows her stuff,* he thought, *Butch is nuts.* Mac then spotted George Saber sitting off in the corner with another man. His instincts screamed for him to veer away, but morbid curiosity screamed louder. With each step toward George, he felt like he was witnessing another terrible car wreck, only this time it was his future. *You need to get as much insight as you can about where the legal side of things might land with the kids,* he thought.

George and his friend looked up as they approached.

"Do you mind if we join you?" Mac asked, gesturing toward Butch with his head.

"Of course," George said, "this is Andrew Souza."

Taking a seat, Mac placed his tray onto the table and shook Andrew's hand. Before he could even place a napkin into his lap, Mac turned to George. "That was quite the story you shared the other day in group session."

George tilted his head sideways.

"About all your troubles in court," Mac explained.

George shook his head, his face immediately returning to an angrier place.

"Sorry to bring it up," Mac said. "If you don't want to talk about it..."

"Are you kidding?" George said. "Talking about it is the only thing that's stopped me from killing someone."

Mac nodded, thinking, *I hope he means that figuratively.*

George said, "I'll never forget when my jackass attorney whispered, 'The judge went easy. You've been given standard visitation.' Went easy? I thought, more pissed than I ever imagined I could get. And to add insult to injury, I was still paying the mouthpiece to defend rights that were never mine to begin with."

"Ain't that the truth," Andrew blurted, indicating that he'd experienced a similar situation.

"Not long after my ex and I left court," George went on, "reality set in. I took my kids for our court-ordered visits, only to drop them off a few hours later. And believe it or not, things got even worse."

"Oh no," Mac blurted, more for himself than for the man telling the story.

George nodded. "Yup, she called the shots from then on. And because of one simple chromosome, my role in my kids' lives was now limited."

"That sucks," Butch said, though he was clearly more interested in what remained on his plate than the bleak table conversation.

"And so it went," George said. "I'd drop my kids off after our quick visits so another man could bounce them on his lap."

New boyfriend? Mac thought, his stomach kicking up enough acid to make him stifle a gag. He'd never even considered the possibility of Jen finding a man.

"Yup, each new boyfriend was given all the time he wanted with my children," George said. "At first, it killed me, but I decided that whatever was best for my kids had to come first." He threw his fork into his plate. "It stung something terrible all the way to Christmas."

"Oh, the Christmas story," Andrew sighed, as though issuing a warning to the others.

Mac steeled himself to hear more. *You need to know this*, he told himself.

George took a deep breath. "I waited in my old driveway for four long hours, while three inches of snow covered my windshield, as well as all my screaming from inside my truck. When my ex and the kids finally pulled into the driveway, the old lady snickered, 'I must have lost track of time.' The kids were dead tired and half-asleep. And the ex...well, she just grinned, knowing there was nothing I could do about it. It took all the strength I had left to hide my tears from the kids." He sighed heavily. "I hadn't planned on giving my ex anything for Christmas—like a broken nose—and was doing my best to stick to the plan."

Though it was anything but funny, Butch laughed.

"For months, I tried to contend with my children's misguided guilt of their parents being separated. It wasn't easy. I only had a fraction of my ex wife's time to soothe them. In the meantime, nothing seemed to ease the bitch's spite. She had no qualms about using our kids as pawns in her constant games. She had custody, so the kids were used as negotiating tools." He looked Mac in the eye. "And while I was fighting for fair visitation, she was going for money—as much as she could get."

"They take everything, the dirty bitches," Andrew blurted again, without explanation.

"Which isn't anything compared to how she bashed my character," George hissed, his bottom lip curled over his teeth, "and used our kids as her sounding board." He shook his head sorrowfully. "I mean, I understand being angry, but this never made any sense to me. Wouldn't every derogatory word directed toward me insult half of who my kids are?"

Mac nodded, feeling the same sorrow. *Oh, that sucks,* he thought, picturing his sister-in-law's smug face and wondering if the same thing was going on at home while he was eating lunch with these broken men.

"On the flip side," George continued, "I could never reply in the same manner without compromising the honor I wanted to instill in my kids." He exhaled deeply. "Boys don't talk badly about their moms and understand respect. Knowing this, I never matched my wife's vicious slander—even though she made it a sport to stain our kids' last name."

When a person can demonize someone, Mac thought, *it obviously frees up their conscience to justify anything they do or say about that person.* His heart fluttered nervously. *I suppose no one looks in a mirror and sees a bad person looking back.*

"Words like abandonment were constantly used to mold me into a monster," George added, "justifying the worst acts of greed and cruelty against me."

Mac felt nauseous at the word *abandonment.*

"I was at the mercy of someone who was consumed with a hateful vengeance. And through it all, she swore that she needed to protect our children, to put them first. Imagine that," George asked, "having to protect my kids from me—their own father?"

As if he were a jack-in-the-box, Mac sprang to his feet, his lunch nearly untouched. "Sorry," he said, struggling to conceal the dark emotions that swirled in him, "I have a session with Dr. Fiore and I can't be late again."

Each man studied him, their faces betraying their lack of belief.

"I'm sorry if I said something..." George began

"Not at all," Mac lied. "I just need to go."

"I'm guessing that you need to make things right with your kids again," Andrew blurted, looking at Mac. "There's no secret to it, pal. Just make yourself available and let them know they mean more to you than anything else in the world." He studied Mac's face. "But you have to mean it, or they'll know that too."

"You clearly have no idea who I am," Mac said, taken aback.

"I don't need to know who you are," the crass man said, "your kids do."

"And they do!" Mac roared, surprising himself with the rage that still simmered just beneath the surface. *At least I think they still do.* Without another word, Mac made a beeline to the gray trash can and dumped the barely eaten meal from his tray.

As the long weeks turned into months, Jen had never felt so exhausted. Struggling with the heavy stresses of everyday life as a single mom, she was sitting at the kitchen table when her cell phone rang. She picked up the phone and looked at the caller ID. "Roland Dube," she said aloud, preparing to answer it. But she didn't. *I can't,* she thought. *I just don't have the energy for another Mac update right now.* She screened the call, letting it go to voicemail. Two minutes passed when she checked the phone again. *No voicemail,* she thought. *Good.*

She dialed her sister's number.

"Hello?" Diane answered.

"Hi Di."

"Oh, hey Jen," Diane said, sounding happy to hear from her. "Mom said you didn't attend the awards ceremony?"

"No, I didn't."

"Why?" Diane said. "You should be proud that…"

"I'm very proud of the journalism award, Di," Jen interrupted, "but I need to be home with the kids."

"I could've babysat."

"You don't understand," Jen said. "Brady asked me a few weeks ago what would happen to him and his sisters if I left them too. 'Will Grandma take care of us?' he asked."

"Oh no," Diane said, "you didn't tell me that."

"Because it's not uncommon, Di," Jen said, shaking her head. "Mac hasn't lived with us for months, but sometimes it feels like he never left."

"How so?"

"A few weeks ago, I took the training wheels off of Brady's bicycle…" And the memory returned.

On the Anderson's thawed lawn, Brady fought to balance a two-wheel bicycle. Jen ran behind him, while Jillian and Bella stood off to the side, looking on. All three kids were happy; there was even a little laughter in the air.

"Not bad, Brady," Jillian called out to him, "but when Dad taught me to ride a bike, he…"

A dirty look from Jen halted the comment. Bella ran into the house, crying. The others were left to face a horrible moment of silence. Jen felt like crying. *It's hard enough juggling work and raising kids alone*, she'd thought, *but when there's bitterness and anger involved, it can be unbearable.*

∞

Jen returned from the stinging memory. "And at gymnastics, when Bella slipped off the pommel horse and fell hard onto the matt, spraining her arm, who do you think she yelled out for?"

"Mac?" Diane answered, reluctantly.

"You got it," Jen said, her mind immediately rewinding again.

∞

The entire gym was preparing for an upcoming meet, the floor of padded, blue mats swarming with tiny acrobats.

"Don't worry," Bella had told her mother, "it's just a routine maneuver."

Jen had laughed, pleased that her daughter was using words like *maneuver.*

But it was hardly a routine maneuver. And when Bella slipped off the horse and crashed to the matt, spraining her left arm in the process, she instinctively screamed out in pain. "Daddy!"

Jen rushed to her aide. "I'm here, baby. Mama's here."

"I want Daddy," the little girl cried. "I want my daddy."

∞

Back in the present, Jen cleared the emotion from her throat. "That's right, Diane, she called for her daddy." Jen took a few deep breaths to keep the emotional storm at bay. "Trust me, Di, I may hide it well from the kids but it's been a living hell trying to move on."

Diane exhaled deeply but never dared to utter another word.

Jen looked up to find Jillian standing in the doorway, listening. "Diane, I need to go. I'll talk to you tomorrow." She hung up the phone. "What's up, Jill?"

Clearly upset, Jillian threw a piece of paper onto the kitchen table.

Jen read it and looked up. Choosing her words lightly, she said, "If...if you want to go to the father daughter dance, I'm sure..."

"...that Dad will miraculously appear?" Jillian snapped. She stopped before starting to cry and stormed out of the kitchen.

Jen caught up to her in the living room. "Jill," she said gently, "I'm sure it would be all right if I went to the dance with you."

"No Mom, it's for girls who have fathers and I don't have one of those anymore," she said, shaking her angry head. "Maybe it's for the best anyway," she added, snickering, "because if Dad went, I'm sure most of the other kids wouldn't."

In a room filled with souls in much worse shape than himself, Mac stood in the Presbyterian med line. Nurse Mal handed him a paper cup containing two pills. "Bottoms up," she said with a wink. Mac tipped the cup to his mouth, drank from a water fountain to wash them down and returned the wink to his spunky caretaker. Even though Mac was starting to feel healthier—with his Xanax dosages being closely monitored—he was still suffering.

"How's it going?" Mal asked. "Is it getting any easier?"

Mac shook his head. "I'm still getting the panic attacks pretty bad." He sighed. "I never realized I could experience so much pain."

"Oh, there's enough pain in this world to go around," she told him. "Believe me, I've met pain many times in my travels. And he's a selfish bastard, stealing away time and energy and hope." She shook her head. "But there's no way around him, Mac, or over him or under him." She gazed into Mac's eyes before winking at him again. "To get past pain, you have to go straight through the son-of-a-bitch."

Mac nodded. He understood only too well.

"Just remember," she added, as he started to step out of the line, "everyday above ground is a good day."

I'm starting to believe that again, too, Mac thought, gratefully.

An hour later, Mac sat across from Faust, engaged in another intense therapy session. "So I understand that you've been engaged in some vigorous exercise regiments," the doctor prodded.

Mac nodded. "I've been trying to overwhelm the panic attacks by releasing large amounts of adrenaline."

"Has it helped?"

"It does," Mac said, "at least for a while." Unfortunately, Mac was also learning that his will was an ineffective weapon against this ruthless enemy.

"Very good," Faust said, jotting down some notes. "And when you're not exercising?" he asked.

"Just by thinking of the symptoms, I start to feel them," Mac said, shaking his frustrated head, "so I do everything I can to avoid those thoughts."

"Which, of course, only forces your mind to visit them more often, kicking off the vicious cycle that you can't stop, right?" Faust added.

Mac nodded. "Exactly," he said, "and even though we're starting to get the symptoms under control, it takes everything out of me."

Faust wrote down another note. "I'm not sure you realize this, Mac," he said, "but you certainly don't suffer alone. In today's fast-paced, stress-filled world, the number of panic sufferers is staggering, almost epidemic."

Oddly enough, Mac felt some relief with having the company. *At least I'm not alone*, he thought, feeling bad for thinking that way.

"Try this," Faust suggested. "Instead of using the time you normally spend worrying, why don't you learn as much as you can about anxiety and panic attacks."

Makes sense, Mac thought.

"It won't take you long to figure out that you really do have to venture within yourself in order to heal."

I think I already get that, Mac thought, nodding.

"In many ways, this is a journey only you can make," Faust added.

"But at least now I know I'm not alone in making it," Mac said aloud.

Faust smiled. "You're never alone, Mac," he promised.

Mac thought about his friend Brandt's letter and smiled. "I know that."

Mac knelt beside his bed, as he did each night, and prayed with all the strength and conviction he possessed. Once finished, he blessed himself, grabbed the framed photo of Jillian, Bella and Brady off his nightstand and kissed his children goodnight. Lying in bed, he began working out many of his problems in the solitude. *Jen was only protecting our children*, he finally understood, *and being the great mother she's always been.* And to his surprise, he realized that he missed her too.

Chapter 16

Mac was discovering that the formal classes on anxiety disorders were well worth the time and effort, teaching him many things. The horrid condition of panic disorder transcended all barriers: race, religion, economic. No one could ever forget the first time they stood face-to-face with this sadistic demon. *Ain't that the truth*, he thought.

The relaxation exercises seemed so much like childbirth classes that, at first, Mac considered them a waste. But being desperate for peace, he stuck with them. *Thank God!* With one hand on his belly, he learned to watch his abdomen rise and fall with each breath. *I never realized it,* he thought, *but it's been years since I've breathed from my diaphragm.*

After learning the value of affirmations, transcendental meditation had him chanting one-syllable mantras, while he breathed in and out like a baby. He'd tighten each muscle in his body and then allow them to relax. He did this until his limbs felt like rubber bands and the rest of him felt submerged in Jell-O. The instructor whispered, "Imagine the safest place in the whole world. Now, imagine a staircase that leads down to this wonderful place. There are ten stairs. As you descend each step, you will breathe in deeply and exhale, feeling more relaxed with each step down."

Mac said the word *ten* in his mind, took a deep breath and imagined stepping down. *Nine*, he thought, took in a deep breath, exhaled and stepped down. He was definitely more relaxed. By the time he hit the number one, he felt paralyzed, completely serene—*like I'm out on the water, sailing.* There was no longer a need to think—*just be.*

For twenty glorious minutes, Mac imagined spending time in his favorite place—adrift on a sailboat with his three children. When it was time to return, on cue, the instructor helped him breathe his way back up the staircase.

Slowly, he opened his eyes and smiled. Although the trip had taken him through countless days of hell, he'd finally returned with an answer. *With all the responsibilities, the obligations and the important things I needed to remember each day,* he realized, *I forgot to breathe.*

That afternoon, Mac took a leisurely stroll through the Presbyterian grounds with Faust.

"It's great that Butch and you have gotten close," the doctor said, "but I haven't seen you making any real friendships with the other patients."

Mac grinned. "It's like I always tell my kids—I'd rather have a silver dollar in my pocket than twenty nickels."

The first few drops of rain fell from the darkening sky.

"That's good, Mac," Faust said, chuckling, "I like that. Although I can't imagine that Butch has ever been described as a silver dollar before."

"Getting to know Butch is like wondering why kids who play T-Ball wear batting helmets," Mac said, chuckling.

"How so?"

The rain immediately picked up in speed and volume.

"It's because they hit themselves in the head with the bat." They shared a laugh before Mac turned serious. "Listen, my court date is quickly approaching, Faust," he said, reminding his captor of his legal battle, "and I know I can't leave, but..."

Faust nodded. "I'll call the court and explain, okay?" he said before scurrying off to get out of the storm.

"Sure," Mac said, suddenly standing alone in the yard.

With a short stack of letters protruding from his back pants pocket, Mac tilted his face toward the heavens. The rain drenched him from head-to-toe. He checked his watch and the tears began to mix with the weather. He lifted his face back toward the sky. "Please God, help me go home," he yelled, knowing there was no choice but to honor Faust's contract. *I can't leave*, he thought, *but what I wouldn't do to bust through those front gates and sprint all the way to that courthouse.* But he'd learned the hard way. *I have to do it right this time.*

As quickly as it had come on, the storm blew away. Alone in the yard, Mac bathed in the fresh air that followed. Light peeked out from the dispersing clouds, its soft rays being trapped in the small puddles left behind. *We don't get what we wish for, Mac,* he reminded himself, *we get what we work for*—steeling himself for the final push to get home.

As the intermittent rain tapped against the windows, Jen stood before Judge Tremblay, the disciplinarian who'd imposed the one-year restraining order. The judge appeared to be in her usual foul mood.

This woman is one tough cookie, Jen thought, already feeling intimidated.

The stern woman finally looked up from her bench, leaned down and spoke in a business-like tone. "Mrs.

Anderson, your husband's clinical psychologist contacted me to report that Mr. Anderson is currently enrolled in an inpatient treatment program and will not be able to join us today."

"That's correct," Jen said.

The judge nodded. "That being said, I think the restraining order remains in the best interest of your family for another year. Once your husband is released from treatment and decides to show some interest toward reuniting with his children, we can take another look."

"Ummm...okay," Jen said, taken aback by the frigidness of the process.

"Although it's good that he's in treatment," the woman said, robotically writing notes into a manila folder, "for the time being, I'll extend the order for another full year. Mr. Anderson can petition the court for a hearing when he's ready to do so."

While the rain continued to pelt the courtroom's giant windows, Jen nodded.

The judge signed a document forbidding Mac from his children for an additional year.

Another year, Jen thought, a torrential downpour of mixed thoughts making her feel like she'd been tossed upside down into a whirlpool.

It was late when the kids and their inebriated grandmother were tucked into bed. Jen sat on the couch with her sister, Diane, explaining her recent court appearance.

"So, Judge Tremblay extended the restraining order?" Diane said.

Jen nodded. "She said she thinks the restraining order remains in the best interest of our family, or until Mac decides to show some interest in the kids."

"But Mac didn't appear in court because he's in inpatient treatment, right?"

Jen nodded again. "The judge knew that and, from what I could tell, she couldn't have cared less."

"Wow," Diane said, "even I couldn't be that cold."

"As of right now," Jen said, "Mac's forbidden to see the kids for another full year."

"Which is a good thing, right?" Diane said.

Jen started to shrug but was able to restrain the impulse. "It is," she said, sounding resolute, "at least until he gets well."

Diane stood to leave. "Wow," she repeated under her breath, "another full year."

Once her sister was out the door, Jen returned to her seat on the couch. She looked up at the fireplace mantle where a row of family photos had once smiled. Only a single picture including Mac remained. Any other reminders of him were too painful and had long been removed. Grabbing a pen and pad, she started another letter to her long lost husband.

Dear Mac, I pray this letter finds you well. I cannot begin to explain how sorry I am for everything that has happened. Most of the time, I can't make sense of any of it. But what I do know is... She stopped and, after quietly reading the newest letter, she threw it onto the floor where all the others ended up. Collapsing onto the couch, she hugged one of the throw pillows. *I'm still not sure how all of this could have happened?* Although she could still feel the pain, it had become dulled over time. And for the first time, she recognized there were no tears to follow.

∞

Mac read aloud, "I tried to save you, I swear I did. You were so young, with your whole lives ahead of you. I'm so sorry that was taken from you. Please forgive me, boys." Although his eyes were filled with tears, his breathing was deep and even. He looked up from the wrinkled letter.

"That's wonderful," Faust said. "Not so long ago, you would have never been able to share that with me."

"I know," Mac admitted. "It's the first time I've read it aloud."

"How does it feel to hear those words?" Faust asked.

"Like I don't have to bury it way down deep anymore," Mac said, nodding. "I don't have to pretend it never happened." He took a deep breath and exhaled slowly. "But it did happen. God knows I would have done anything for it not to have, but it did. And there's nothing I can do about that."

"That's right," Faust whispered.

"I'll always feel sad when I think about it—that I know. But I'm done with trying not to think about it."

"Very good," Faust said.

"Although I'll pray for those boys for the rest of my days, something deep inside tells me they've already forgiven me."

"And you," Faust asked. "Have you forgiven yourself."

"I have," Mac said without hesitation.

"Excellent," Faust, standing to leave. "You should be very proud of the work you've put in."

"I am," Mac said.

With a genuine smile, Faust left the room.

Mac sat quietly for a while, contemplating just how far he'd traveled in the healing process. Although he'd counted every tormented minute it took to get to where he was, he was now a world away from the horrifying place he'd started.

∞

Feeling completely spent, Mac returned to his small room. Trying to focus on his treatment and not on how much he longed to be with his children, he eventually fell asleep. But his subconscious had different priorities, escorting him back in time.

∞

Jillian—then ten years old—had returned home heart-broken from school.

"What's wrong?" Mac asked her.

"Some kids at school were laughing at me, saying there's no such thing as Santa Claus."

"No such thing as Santa Claus?"

"Well, is there?" she asked, searching her dad's eyes for the truth.

Mac took a deep breath and gathered his thoughts, knowing full well this was going to be a defining moment in their relationship—as well as his daughter's young life. Just like his father before him, he answered Jillian's question with a question of his own. "What do you think, Jill?"

Jillian thought about it for a moment and shrugged. "I don't think Santa's real," she said and looked at her dad, her eyes filling with the tears of betrayal.

Mac shook his head. "I think you're all wrong," he told her and stood. "Come with me. I need to show you something." He led his girl into the basement.

Climbing over a pile of boxes, he finally reached the box that was filled with Bella and Brady's Christmas presents.

"Who are these for?" Jillian asked, peering into the box.

"Your brother and sister," he told her honestly. "And I need your help wrapping them, okay?"

Jillian nodded and they began their work right away.

As they wrapped the toys, Mac explained, "Santa Claus is the spirit of Christmas, Jill, the spirit of giving from your heart as an expression of love. Santa Claus is a reminder that there are more important things in the world than the worries of everyday life."

Jillian's eyebrows danced in confusion.

"Santa Claus is the spirit of true fellowship," he added, "of feeling connected to the human race and celebrating that bond through simple acts of kindness and generosity." He then watched the struggle behind Jillian's innocent eyes, as she tried to understand.

"Who are these presents from?" she asked, sticking a new tag onto one of the gifts.

"From you," he told her, "but write *Santa Claus* on the tags."

Her eyes flew up.

"Santa Claus lives in all of us, Jill," Mac explained with a nod, "so the kids at school are wrong."

Although it took Jillian a few days to reconcile this new truth, it all came together on Christmas morning. As Bella and Brady unwrapped their Christmas presents, Jillian watched her siblings closely. Filled with joy, her smiling eyes twinkled with the love of the jolly old elf, himself.

Long after I'm gone, Mac had thought, *Santa Claus will live on in my children.*

∞

It was one of the greatest gifts I've ever received, Mac thought in another area of his brain when he realized he was standing in that long, dark tunnel of depression again. *What if it's one more step?* he asked himself. In the blink of a blinded eye, the smallest ray of light permeated the blackness that consumed him. Cautiously, he stood and slowly walked to the light. With each step, the light's intensity increased—and he began to run. The brightness warmed his face and for the first time, he could smile. Reaching the end of the tunnel, he looked back. Although it was a pain that would linger in his memory, at last the brutal maze had been conquered.

Mac awoke panting. He looked around. The answer was simple and had been with him throughout the entire journey: *Hope has always been the only escape.* Stifling a yawn, he glanced out his hospital window and smiled.

"Mom," Bella said, entering the kitchen with her little brother two steps behind her.

"Yes, sweetheart," Jen said, focused on proofreading her newest piece on her laptop.

"Brady says that Daddy has brown eyes, but I think they're blue."

"They're dark brown," Brady said, nodding vigorously.

Jen closed her laptop and looked up, giving her full attention. "They're brown, babe," she said gently.

Bella gasped. "I was trying to remember what Daddy's face looks like but I can't anymore," she said, ready to cry. "I...I don't remember what Daddy looks like." The tears began to fall.

Jen grabbed the little girl, placing her on her knee. "You have to put it into context," Jen said. "Don't just try to picture Daddy's face. Instead, try to remember an experience you had with him and then you'll be able to see him."

"Or don't even bother," Jillian muttered, standing in the door's threshold. "That's what works best for me."

Jen's head snapped toward her teenage daughter. "Don't ever tell her that, Jill."

"Well, it's true," Jillian said. "Do you want me to lie, Mom?"

"You're being ridiculous," Jen said, clearly frustrated.

Jillian shook her head and smiled; it was not the kind of smile inspired by joy. "I'd say you guys are the ones being ridiculous." She turned to walk away. "Why even bother trying to remember anything about him?"

"Jill, don't..." Jen started to say.

"I can see him!" Bella called out, interrupting her mother.

"You can?" Brady asked his sister, sounding as fearful as he was excited.

"On the sailboat," Bella said, "the last time we went out. I can see him smiling at us." Instantly, her smile disappeared, and the crying continued. "I can see him smiling," she whimpered.

"Oh babe," Jen whispered, hugging her daughter tightly.

At last, Mac's treatment was complete and he was released a free and healthy man. "Did you write the letter, Faust?" he asked, anxiously.

Faust nodded. "I did, Mac."

"And sent it to my attorney?"

The doctor nodded again, extending his hand for a shake. "I'm proud of you," Faust said.

Mac was taken aback. These were the very four words he'd always longed to hear from his father but never did. Somehow, coming from this wise man, they had the same effect he'd always imagined. Mac walked past the handshake into a hug. "Thank you, Faust," he told his confidant, "for everything."

"You're welcome, Mac," the doctor replied, his kind eyes confirming that he meant it.

Mac swallowed hard. "I hope we..."

"...never see each other again," the doctor said, finishing Mac's thought.

"Exactly," Mac said.

"I understand," Dr. Faust said, "and I doubt we ever will unless I need to hire the best man in advertisement." Without another word, he left the room.

It only took seconds for Mac to pack his things. His entire wardrobe now fit into a paper bag: he owned three pairs of jeans and twice as many t-shirts. *Material things no longer matter*, he realized and, although he was more than anxious to reunite with his children, he felt better than he had in a very long time.

It was nearly dusk when Mac stepped into Attorney Roland Dube's office.

"My God, Mac, you look great," Roland said, standing up from behind his desk. "How are you?" They shook hands.

"Except for not seeing my kids for over a year, I've never felt better," Mac said.

"Great. Glad to hear it."

"I need to see my kids, Roland. I really do," Mac said, not mincing words. "How soon can we get into court to make that happen?"

Roland shook his head. "Ummm...Mac, I don't mean to piss on your parade, but I'm not sure this would be the best time to file a motion."

Mac felt like he just took a right hook to the jaw. "What? I've spent months doing everything that was asked of me," he said, getting angrier with each word, "and you're going to tell me that it's not a good time?"

The lawman lowered his tone. "Mac, hear me out on this. You know I'd never steer you wrong, especially where the kids are concerned. You know that, right?"

"I'm sorry, Roland, go ahead."

"I think it's wonderful that you've received help," Roland said, "that you've gotten well again, and so will the judge, but..."

"But what?"

"But you've spent an extensive period of time estranged from your children. And I'm sure that time has been equally difficult for them. The way the court is going to see it..."

"Roland, please!" Mac squealed.

"Fine," the lawman said, surrendering with a nod, "I'll file for an emergency hearing first thing in the morning."

"Thank you," Mac said, feeling relieved.

"You're welcome, Mac," Roland said, "but you need to be prepared for whatever decision the court renders."

"I understand," Mac said. "Whatever gets me closer to getting back to my kids."

"Look Roland," Jen said, standing in front of his desk and making him squirm with discomfort, "I need to know what Mac's plans are for the kids." She pulled a letter out of her purse; it was from the court. "It states that I may appear next week, as Mac is appealing the no contact order. Can you please tell me what's going on?"

"Sure," Roland said, clearly crawling out of his skin for having to speak to her in person. "I filed a motion on behalf of Mac to have the no contact order dropped with regards to the children. This way here, we can get visitation set and..."

"Should I go?" she asked.

"You absolutely can, especially if you want to object to the motion." He leaned in toward her, trying to gauge her reaction.

She said nothing.

"But I don't think it'll matter," Roland added, "I doubt highly that the court will allow Mac to reunite with the kids just yet."

"And why's that?" she asked. "He's not better?"

"Oh no, not at all," Roland quickly countered. "He's much better. In fact, he looks great...like his old self again."

Oh, Jen thought, feeling her heart flutter and face flush.

"It's just that Mac will need to provide evidence of stability after finishing inpatient treatment," Roland explained, "a permanent residence, secure employment, established supports within the community—you see what I mean."

She nodded. "I do," she said, still trying to shake off the man's *back to his old self again* comment.

"As I said, you're welcome to attend next week's hearing if you want."

"I...I don't know, Roland," she muttered. "Did Mac say anything about us," she asked, "...about me?"

Roland met her eyes. "Mac instructed me to appeal *only* the no contact order, which currently separates him and the children," he said, shaking his head.

Jen was surprised to feel most of the air leave her lungs. "I never wanted to keep the kids from him," she said, thinking aloud, "I tried explaining that to him in court, but the judge wouldn't let me."

"I know, Jen," Roland said, "I know."

"Thanks for the information," she managed before stuffing the letter back into her purse and hurrying out of the man's office.

∞

It was late, the house cloaked in a welcome silence. Jen adjusted the kitchen telephone to a comfortable position in the crook of her neck. "I don't know what I should do, Joel," she said.

"What does your gut tell you?" Joel asked on the other end of the line.

Jen shook her head. "Roland Dube, our...I mean, Mac's attorney, claims that the court won't allow Mac to see the kids right now."

"Do you believe him?"

She shrugged. "I do," she said. "He's been straight with me this entire time."

"Is Mac better?" Joel asked.

"Roland says he is, but that it's really up to the court to decide." She shook her head again. "This is so crazy. Part of me really hopes that he's well again...that he's back to who he was before he got sick. But another part of me is terrified to have him back in our lives."

"I can understand that," Joel said. "I think anyone could."

"Mac hasn't seen the kids since..." her heart sank, "...since before last Christmas."

"Which was the court's decision," Joel said. "You need to remember that."

"I know."

∞

Mac felt the onset of a panic attack, but within minutes—through proper breathing and thought control—

he quelled the symptoms. At this point, he'd become an expert on anxiety. Following Roland out of the court-room, he struggled to keep his rage at bay. "I hate that vile woman," Mac hissed, as his attorney turned to face him. "She must not have a soul."

"Judge Tremblay is the toughest on the circuit," Roland whispered, "and she definitely doesn't seem to care for you."

Mac continued to take in deep breaths. "I can't believe this," he said, "after everything I've done…"

Roland grabbed his arm. "Listen, I told you that the court was going to consider the significant time you've spent away from the kids." He gave the arm a squeeze. "They've finally settled into stable lives and the judge is making sure that nothing disrupts that."

"I'm never going to see them again," Mac said under his breath, his mind spiraling.

"That's not true at all," Roland said in a louder tone. "As Judge Tremblay just explained, the court is looking for stability on your part. After a lengthy hospitaliza-tion, she wants to see how you interact in society." Both eyebrows rose. "Mac, you need to prove you have the ability to maintain a safe, loving and consistent rela-tionship with your children before the court will ever entertain a reunion."

"And how in the hell…" Mac said.

"By establishing a secure residence," Roland inter-rupted, "gainful employment and an active role within the community. You might even consider attending religious services."

"How long?" Mac interrupted, still working on slow-ing his breathing. "How long do I have to prove myself before we can get back here?"

"Give it a couple more months," Roland said, "a few months away from inpatient treatment; time that would more than prove your credibility to the court."

"A couple more months?" Mac repeated, closing his eyes for a long moment. "You've got to be kidding me," he said, his eyes now laser-focused on his lawyer's. "I need my kids to know that I'm out of the hospital, Roland, that I'm better and that I need to see them."

"Soon enough," Roland said.

"No," Mac countered, shaking his head, "today wouldn't even be soon enough."

"Just a couple short months," Roland repeated, "and then I'll fight like hell for you and get those kids back into your life, okay?"

Just? Mac thought, *Short?* He put up his hands in surrender. "Okay, Roland, okay. I'll stay away. I'll get established and call you in a month." He took a deep breath.

"That's great, Mac. But I'm begging you—please don't mess up now. The court will be notifying Jen that the restraining order remains in place, so stay clear of those kids until..."

"I know. I know," Mac said, "they won't see me until the court allows it." He thought about it. *I'll do whatever's in the best interest of my children,* he decided.

Chapter 17

Mac walked through the front door of the boarding house with some takeout food and a newspaper. He wore a uniform with the name *Mac* embroidered on the front and *Collision Towing* stitched on the back. Sitting down at an old, rickety kitchenette table, he popped a tiny yellow pill into his mouth before washing it down with a sip of coffee. With the paper spread out before him, he circled a few possibilities in the classifieds. Once done, he fingered through the paper before coming upon an article written by *Jen Anderson*. He read it and grinned. *Very nice work*, he thought. After cutting out the piece and folding it up, he pulled out the classifieds.

Mac picked up the phone and dialed. "Hi. Mark Grocholski, please?" There was a brief wait. "Mr. Grocholski, Mac Anderson here. I was over at New Dimensions for some time." He smiled. "Right, I'm the guy." After another deep breath, Mac took the plunge. "Mr. Grocholski, I see you're looking for a new gun slinger over at your firm. Any chance we can set up a time for me to come in and discuss?"

Along with eleven other children his age, Brady sat on the stage in the elementary school auditorium. It was the final weeks of the school year and a spelling bee was in full swing. Mrs. Homer, the English teacher, fired one word after the other at the nervous kids. Two children had already been eliminated before Mrs. Homer reached Brady. "Brady, the word is elephant," she said slowly.

Brady's forehead wrinkled. "Elephant," he repeated. "E L E." There was a breathtaking pause. "P H A N T. Elephant."

"Correct," the excited teacher announced.

From the rear of the auditorium, someone began clapping and only stopped when no one followed their lead. Hushed giggles traveled through the crowd.

Jen turned to her mother. "Looks like Brady has a big fan," she whispered.

Sue smiled. "More than one, I'd say," she said, waving at her grandson.

Jen turned around. There was no one there.

Seated at his small kitchen table, Mac wrote another letter; not because he wanted to but because he needed to.

> *Jen, I'm writing this letter, knowing that I may never send it to you. But I need to get this all out...for me. When I first got sick, I vowed that I'd protect you and the kids from the nightmare I was suffering from...every second of every day. I realize now that this was a terrible mistake on my part. Although the kids didn't need to know what I was going through, I should have shared every ugly detail with you. Even if it still tore our marriage apart, at least you would have known the truth about why. But I feared you would discover that I wasn't the man you thought I was. The more I got*

sick, the deeper I went within myself and the more I felt alone. And that's when I felt like you'd abandoned me. Crazy, I know, because you didn't know the extent of what was going on with me, even though you asked again and again. Once I started spiraling, I couldn't stop. Even the smallest things infuriated me. Every time you talked about returning to work, I felt like I was losing control of my life—of our life together. I'm more sorry for that than most other things. You absolutely deserve to have a successful career. I wouldn't have had mine if it wasn't for you. I'm sorry for not being supportive. I really am. And then when the world came tumbling down and everything came to a head, I thought you'd betrayed me, but I was no longer tapped into logic or reason. I'm so sorry for putting my hands on you and making the threats I did. I've loved you more than my own soul from the moment we met all those years ago. I would never hurt you or our children. And once I lost them, I lost the rest of my mind. To say I hated you would be an understatement. I never knew I was capable of such dark emotions and even darker thoughts. But the more time that passed, the more I realized it was me. It was me all along. I'm sorry, Jen. I love you. And I miss you terribly.

He signed it, *You Live in My Heart, Mac.*

After reading it through twice, Mac folded the letter in half and placed it into a book. *I needed a new book mark anyway,* he thought.

The auditorium was jam packed with proud parents and heckling siblings. More nervous than she'd ever been, Bella prepared to make her debut as a solo dancer. She peeked out of the heavy red curtain. Her mom and the rest of the Anderson entourage were seated up front. *Everyone's here*, she thought, catching herself. *Well, almost everyone.* She trembled from nerves. *I wish my number was up first and not halfway through the show,* she thought. *I just want to get it over with.*

Before she knew it, the lights went down, the music went up and Bella tap-danced her way straight into the hearts of an applauding crowd.

Toward the end of her routine, a photographer—wearing a fishing hat and bifocals—pointed his camera at her and clicked off several shots. With a wink, he whispered, "Beautifully done." The stranger took one last photo before walking away.

Goose bumps covered Bella's sweaty body. She bowed twice and, as she exited the massive stage, she scanned the crowd for the cameraman. "It can't be," she whispered under her breath. "There's no way."

Impeccably dressed, Mac felt a jolt of adrenaline surge through his body. It was similar to panic, but different enough to actually enjoy. While his colleagues at Grocholski Advertising filled the conference room, he shook off the jitters of presenting his first proposal to the new company. He was at the bottom of the food chain again, but he couldn't be happier. "Ladies and gentlemen," he announced, "allow me to introduce the new look for Harvey's Super Stores."

He removed the white cloth that covered the giant easel, revealing a colorful collage of drawings and catchy phrases. The room erupted in cheers. Harvey Patterson, the client, clapped the loudest.

After an impressive detailed presentation, the room cleared out.

Mark Grocholski—or Grock, as he insisted everyone call him—and Harvey Patterson stayed behind. "Mac, since we opened the very first store back in 1986," Harvey said, "I've entrusted all of my advertising to this firm. To be quite honest, though, this is the best material I've seen. I couldn't be happier." He glared at Mac's boss. "Whatever you're paying this guy, Grock, it can't be enough."

Winking at Mac, Grock replied, "It's funny you should mention that, Harvey. I was planning to offer Mac a position where he can run his own creative team." He looked Mac square in the eye. "So what do you think?"

Mac shook his boss's hand. "I think I've finally returned to a very important piece of my life," he said. "Thank you."

"So is that a yes?" Grock asked.

Mac smiled. "It's a definite yes."

It was opening day on the softball diamond. Jillian took the pitcher's mound, prepared to use all the moves her father had taught her. As the crowd cheered her on, she struck out the first three batters. She then got on deck to hit. As she approached the plate, Jen yelled, "Come on, Jillian. You can do it!"

"Come on, Jill!" Bella screeched.

"Hit a home run!" Brady added.

Jillian didn't even acknowledge her family's screams. Instead, she concentrated and fouled off the first fastball.

On the second pitch, Jillian caught all of it and tagged it. Bouncing once, the scorched softball went over the fence for a stand-up double. The umpire waited several moments for one of the younger spectators to throw the ball back onto the field. It never came.

While standing on second base, Jillian searched the many different faces in the crowd. Although everyone was smiling, she just couldn't bring herself to do the same. *The only person I wish had seen that double is far, far away from here,* she thought, angry at herself for allowing such a thought.

Finally, the ump plucked a new ball from his pocket and handed it to the catcher. "Play ball!" he yelled.

The game resumed.

∞

Jen answered her front door an hour later. It was her sister.

"Where are the monsters?" Diane teased.

"Jill's still at the softball field with her friends," Jen said. "She should be home soon. The other two are in the backyard playing quietly, thank God." Jen smiled. "What a game Jillian had."

They sat on the couch. "Oh yeah?" Diane said.

"I'll let her tell you about it when she gets home," Jen said.

Diane nodded. "Sorry I couldn't make Brady's spelling bee. Mom called and told me that some guy in the back was clapping for him. That's kind of creepy."

"It was the strangest thing," Jen said. "Brady didn't seem to mind, though. He was happy to have a fan."

"Who was he?" Diane asked.

Jen shrugged. "Probably one of the teachers. When we got back there, he was gone."

"Mom said Brady came in second place?"

Jen laughed. "Yeah, and of all words, he misspelled *cheese*."

As Diane laughed, a tornado named Bella blew into the room. She approached her aunt and kissed her. "Thanks for coming to my dance recital, Auntie Diane," Bella said.

"I wouldn't have missed it, sweetheart."

"It's a good thing you got your ticket online," Jen joked. "They actually sold out."

Diane's eyebrow stood at attention. "You're kidding me? I realized the place was packed but..."

"Oh, these dance recitals are a big to-do," Jen said. "It's dog-eat-dog for good seats."

Diane laughed.

"I thought you were playing outside?" Jen asked Bella.

"I just came in to get a drink. I'm going back out."

"Take it easy on your brother," Jen told her.

"Not a chance," Bella yelled over her shoulder, as she left.

Jen and Diane were laughing when Jillian came into the house, wearing her softball uniform.

"How was the game?" Diane asked.

"We lost by one," Jillian reported before kissing her aunt.

"Well, that stinks," Diane said, looking at her sister—confused.

"The good news is," Jillian said excitedly, "I hit a double. It bounced over the fence and rolled into the woods. They stopped the game for a few minutes..." She shrugged. "...but nobody could find the ball."

"Why?" Diane asked. "Did you want to keep the ball?"

Jillian snickered. "Not for a double, Auntie Diane."

∞

It was a warm Sunday afternoon when Mac—and a dozen adolescents—arrived at the soup kitchen of Our Lady of Grace Church. For several weeks, he'd become heavily involved in the Youth Group. While other adults took the kids on outings to have fun, Mac opted to show the teenagers that some of the greatest joys in life could be found in helping others—folks who could never return the goodness.

With his sleeves rolled up, Mac began serving potatoes to the homeless and downtrodden. Offering a smile to each one, he occasionally shared a laugh with some. And while he did his part, Steph Grossi, one of the pre-teens from the Youth Group, said, "Mr. Anderson, I have a strange question."

"Then prepare yourself for a strange answer," he teased.

She giggled. "Seriously though, why is it that being here makes me feel better than almost anywhere else I've ever been?"

Mac smiled. "It's pretty simple, Steph. There's no better feeling than having purpose and that's exactly what you feel when you're here." He drifted away in thought. *Just wait 'til you have kids. I swear there's no better feeling in the world.* Grinning, he peered into Steph's eyes. "I've found that the greatest reward we can give ourselves is to give to others. Trust me, I've learned that the hard way." He nodded. "And I've also found that when you help someone dig themselves out of their troubles, you can usually find a place to bury your own."

"Thanks, Mr. Anderson," she said.

Mac continued to spoon out more than potatoes— offering love and compassion to those who needed it, while teaching others to do the same. *Life is becoming purposeful again*, he realized, *thank God.*

Drew, Brady's best friend, was in town visiting with his grandparents for a full week. At Brady's relentless pleading, Jen finally agreed to throw his eighth birthday party a few weeks early.

The same banner from the year before hung in the living room. A small contingency—Jen, Sue, Diane, Jillian, Bella, Brady and Drew—were gathered for the quiet celebration.

Jen entered the living room with the candle-lit cake and started in on a strong rendition of, "Happy Birthday to you. Happy birthday to you. Happy birthday, dear Brady. Happy birthday to you!"

Making a closed-eyed wish, Brady blew out the eight candles. Everyone applauded. Jen handed the boy his present. He slowly unwrapped the gift. It was a remote-control race car.

"Whoa, so awesome!" Drew said.

"It's the race car you wanted, Brady," Bella said.

Brady nodded but said nothing. He was clearly upset.

"What's the matter, buddy?" Jillian asked.

Jen was surprised. "It's not the car you wanted?"

"What I really want is...is to go sailing with Dad." He broke down crying and ran out of the room.

While both Jen and Drew hurried after him, Diane looked at Jillian and Bella. "Guys, your mom's trying the best she can and you should..."

"...be happy that our dad abandoned us?" Jillian asked in her sarcastic tone.

"I...I didn't say that, Jill."

"We miss Daddy, Auntie Diane, that's all," Bella said through her sniffles. "We just miss him really, really bad."

Jillian stormed out of the room.

Diane pulled Bella in for a hug, where the young girl sobbed mournfully.

∞

Mac sat on the very park bench that had hosted him at his worst. This time, instead of a vodka bottle, he held a pen and a pad of paper, and wrote a birthday letter to his little boy.

Dear Brady,

Happy Birthday, my boy. What I wouldn't do to be there with you in person right now to help celebrate your eighth birthday. You have no idea. But please know that my thoughts are with you, son, and so is my heart. I'm singing for you today and wishing you all the best this world has to offer. You deserve it, buddy!

It's very important that you know what you mean to me, Brady. Everything... that's right, you mean absolutely everything to me. My life would be so empty without you in it.

As I think about you today—as I do every day—I need to ask you to please not be in too much of a hurry to grow up. It'll happen soon enough.

I'm very proud of you, Brady. You've always been a good boy who listens well, which is so important as you grow older. You can't learn anything when you're talking, only when you're listening, right? Remember that. And never be afraid of your feelings, my boy, or being able to express them.

Holding things inside is usually the worst thing you can do, believe me.

Although you can't see me today, I am with you. I am always with you. Happy Birthday, buddy. I can't wait until we go sailing again! Soon...

You Live in My Heart—Always,
Dad

∞

Nine endless weeks had passed. Dressed in a new suit and tie, Mac took a seat near his attorney. He glanced over at Jen, but quickly looked away when their eyes locked.

Roland picked up on it. "Maybe you should give Jen a shot and talk to her," he told Mac, "see why..."

"Roland, I've spent a year healing to get back to my kids," Mac interrupted, "and I really need us to focus on that right now."

As Roland started to respond, Court Officer Beaupre announced, "All rise. This court is now in session, the Honorable Judge Dana Rowe presiding."

Out of the corner of his eye, Mac spotted Dr. Faust Fiore sitting in the gallery. *Thank you so much,* Mac told the man in his head.

Faust winked at him, as though he'd read his mind.

Judge Rowe entered the room, as did social worker, M.J. Connell. Everyone stood. Judge Rowe peered over a pair of eyeglasses that were sitting on the bridge of his slender nose. He finished reviewing the paperwork before him and then glanced thoughtfully at Mac. "Mr. Anderson," he began, "from what our records indicate, you have not seen your children for nearly a year. Is that correct?"

Mac stood. "It is, your Honor."

"And you have come before this court today to appeal an active no contact order that currently prevents you from visitation?"

"Yes, your Honor, I have." He took a deep breath. "May I please speak?"

The judge waved his hand, giving Mac the floor.

"Your Honor" Mac began, "many months ago, I was convicted of domestic assault, for which I admit I was guilty. Though I will never be proud of that fact, only in the last year have I been able to understand why I acted as I did." He breathed deeply. "You see, your Honor, I've been diagnosed with Post Traumatic Stress Disorder. As a result, I've lost my career, my home, my marriage, but worst of all, nearly nine months of my children's lives, time which we can never get back." Tears filled his eyes. "I can't imagine that receiving the death penalty could have felt worse. I'm sorry for what I did, but...but I think I've been punished for my illness long enough." He paused. "Your Honor, in these past months, I've done everything this court has asked of me and more. My only motivation to overcome my illness and reclaim my life has been to reunite with my three children." He nodded with conviction. "I love my kids more than my own soul and I beg this court, regardless of the circumstances or conditions set before me, to please allow me back into their lives, back to where I belong." He paused again to collect himself. "I was sick once, very sick, and I understand there was a need to protect them. But not anymore. I take my medication and I've worked through the root of my issues." He peered into the judge's eyes. "Most of all, your Honor, I believe my children and I should be reunited because I was never just their father—I've always been their dad. You see, I know in my heart that they need me just as much as I need them. Please, your Honor, please let me see my kids. Let me love them again, in ways that only they can understand." He whispered, "Please..."

Except for several sniffles—Jen's being the loudest—the courtroom remained silent. Judge Rowe shook his head. This one simple act struck fear in Mac's heart. *Oh, dear God...* As if he were about to be electrocuted, he squeezed his fists and gritted his teeth.

"Mr. Anderson, your passionate plea has touched the heart of this court," the judge explained, "but you must understand that the welfare of your children is paramount."

Mac nodded. *Please God!* He felt like he was going to pass out. Out of the corner of his eye, he saw Jen slide to the edge of her seat. Her face was bleached white.

"Mr. Anderson," the judge continued, "I apologize for the pain you've endured this past year. It's quite evident to me that you've suffered tremendously."

Mac nodded again, awaiting the worse.

"I apologize because, although I agree that your children needed to be protected at a time that you required psychological help, I'm not sure that a no contact order was in the best interest of anyone involved—you or your children."

Thank you, Lord, Mac thought, his eyes swelling with joyous tears. *This judge actually understands compassion.*

"You see," Judge Rowe explained, "that's the problem with family court—the laws are vague and those passing judgment are compelled to play it safe." He shook his head. "Family court should, whenever possible, keep the family unit intact. And that clearly did not happen in this case." He paused to write something down. "Mr. Anderson, I am going to grant your appeal and revoke the no contact order."

"Yes!" Mac blurted, nearly leaping out of his skin. At last, he could breathe again.

"...with several conditions," the judge added.

Mac nodded.

"…that you reunite with your children under the initial supervision of the Department of Social Services," the judge said, smiling at Mac. "We need to ensure that your behavior is appropriate and your interaction with the children is acceptable. If what you've said to this court today is true, then I can't imagine this will pose a problem."

"I understand, your Honor." Mac had to force the words past the lump in his throat. Tearfully, he smiled back. "No problem at all."

"Your assigned social worker will report back to me on your progress and we'll revisit the need for supervised visitation at that time."

"Thank you, your Honor. Thank you so much!"

The judge leaned forward. "No, Mr. Anderson, thank you. In all sincerity, you should be commended for the work you've put in and the devotion you've shown toward your children. I've seen many similar cases come before me and not every father is willing to dedicate himself the way you have." He looked at Jen. "The first visit will be scheduled for this coming Monday at 6:30 p.m. Will there be a problem with this, Mrs. Anderson?"

Mac cringed. *Here we go…*

"No, not at all," Jen squeaked. She, too, was clearly overwhelmed with emotion. "I'm absolutely delighted, your Honor."

For the first time since he could remember, Mac looked at his estranged wife—stepping into her eyes. When he did, Jen returned the gaze and stared straight into his soul. She smiled sweetly. He swallowed hard. *There are still deep feelings*, he realized, surprised by this.

Jen's eyes never left her husband's. "And I know the kids will be too," she added. "They've really missed their dad." Her face was awash in tears.

Mac swallowed hard again.

"Very good then," Judge Rowe said, wearing a smile while he jotted down another note. "Mr. Anderson, on Monday at 6:30 p.m., you will be reunited with your children. We can..." The rest spilled out as some undiscernible buzz.

Mac turned to Roland and hugged him.

"One last thing, Mr. Anderson," Judge Rowe said.

Mac broke off the hug. "Yes, your Honor?" he asked, reluctantly.

"This court would like to extend its best wishes toward a successful reunion with your children."

Mac was overjoyed. "Thank you, your Honor." He'd never been happier. He turned back toward Jen. She winked at him, releasing a swarm of butterflies in his gut. *It doesn't make sense*, he thought, *after everything we've been through.*

Mac met Faust outside of the courtroom.

"Congratulations," the doctor said, "it looks like our court system finally got something right."

Mac felt overwhelmed with gratitude. "Thank you for coming today, Faust," he said.

"I was here in case you needed a closing pitcher," Faust said, "but I just witnessed a no-hitter...a perfect game."

Mac chuckled and shook the man's hand. *Hopefully, for the last time*, he thought.

"Goodbye, Mac Anderson," Faust said, "be sure to take good care of yourself..." He smiled. "...and your family." He walked away.

As Mac floated down the courtroom's granite stairs, he thought back on all that had happened. As tragic as many of the twists and turns had been, he'd learned a few invaluable lessons along his crooked path. Each aspect of life was like a single domino. One of the tricks to keeping everything standing was to make sure that the dominos were spaced far enough apart. This way, if one fell then the rest didn't have to come tumbling down along with it. *It's amazing,* he thought. *One single event, no matter how simple and meaningless at the time, can easily trigger a terrible chain reaction—a series of more events that can just as easily tear a life down to its foundation.* The theory was simple. If one domino went down, then the best reaction was to concentrate on saving the others. Mac thought about his ancient car accident and shuddered. *One twisted moment, all those years ago, spun my entire world out of control.* Strangely enough, he still couldn't recall the morning when he awoke to discover that all his dominoes were lying on the ground. *We're each hanging on by a thread,* he decided. Inhaling deeply, he looked up at the baby blue sky. *But I'm standing in the sunlight again...Thank God.*

Chapter 18

Mac arrived at the Department of Social Services building at 5:30 p.m., a full hour earlier than scheduled. He was excited and nervous at the same time. M.J. Connell, the DSS caseworker assigned to the Anderson case, met him with a smile. Mac had three shoeboxes tucked under his arm.

"Aren't you a little early, Mr. Anderson?" M.J. commented.

Mac smiled; it was bittersweet. "Actually, I'm nearly a year late," he said.

M.J. chuckled, rubbing Mac's arm in a display of compassion. She escorted him into a small conference room. "Why don't you take a seat and try to relax," she said. "The men's room is down the hall on your left and there's a soda machine right across from it, in case you get thirsty."

Although Mac nodded, his focus was hardly on the kind woman; he was scanning the hall for his children. Rubbing his leaky palms on his pants, he took a few deep breaths.

Laughing again. M.J. kept her hand on his arm for a long moment. "Hey, don't look so serious. You're going to do fine." She nodded. "Try to get comfortable. When your children arrive, I'll bring them right in. Fair enough?"

"Better than fair," he said. "Thank you."

The woman glanced down at the three boxes. "New sneakers for the kids?" she asked.

"No, just three pairs of shoes the kids never saw me wear," he said, offering no further explanation.

M.J.'s forehead creased. Mac opened one of the boxes. She peeked in, her forehead wrinkling more. She looked up at him for a second and then back into the boxes. Suddenly, she gasped for breath, while her eyes filled with tears.

He smiled. *I just hope the kids have the same reaction,* he thought, placing the boxes under the conference table.

M.J. patted his arm one last time. "You're going to do better than fine, Mr. Anderson," she said. "You're going to do great." She left, wiping her eyes and nodding as she went.

Mac sat alone—again. He spent the long minutes glancing at his watch, pacing the floor and sticking his head out the door to check the hallway. After a dozen or so cycles of this, he walked to the window and looked out again. *Where are my children?* he thought, a pang of nausea slapping the interior wall of his stomach. *What if...* he was just starting to think when he spun on his heels and caught the sight of Jillian, Bella and Brady standing in the doorway. He nearly dropped to his knees. *Oh my God*! He started toward them, spreading his arms wide for some long-awaited hugs.

The kids, however, looked frightened—and never budged.

"Jillian, Bella...Brady," Mac said softly, "my God, have I missed you guys. Come give Dad a hug."

Sluggishly, the kids started for him, clearly more afraid than excited.

Jillian was the first to offer a pathetic half-hug.

"Hi slugger, how have you been?" Mac asked.

Jillian didn't respond, avoiding all eye contact.

"Jillian, I..."

"I'm here for them," the teenager snapped, gesturing toward her younger siblings. "Not for you."

Swallowing hard, Mac looked toward his younger children.

Bella took a half-step toward him before she stopped, choosing to stand firmly beside her older sister.

"Oh, princess," Mac said, reaching out for her, "has Dad ever missed..."

Bella's nervous smile quickly turned into sorrowful tears, halting Mac from embracing her.

Brady stood with M.J., half of his body concealed behind her leg.

M.J. bent down to address the small boy. "Brady, aren't you going to give your dad a hug?"

The small boy began to hyperventilate until the real bawling began.

"Okay guys," M.J. said, standing erect and gently facilitating the tense reunion, "it's been a while since you've seen each other, so why don't you all take a seat at the table and try to relax."

Panic—Mac's old nemesis—struck his heart. *At their young ages,* he considered, *maybe too much time has passed?* He could feel the great distance that now separated them. He could also feel the weight of all the months they'd lost. *What a waste,* he thought. For a second, he didn't know what to say. Jillian and Bella were staring at him like he was an apparition from the past and an unfriendly ghost at that. Mac wiped his eyes and took a seat at the table. He gestured for his children to do the same. "Let's just sit and talk," he said.

Reluctantly, each one sat. M.J. remained in the doorway, watching on.

Mac took a deep breath. "Guys," he began, "I need you to know that I never meant to hurt you."

"You left us," Jillian roared, quickly speaking for them all. "We needed you and you left us!" The tears were clearly blinding her from trying to stare her father down.

Mac shook his head, fighting off the impulse to break down and sob. Although his carefully chosen words were garbled with emotion, he explained, "No Jillian, I never left you. This past year, I know there have been times when you needed me and I wasn't there, but..." He paused, struggling to speak. "...but I swear, I never left you."

All three children began weeping—tears of resentment, longing, sorrow, confusion and anger pouring from their eyes.

Mac took another deep breath, reached beneath the table and revealed three shoeboxes. On the top of each box, in big bold letters, were the names *JILLIAN, BELLA, BRADY*. He slid each box to its rightful owner. "Here," he said, "I'm praying this helps you to understand."

The kids looked at each other, confused.

"No guys," he repeated in a whispered cry, "I *never* left you."

Jillian was the first to crack the lid on her box. Her eyes went wide. She reached in and pulled out a giant pile of letters bound by an elastic band. She looked around and found Bella and Brady holding the same sized pile. Jillian began fanning through her pile, taking note of the different dates. She looked at her siblings again, and then at her father.

Before she could inquire for them all, Mac explained, "Once I got to the hospital to get well, I wrote you guys every day. At first, I sent them to the house, but when you never wrote back I realized Mom wasn't letting you read them."

"Mom kept your letters from us?" Bella asked angrily.

"No honey, it wasn't like that. Believe me, I was angry at first too. But then I realized that Mom was doing the only thing she could do at the time—and that was to protect you guys. She didn't know when I'd come back...if I'd ever *come back.*" His eyes leaked. "Your mom didn't know that I was fighting to get well...that I was fighting with everything inside of me to get back to the three children I love."

Still entrenched in bitterness, Jillian pulled a bruised softball from the box and looked at it, confused.

Again, before she could utter a word, Mac explained, "This past season, first game in, you guys played the Tigers."

The teenage girl swallowed hard. "Yeah?"

"In the first inning, you cracked the sweetest double I've ever seen in my life," he said. "It hopped the fence and rolled into the woods."

"Yeah, I remember," she said, "the umpire stopped the game, but no one ever found the ball."

Mac's eyes filled to the point that he couldn't see. "There was no way they could have, Jill," he whimpered, nodding, "because I caught it."

Jillian's body began to convulse. Obviously trying to remain strong, she dove back into her box, only to pull out wrapped gifts and cards; it was everything she believed her father had missed. The entire box was filled with her dad's love.

Bella removed two photos from her shoebox. "These are from my dance recital," she said. "I remember a man taking these, but he..."

"...was wearing a funny looking hat and moustache?" Mac asked.

She nodded. "Oh, Daddy," she whimpered.

"You smiled right at me, princess," Mac said, "and you never looked so beautiful."

Brady held up one of the treasures from his shoebox. He looked at his father.

Laughing, Mac told him, "That's the program from your Spelling Bee, Brady."

"You were there, Dad?" the boy asked.

"Of course I was, son. I wouldn't have missed it for the world." He grinned through the tears. "And I also learned that you've been eating too many artificial snacks since I've been away." He laughed, spelling, "C.H.E.E.Z.E.?"

Everyone laughed, especially Brady. He looked at his sisters. "Dad saw me too," the boy squealed.

"And I was never so proud of you," Mac added, beaming. "There's nothing wrong with second place, Brady. I could tell that you studied hard to get there."

From each of their boxes, the three kids retrieved items and began calling them out, excitedly—talking over each other.

"My report card…" Jillian said.

"Christmas presents?" Bella said.

Brady nodded. "And Easter candy!"

"More letters," Bella yelled.

"And pictures of me," Brady yelled back.

"And a birthday card," Jillian concluded, choked up. Each box was a complete account of the last year of their lives. Jillian stood and approached her emotional father. "Oh Dad, I love you so much," she said.

Mac grabbed his eldest girl, pulling her to him. He hugged Jillian tight, allowing her the opportunity to let out all the pain. *The last thing I wanted was for my girl to sprint past her childhood*, he thought.

Jillian bawled like a baby.

"I'm so proud of you, Jill," Mac whispered. "You helped Mom take good care of our family while I was away. But it's time for you to be a kid again, okay?"

She nodded, unable to respond through the sniffles.

Mac looked at them all. "I'm not sick anymore, guys. Dad's back and I'm never going away again."

Bella and Brady followed Jillian's lead and swarmed upon their father, smothering him in hugs and kisses.

Mac cried openly with his children, weeping the same way he had on the days that each of them were born. He sobbed hard for the time they'd lost, as well as the opportunity they now had to start over. "Nope, I never left you guys," he whimpered. "I was always with you. Always..." He slapped his chest and inhaled deeply. "...because you live right in here."

The kids all slapped their chests before smothering their beloved father in more hugs and kisses.

Brady saluted. "Aye Captain, right in here." He slapped his chest again.

Laughing and crying joyfully, they returned to their unbreakable huddle.

It was early autumn. Mac and his three children were adrift on the lake. There were no other boats on the water. Everyone was beaming with smiles. Life was good again, nearly returned to the way it had been a year before. Even Brady was wearing his tightly-fitted sailor's hat.

Jillian cleared her throat. "Dad," she said, "we got you something. A welcome home gift."

Mac smiled.

Jillian turned toward her little brother. "Go ahead, Brady, give it to him."

The young boy reached into his pocket, retrieved an old dirty bottle cap and handed to his father.

It's the treasure we buried at the park, he realized, his eyes swelling with love. He lifted the bottle cap and peered into the eyes of all three children. "Thank you, guys. I'll keep this good luck charm with me forever."

Each of them beamed.

"Maybe it'll help you on your big date," Bella teased, making her sister and brother giggle.

"You guys are too much," Mac said, joining in the laughter. "I've already told you, we're only going out to dinner."

"Sure, Dad," Jillian teased.

"Yeah, sure," Brady echoed.

Bella jumped in. "I don't know, Dad. Mom bought a new dress and she's been starving herself for two weeks to fit into it."

"She has?" Mac asked, blushing.

The kids picked up on it. "Ooooh..." they sang in chorus.

Mac tried to return to seriousness. "Guys, don't get your hopes up. A lot's happened between your mom and me." He half-shrugged. "I'm not sure..."

"But a lot more good things happened before you got sick, right?" Jillian quickly interrupted.

"Geez, I don't know," Mac said, at a loss.

"Come on, Dad, where's your faith?" Bella asked.

Instantly, Mac's breathing turned shallow, as his mind returned back to Presbyterian Hospital.

∞

"Mr. Anderson?" Dr. Fiore said, waiting for Mac to return to reality.

"Huh? What?" Mac said. "Oh yeah, I'm sorry."

The doctor smiled. "Looks like you were quite a ways from here. Where'd you go?"

"To where my kids are...or were anyway."

The doctor picked up on the melancholy. "Can't wait to get back to them, right?"

"I wish," Mac said, sadly. "The judge took them from me and I'm not sure I'll ever be able..."

"Whoa there," Dr. Fiore said, cutting him off, "where's your faith?"

"Faith?"

"Yeah, *faith*. You don't honestly think this is the end of the line for you, do you?" He shook his head. "Oh no, this is just another starting point, Mr. Anderson—that's all." He nodded. "You'll be with your kids again. Just by the look in your eyes, I can guarantee it."

"You must know something I don't, doc," Mac said gratefully, "but I hope you're right."

"Sure, I'm right," the man confirmed, smiling. "Besides, how can anyone take something from you when it lives right in here?" Dr. Fiore slapped his chest.

Mac looked up to find his three beautiful children grinning at him. Jillian patted him on the back, pointed to Bella, Brady and herself and said, "Yeah Dad, if we can start over, who says it can't happen for you and Mom?"

Mac offered each of them a hug. His children had witnessed his return from the ashes, along with the countless hours it took to make that happen. What many people would see as impossible, they could now see as possible, even probable. *At least Jen and I never fought apathy or indifference,* he thought, grinning. *The passion has always been there.* He also knew he could only reclaim true happiness through forgiveness—*by choosing love over hate, peace over war.*

All three kids awaited his reply.

"Nobody says, that's who," Mac said. "I suppose we've all learned that anything's possible, right?"

Brady saluted. "Aye Captain, anything." The young boy slapped his chest, causing the rest of them to do the same.

While Mac sat amazed at the many spiritual signs, his eyes swelled with love. "I love you three more than anything in the world," he vowed.

"We love you too," Jillian said.

As he struggled to regain his composure, he stood and began working the main sail.

"I hope you're going to bring Mom flowers for your date?" Bella said.

Mac grinned. "I've been thinking about giving her a book mark instead," he said.

The kids looked confused.

Mac allowed it. "Have you guys ever heard of a place called Gooseberry Island?" he asked.

All three children shook their heads. "No, Dad."

Mac smiled. "Then let's sail over there and discover it together."

He and his children laughed well past the setting sun. *Ours is a love that can never be destroyed,* he thought, *and with enough hard work, dreams really can come true.*

Acknowledgments

First and forever, Jesus Christ—my Lord and Savior. With Him, all things are possible.

To Paula, my beautiful wife, for loving me and being the amazing woman she is.

To my children—Evan, Jacob, Isabella and Carissa—for inspiring me.

To Mom, Dad, Billy, Julie, Caroline, Caleb, Randy, Kathy, Philip, Darlene, Jeremy, Baker, Aurora, Jenn, Jason, Jack, the DeSousas—my beloved family and foundation on which I stand.

To Sue Nedar and Roland Dube for helping me breathe souls into these characters. It was the thrill of a lifetime to see these characters come to life on stage. And to the amazing cast, who played the original roles, your gift was priceless and will never be forgotten.

To Lou Aronica, my mentor and friend, for helping me to share this story with the world.

About the Author

Steven Manchester is the author of the #1 bestsellers *Twelve Months, The Rockin' Chair, Pressed Pennies,* and *Gooseberry Island,* the national bestseller *Ashes, and* the novels *Goodnight, Brian* and *The Changing Season.* His work has appeared on NBC's *Today Show*, CBS's *The Early Show*, CNN's *American Morning*, and BET's *Nightly News*. Recently, three of Manchester's short stories were selected "101 Best" for the *Chicken Soup for the Soul* series.